CLAUDE SIMON

THE
FLANDERS
ROAD

Translated by Richard Howard

Introduction
by
JOHN FLETCHER

JOHN CALDER · LONDON
RIVERRUN PRESS · NEW YORK

This edition first published in Great Britain in 1985 by
John Calder (Publishers) Ltd
18 Brewer Street, London W1R 4AS
and in the United States of America in 1985 by
Riverrun Press Inc
1170 Broadway, New York, NY 10001
Second impression 1986

Originally published in French in 1960 by Les Editions de Minuit under the
title of *La route des Flandres*, and first published in Great Britain in 1962 by
Jonathan Cape Ltd.

British Library Cataloguing in Publication Data
Simon, Claude
    The Flanders road.
    I. Title   II. La route des Flandres. *English*
    843'.914   [F]   PQ2679.I46

    ISBN 0-7145-3994-5

SUBSIDISED BY THE
Arts Council
OF GREAT BRITAIN

Library of Congress Cataloging in Publication Data
Simon, Claude.
    The Flanders road

    Translation of: Route des Flandres
    1. France — History — German occupation, 1940-1945 —
Fiction.   I. Title.
PQ2637.I547R613   1985   843'.914   85-8358

    ISBN 0-7145-3994-5 (U.S. : pbk.)

Printed in Great Britain by Heffers Printers Limited, Cambridge.

INTRODUCTION

In the extreme north-eastern corner of France, close to the Belgian border, a road runs dead straight for a few miles over undulating terrain, a rural landscape of meadows and hedges with small copses dotted here and there. The villages and small towns are built of drab brick and slate. It is solid farming country, with little to attract the tourist. The road in question runs more or less east to west, from Solre-le-Château to a place called *Les Trois Pavés*, where it joins the N2, which links Avesnes-sur-Helpe to the south with Mauberge in the north, and ultimately takes you to Brussels, Antwerp and the Hook of Holland.

Before it joins the N2, the straight road I am talking about, the D962, passes close to a village called Sars-Poteries which, as its name implies, is a small industrial centre containing several ceramics workshops. It was on the outskirts of Sars-Poteries that, in the middle of May, 1940, the event occurred which lies at the heart of this epic novel. The weather then was perfect: day after day of warm sunshine with virtually clear skies from dawn to dusk. It was ideal weather for the German panzer divisions, which were pouring across the ill-defended Meuses river, and for their supporting aircraft. It was vile weather for the hapless French cavalry who were trying to stop tanks with frightened, disoriented troops mounted — of all things — on *horseback*. From the German point of view the campaign was a dazzling, almost unbelievable triumph; for France, a humiliating rout which was to determine the course of history in Europe for the rest of the century, as there can be little doubt that if the French had been less soundly and decisively beaten at the battle of the Meuse, the rest of the war and its aftermath would have turned out rather differently.

One of the luckless troopers retreating from east to west in the carnage and confusion of those sundrenched spring days was Claude Simon, a conscript then aged twenty-six. He was riding

3

with another trooper behind two officers, a captain and a lieutenant, and as they were leaving Sars-Poteries on the road to Avesnes the captain was shot dead by a sniper hidden behind a hedge. The others made their escape as best they could. Simon was eventually rounded up with thousands of other French soldiers and sent to a POW camp in Saxony, from which before long he succeeded in escaping. For many years the memory of that episode on a road in Flanders ripened in his imagination, and in 1960 he published this novel, which develops the incident into a deeply moving meditation on war, on human suffering, on time, and on mankind's craving for love and for the illusory permanance it affords. Sensitively translated by Richard Howard, this book — first published in English in 1961 — is reissued at a time when Claude Simon is felt by many to be one of the world's greatest living novelists, as the reaction to the failure of the Swedish committee to award him the Nobel Prize for Literature in 1983 demonstrated. The unprecedented scandal provoked by one of the committee's members declaring publicly his disagreement with the decision to pass over Claude Simon in favour of William Golding caught the headlines and aroused the sympathy of many who feel that the committee had made a mistake.

When *The Flanders Road* was published in France, the lieutenant on the fateful day in 1940 — by then a retired colonel of dragoons by the name of Cuny — wrote to Claude Simon to compliment him on the accuracy of the descriptions in the novel of the events leading up to the murder of his brother officer (called in real life Captain Rey). It was a remarkable and indeed moving testimonial not only to Simon's powers of recall but also to his skill in recreating the experience which he and Cuny shared. Like all great novelists Simon possesses the gift of making the ordinary memorable and the extraordinary seem natural. It would be difficult to improve, for instance, upon his tellingly graphic descriptions of the rout, what he here calls 'that disaster, that blind patient endless debacle', and of the detritus spread over mile after mile which characterised it, 'exuding not the traditional and heroic odour of carrion, of corpses in a state of decomposition, but only of ordure, simply stinking, the way a pile of old tin cans, potato

4

peelings and burnt rags can stink, and no more affecting or tragic than a pile of rubbish . . .'

So far as I know Captain Rey was a stranger to Simon, someone he met by chance during the confusion of the retreat from the Meuse. For this is a work of fiction, and Captain de Reixach (the name given in the novel) is not a real historical person: only the Flanders road, running 'almost exactly east-west', truly exists. The rest is imaginative reconstruction of a high order: an achievement which Tolstoy would recognise as being in the tradition of *War and Peace* and of its consummate balancing of the microcosm — individual Russians with their emotions and sufferings — and the macrocosm: the conflict of nations, the struggle (just as epoch-making in its way as Hitler's *blitzkrieg*) between Tsar and Emperor.

The ambush on the Flanders Road in which Rey/de Reixach dies is in any case not the only important element in the story. There is also the steeplechase, in which de Reixach insists on riding in place of his jockey Iglésia (later his wife's lover and later still his orderly in Flanders), and his humiliating failure in the saddle, which represents in little the infinitely more serious defeat of the mounted troops in the battle with which, almost exactly half-way through the novel, the race is textually 'spliced'. There is, too, the powerfully erotic account of the night of love which Georges, the demobbed trooper who is the author's representative in the story, spends with de Reixach's widow Corinne in a doomed attempt to 'pursue upon her body in his body' the reconstruction, the imaginative recreation, the reliving, of the traumatic episode on the Flanders road. And there is, finally, the ancestral portrait, the painting which seemed to Georges in his childhood to show an eighteenth-century forbear bleeding from the temple because the latter had read too much Rousseau and had been cruelly disappointed by human frailty when he returned unexpectedly from the wars and found his young wife energetically making love to a farm boy endowed with a 'muscular back', as Corinne was later to copulate frenziedly in the stables with Iglésia. The difference, Georges thinks, is that the disciple of Jean-Jacques blew his brains out with his own shotgun, whereas in May 1940, as befitted a less

5

heroic and self-conscious age, Captain de Reixach chose instead to ride into a German ambush and disguise his suicide as death in action.

Or was it really so? asks the text in the closing pages, in a striking attack of self-doubt which shows that Simon is as much a disciple of Faulkner as he is of Tolstoy, and a true member of the *nouveau roman* movement which has induced us to recognise that words are not safe, and that literature is a quest rather than a discovery. Just as John Fowles (another contemporary novelist engaged in warning us that writing is exploration, not cartography) advises the reader not to assume that any of the possible endings of his novel *The French Lieutenant's Woman* is the 'right' one, but to accept them all simultaneously, Claude Simon implies that Captain de Reixach could equally well have been killed by accident (because the enemy sniper would naturally pick out the senior member of the group). After all, when Georges grew up and got to know the family portrait better, he realised that the 'blood' pouring from his ancestor's temple was something much more probably, and even frankly banal: a crack in the impasto of the picture which had widened so much over the years as to reveal the brownish primer underneath.

So it is, the novel suggests, with all human endeavour abandoned 'to the incoherent, casual, impersonal and destructive work of time', the gnawing of termites which reduces all things to the same dust from which they originated, just like the dead horse which is the novel's central symbol: inexplicably covered in mud despite the dry weather, it is already being absorbed by the earth out of which it was created. Claude Simon proposes an unsentimental stoicism in the face of this enduring strength of the natural world as compared with the puny efforts of mankind to secure permanance through love and literature. As Georges his spokesman tells the professor his father, if all that written in the volumes held in the great Leipzig library was so signally incapable of preventing the evil which led directly to the library's destruction, then perhaps it was not worth much, or at least not to be weighed in the same scale as those 'objects of prime importance' to POWs, such as warm clothes, footwear, soap and cigarettes. But though Simon is

6

unsentimental over matters like these, he is not lacking in humanity: the scene in the POW camp, where the gambler faints with hunger because he pays his daily rations over to the banker, is conveyed with discreet but powerful feeling. The 'someone' who is watching and who says 'You bastard' to the banker is also someone close to the narrator, and indeed someone who voices aloud what the reader feels. And while showing that certain people will always exploit the weakness of their fellows, the text at the same time reveals the dignity of the gambler, who prefers to starve rather than suffer the humiliation of being seen to default on his debts.

A final word about Simon's style. This will hold no terrors for the reader who has read Faulkner, from whom Simon learned so much: especially the trick of avoiding a precise narrative tense (by using the present participle instead of a finite verb), the elaborately rich similes, the explanatory parentheses, and the generous profusion of adjectives. And a useful tip: if you get lost, do not despair. Simon opens parentheses liberally, but he never omits to close them, so if you are bogged down in an aside, skip to the next closing bracket, and start again. Although the prose is dense and rich, and works largely by association of ideas rather than chronological sequence, it is never perverse, never out to baffle the reader on purpose; on the contrary, as Simon once said, far from evolving a difficult style in which to wrap up simple things, he has forged for himself an instrument, which is as straightforward as he can make it, to render intelligible matters which are infinitely complex.

JOHN FLETCHER

1

I thought I was learning how to live,
I was learning how to die.

LEONARDO DA VINCI

HE was holding a letter in his hand, he raised his eyes looked at me then the letter again then once more at me, behind him I could see the red mahogany ochre blurs of the horses being led to the watering trough, the mud was so deep you sank into it up to your ankles but I remember that during the night it had frozen suddenly and Wack came into the bedroom with the coffee saying The dogs ate up the mud, I had never heard the expression, I could almost see the dogs, some kind of infernal, legendary creatures their mouths pink-rimmed their wolf fangs cold and white chewing up the black mud in the night's gloom, perhaps a recollection, the devouring dogs cleaning, clearing away: now the mud was grey and we twisted our ankles running, late as usual for morning call, almost tripping in the deep tracks left by the hoofs and frozen hard as stone, and a moment later he said Your mother's written me. So she had done it in spite of the fact that I told her not to, I could tell I was blushing, he stopped and must have tried to smile but probably that was impossible, not being friendly (he certainly wanted to be friendly) but eliminating that remoteness: the effort merely stretched the hard little pepper-and-salt moustache somewhat, he had that tanned lustreless skin of people who live outdoors most of the time, something of the Arab in him, probably the traces of one Charles Martel had forgotten to kill, maybe he claimed descent not only from His Cousin the Virgin, like his neighbours the petty nobility of the Tarn, but even from Mohammed into the bargain, he said I think we're cousins more or less, but in his mind I suppose that as far as I was concerned the word probably meant something more like mosquito insect midge, and I could feel myself blushing with fury again the way I had when I first saw that letter in his hand, recognized the stationery. I didn't answer, he must have seen how furious I was, I wasn't looking at him but at the letter, I wished I could snatch it away and tear it up, he gestured with the hand that was holding the letter folded, the corners fluttered like wings in the cold air, his dark eyes showing neither hostility nor contempt, cordial even, but distant too: perhaps he was only as annoyed as I was, resenting my irritation while we went on with our little ceremony standing there in the frozen mud, both of us making that concession to custom to convention out of regard for a woman who unfortunately for me was my mother, and finally he must have understood for his little moustache moved again while he was saying Don't hold it against her It's only natural for a mother She was right Personally I'm delighted to have the chance If you ever need, and I Oh thank you Captain, and he If something goes wrong don't hesitate to come and see, and I Yes Captain, he waved the letter again, it must have been around ten or fifteen degrees that early in the morning but he didn't even seem to notice it. After they had drunk all the water they wanted the horses trotted off again in pairs, the men running between swearing and hanging on to the bridles, you could hear the noise the hoofs made on the frozen mud, he repeating If something goes wrong don't I'll be happy to do, then folding the letter putting it in his pocket looking at me again with an expression that in his mind must have been a smile and that merely pulled the pepper-and-salt moustache to one side again after which he turned on his heel and walked off. From then on I simply made sure I did even less than I was doing already, I had reduced things to essentials, unhooking the stirrups when I dismounted, unbuckling the harness after I had changed the water once or twice and then taking off the whole bridle, dipping it in the trough while the horse was still drinking, and then the horse went back to the stable by itself while I walked beside it ready to grab an ear, and after that all I had to do was wipe off the steel and now and then use sandpaper when it was really too rusty, but it didn't matter much anyway since my reputation on that point had been established long since and no one bothered me about it any more and besides I suppose that as far as he was concerned he couldn't have cared less and to pretend not to see me when he inspected the platoon was a favour he did my mother without too much bother, unless the polishing was also one of those futile and irreplaceable things for him, one of those reflexes and traditions so to speak ancestrally maintained at Saumur and then later reinforced, although according to what people said she (in other words the woman in other words the child he had married or rather who had married him) did everything she could in their four years of marriage to make him forget or in any case forswear most of these traditional traditions, whether he liked them or not, but even supposing he had given most of them up (and probably not so much because he loved her but because he had to or better still because he had to because he loved her) there are some things that the worst renunciations the worst capitulations can't make you forget even if you want to and usually such things are the silliest or the most senseless ones the things you can't reason about or have any control over, for instance his reaction of drawing his sabre when that burst of gunfire came from behind the hedge: there was a second when I could see him that way his arm raised brandishing that useless ridiculous weapon in the hereditary gesture of an equestrian statue which had probably been handed down to him by generations of swordsmen, a dim figure against the light so that it looked as if he and his horse had been cast together out of one and the same material, a grey metal, the sun glinting for a second on the naked blade then everything – man horse and sabre – collapsing together sideways like a lead soldier beginning to melt from the feet up and leaning slowly to one side then faster and faster, vanishing sabre still held outstretched behind the carcass of that burnt truck abandoned there, indecent as an animal, a pregnant bitch dragging her belly on the ground, the punctured tyres slowly rotting, giving off that smell of scorched rubber the sickening stink of war hanging in the brilliant spring afternoon, floating or rather stagnating, viscous and transparent

13

but somehow visible like putrid water in which the red brick houses the orchards the hedges had been standing: for an instant the sun's dazzling reflection caught or rather condensed all the light and the glory on that virginal steel . . . Only, it was a long time since she had been a virgin, but I suppose that wasn't what he asked, desired of her the day he had made up his mind to marry her, undoubtedly knowing perfectly well from that moment on what lay in store for him, having accepted in advance having assumed having so to speak consumed in advance that Passion, with this difference that the site the centre the altar wasn't a naked hill but that smooth and tender and hairy and secret crease in the flesh . . . Yes: crucified, agonizing on the altar the mouth the cave of . . . But after all wasn't there a whore at the other crucifixion too, presuming that whores are indispensable in such things, women in tears wringing their hands and penitent whores, supposing that he had ever asked her to repent or at least expected hoped that she would that she would become something else than what she had the reputation of being and so expected of this marriage something else than should logically follow from it, even foreseeing or at least having perhaps imagined as far as that final consequence or rather conclusion, that suicide which the war gave him the opportunity of perpetrating so elegantly that is not melodramatic spectacular and nasty like the housemaids who throw themselves under the Métro or the bankers who dirty their whole office but disguised as an accident if you can still consider being killed in the war an accident, somehow taking advantage with discretion and a sense of the opportune of the occasion provided in order to finish off what should never have begun four years before . . .

I understood that, I realized that all he wanted hoped for in that moment was to get himself killed and not only when I saw him there planted on his horse fixed clearly exposed right in the middle of the road without even bothering or seeming to bother to get his horse under an apple tree, that fool of a little second-lieutenant thinking himself obliged to do the same thing, probably supposing that it was the last word the *ne plus ultra* of elegance and chic for a cavalry officer without suspecting for an instant the real reasons that impelled the other man to do it, in other words that it was a question neither of honour nor of courage and still less of elegance but a purely personal matter and not even between him and her but between him and himself. I could have told him, Iglésia could have told him even better than I. But what was the use. I suppose he must have been convinced that he was doing something absolutely sensational and besides why should we have disabused him since that way at least he would die content even ecstatic, dying beside and like a de Reixach, so it was better for him to believe it better for him to be a fool not to ask what was behind that face only slightly bored slightly impatient waiting making us or rather making the campaign service regulations and the orders in case of low-flying aircraft strafing the roads the concession of waiting until they were some distance away and we climbed out of the ditch, turning slightly on his saddle a little exasperated but obliging himself to be patient showing us that still impenetrable expressionless face merely waiting for us to get back on our horses again while they disappeared no larger than dots above the horizon now, then once we were mounted starting again, urging his horse forward with an imperceptible pressure of his legs, the horse apparently starting of its own accord and still at a walk naturally without haste yet not slowly either and not even casually: simply at a walk. I suppose he wouldn't have started trotting for all the money in the world, that he wouldn't have driven his spurs into the horse wouldn't have moved faster if a gun had gone off in his ear and that's exactly what happened there are expressions that are convenient: at a walk then, and that too must have been part of what he had started four years before and had decided, was in the process of ending or rather of trying to put an end to walking calmly, impassively (in the same way that, according to what Iglésia said, he had always pretended to notice nothing, had never betrayed the slightest emotion neither jealousy nor anger) along that road that was something like a death-trap, not war but murder, a place where you were cut down before you had time to know it, the snipers sitting behind the hedge or some bush as though at a county-fair shooting-gallery and taking all the time they needed to get you in their sights, in other words a massacre and for a moment I wondered if he didn't want Iglésia to get his there too, if at the same time he was ending it all for himself he wasn't also taking a longed-for revenge, but all things considered I don't think so I imagine that by then everything had become indifferent to him supposing he had ever had anything against Iglésia since after all he had kept him in his service and now he bothered as much or rather as little about him as about me or about that fool of a second-lieutenant, probably not feeling any further responsibility not so far as we were concerned personally but in regard to his role his function as an officer, probably thinking that what he could do or not do from that point of view no longer had any importance whatever at the stage we had reached: delivered then released relieved so to speak of his military obligations from the moment his squadron had been reduced to the four of us (his squadron itself being virtually all that had managed to survive of the whole regiment along with maybe a few other dismounted cavalrymen stranded here and there around the countryside) which still didn't keep him from sitting as straight and stiff on his saddle as if he had been reviewing his men in the Fourteenth of July parade and not in full retreat or rather rout or rather disaster in the middle of this collapse of everything as if not an army but the world itself the whole world and not only in its physical reality but even in the repre-sentation the mind can make of it (but maybe it was the lack of sleep too, the fact that we had had almost no sleep at all in ten days except on horseback) was actually falling apart collapsing breaking up into pieces dissolving into water into nothing, and two or three times someone shouted at him not to go on (I don't know how many, nor who they were: I suppose wounded men, or men hidden in houses or in the ditch, or maybe civilians who incomprehensibly kept wandering around dragging a broken suitcase or pushing those perambulators ahead of them loaded with some kind of luggage (and not even luggage: things, and probably useless: probably just so as not to be wandering around empty-handed, to have the impression the illusion of taking something of possessing something anything as long as there could be attached to it – the split pillow the umbrella or the coloured photograph of the grandparents – the arbitrary notion of price, of value) as if what counted was to be walking, whether in one direction or another: but I didn't actually see them, all I could see, was still capable of recognizing, like a kind of target, a landmark, was that bony back thin stiff and very straight cambered on the saddle, and the serge tunic slightly shinier over the symmetrical bulges of the shoulder-blades, and I had long since stopped paying any attention – stopped being able to pay attention – to what could be happening along the roadside); voices, then, unreal and whining crying something (a warning, an alarm) and that reached me across the dazzling and opaque light of that spring day (as if the light itself were dirty, as if the invisible air kept in suspension, like contaminated water, that kind of dusty stinking colloidal filth of the war), and he (I could see his head move each time appearing in profile under the helmet, the dry hard outline of the forehead, the eyebrow, and underneath the notch of the eye socket then the firm dry immutable line falling straight from the cheekbone to the chin) looking at them, his expressionless incurious eyes resting for a moment (but apparently without seeing) on the man (or perhaps not even that: only on the place the point the voice came from) who had called to him, and not even reproving severe or annoyed, not even frowning: merely that lack of expression, of interest – at the most maybe astonishment: a little nonplussed, impatient, as though in a salon someone had suddenly spoken to him without having been introduced or had interrupted him in the middle of a sentence with one of those *non sequiturs* (for instance indicating that the ash of his cigar was about to fall off or that his coffee was getting cold) and perhaps making an effort, a show of good will of patience of courtesy to try to understand the reasons or the interest of the remark or if the latter could be related in some way or other to what he had been saying, then giving up any attempt to understand making up his mind without even a shrug of the shoulders probably deciding it is inevitable to meet everywhere always and in any circumstance – in salons or at war – stupid and ignorant people, and that done – in other words decided – forgetting the interrupter, effacing him, no longer seeing him even before looking away, then no longer looking at all at that place where there was nothing, raising his head again and resuming with that little second-lieutenant his calm conversation of the sort two cavalrymen riding through the countryside might be having (in training or on manoeuvres) about fellow cavalrymen about promotion about hunting or about racing. And I felt as though I was there, saw it: the green shade with women in bright-coloured print dresses, standing or sitting on iron garden-chairs, and men in pale riding-breeches talking to them, leaning over them, tapping their boots with their Malacca riding-crops, the silks of the horses and those of the women and the tawny leathers of the boots making brilliant spots (mahogany, mauve, pink, yellow) against the deep-green foliage, and the women of that particular class to which do not belong but which is constituted by (to the exclusion of all others) the daughters of colonels or of men with a particle in their name: rather insipid, rather insignificant and frail, keeping until late in life (even married, even after the second or third child) that virginal look, with their long delicate bare arms, their short white girlish gloves, their boarding-school dresses (until they turn suddenly – in the middle thirties – into something rather masculine, rather horsy (no, not mares, horses), smoking and discussing races or horse shows like men), and the faint hum of voices suspended beneath the heavy branches of the chestnut trees, the voices (women's or men's) capable of remaining decorous, even, and completely futile while speaking the coarsest or even the rawest remarks, discussing copulations (animal and human) money or first communions with the same inconsequent, agreeable and cavalier ease, the voices then melting into the constant and confused trampling of the boots and the high heels on the gravel, stagnating in the air, the iridescent and impalpable clouds of gilded dust suspended in the calm green afternoon smelling of flowers, dung and perfumes, and he . . .

'Oh yes! . . . ' Blum said (now we were lying in the darkness in other words intertwined overlapping huddled together until we couldn't move an arm or a leg without touching or shifting another arm or leg, stifling, the sweat streaming over our chests gasping for breath like stranded fish, the wagon stopping once again in the dark and no sound audible except for the noise of breathing the lungs desperately sucking in that thick clamminess that stench of bodies mingled as if we were already deader than the dead since we were capable of realizing it as if the darkness the night . . . And I could feel them sense them swarming slowly creeping over each other like reptiles in the suffocating odour of excrement and sweat, trying to remember how long we had been in that train a day and a night or a night and a day and a night but that didn't have any meaning time doesn't exist What time is it I said can you see the, What difference does it make to you he said What difference will it make when it's morning Are you so eager to see our filthy prisoners' faces Are you so eager to see my filthy Jew's face they, Oh I said shut up shut up shut up), Blum repeating: 'Oh yes. And then he took that burst of machine-gun fire at point-blank range. Maybe it would have been smarter on his part if'

'No: listen . . . Smarter! God what do you think smart . . . Listen: once he bought us drinks. I mean, not exactly for us, I suppose: because of the horses. I mean he thought they must be thirsty and so at the time . . . ' And Blum: 'Bought drinks?', and I: 'Yes. It was . . . Listen: it was like one of those posters for some brand of English beer, you know? The courtyard of the old inn with the dark-red brick walls and the light-coloured mortar, and the leaded windows, the sashes painted white, and the girl carrying the copper mugs and the stableboy in yellow leather leggings with tongues and turned-up buckles watering the horses while the group of cavalrymen were standing in classical postures: hips arched, one boot forward, one hand holding the crop resting on a hip while the other raises a mug of golden beer towards an upper window where you notice half glimpse behind a curtain a face that looks as if it came out of a pastel . . . Yes: with this difference that there was nothing of all that except the brick walls, only dirty, and the courtyard looked more like a barnyard: an airshaft behind a bar, a tavern, with piles of empty siphon cases and wandering chickens and laundry drying on a line, and instead of a white apron the woman was wearing one of those flowered linen smocks the kind they sell in open-air markets and her legs were bare in slippers and apparently not surprised by what she and we were doing there, as if it had been a perfectly natural thing for each of us to be standing there in full uniform calmly drinking down our beers, he and the second-lieutenant a little to one side as was to be expected (and I don't even know if he drank, I don't think so, I can't see him drinking his pint from the bottle), and we holding our bottles in one hand and in the other the reins of the horses drinking from the trough, and this beside that road along which there was a dead man (or a woman, or a child), or a truck, or a burnt wagon almost every ten yards, and when he paid – for he did pay – I could see his hand slip into his pocket under the resilient grey-green stuff of the elegant jodhpurs, the two bulges formed by the index and middle fingers bent while he grasped his wallet, pulled it out and counted the coins into the woman's hand as coolly as if he had paid for an orange-ade or one of those fashionable drinks at the bar of some paddock in Deauville or Vichy . . . ' And again it was as if I were seeing it: silhouetted against the deep, almost blackish green of the opulent chestnut trees, the jockeys passing while the bell tinkled on their way to the gate line, perched high, monkeylike, on the delicate elegant mounts, their many-coloured silks following each other through the lozenges of sunshine, like this: Yellow, blue braces and cap – the blackish-green background of the chestnut trees – Black, blue St Andrew's cross and white cap – the blackish-green wall of the chestnut trees – Blue-and-pink check, blue cap – the blackish-green wall of the chestnut trees – Yellow, red-and-yellow striped sleeves, red cap – the blackish-green wall of the chestnut trees – Garnet, garnet cap – the blackish-green wall of the chestnut trees – Yellow, green-striped sleeves, red cap – the blackish-green wall of the chestnut trees – Blue, red sleeves, green armband and cap – the blackish-green wall of the chestnut trees – Violet, cerise Cross of Lorraine, violet cap – the blackish-green wall of the chestnut trees – Red, blue polka-dots, red sleeves and cap – the blackish-green wall of the chestnut trees – Brown with sky-blue stripes, black cap . . . the brilliant silks slipping by, the dark-green wall of leaves, the sparkling silks, the dancing lozenges of sunlight, the horses with dancing names – Carpasta, Milady, Zeida, Naharo, Romance, Primarosa, Riskoli, Carpaccio, Wildrisk, Samarkand, Chichibu – the young fillies setting down their delicate hoofs one after the other and picking them up again as if they were scorched, dancing, seeming to be suspended above the earth, without touching ground, the bell, the gong chiming, still chiming, while one after the next the iridescent silks slipped silently by in the elegant afternoon and Iglésia passing without looking at her and on his back that pink silk that seemed to leave the scented wake of her own flesh behind it, as if she had taken one of those silky pieces of lingerie of hers and had thrown it over him, still warm, still impregnated with the odour of her body, and above his yellow, mournful, bird-of-prey profile, and below his little legs bent, knees high, crouching on that golden chestnut with the majestic, opulent gait, with the opulent haunches (even that opulent stiffness of the hindquarters, limbs made not for walking but for galloping, moving one after the other with that rigid distinction, that arrogant clumsiness, the long blond tail swaying, glinting in the sun), and the last silks seen from behind now (dark blue with a red St Andrew's cross, brown with blue polka-dots), vanishing behind the scales, the building with the white-washed roof, the false Norman beams, and she (she hadn't turned her head either, hadn't showed that she had seen him) sitting on one of those iron chairs in the shade, and perhaps in her hand ρne of those yellow or pink sheets with the last odds written on them (but not looking at that either), talking desultorily with (or listening desultorily to, oŕ not listening to) one of those men, one of those retired colonels or commandants never seen except in such places, wearing striped trousers, a grey bowler (and probably stored away somewhere, fully dressed, for the rest of the week and taken out only on Sundays, quickly dusted off, smoothed out and set here along with the baskets of flowers on the balconies and the staircases of the grandstand, and immediately afterward stored away in their box again), and finally Corinne standing up casually, moving calmly – her vaporous and indecent red dress swaying, swirling around her legs – towards the grandstand . . .

But there was no grandstand, no elegant public to look at us: I could still see them silhouetted ahead of us (Quixotic shapes diminished by the light that gnawed, corroded the outlines), ineffaceable against the blinding sunlight, their black shadows sliding beside them on the road like their faithful doubles, now foreshortened, hunched or rather telescoped, dwarfed and de-formed, now stretched, spindly and distended, repeating in miniature and symmetrically the movements of their vertical doubles to which they appeared to be joined by invisible links: four points – the four hoofs – separating and rejoining in alterna-tion (exactly like a drop of water separating itself from a roof or rather dividing, part of itself still attached to the edge of the

gutter (the phenomenon occurring as follows: the drop stretching, becoming pear-shaped under its own weight, distorting
itself, then pinching itself in two, the lower – larger – portion
separating, falling, the upper part apparently moving upward,
retracting as though sucked towards the top immediately after
the break, then immediately swelling again with a new deposit,
a second later what seemed to be the same drop hanging, swelling again, still in the same place, and this continuing endlessly,
like an animated crystal ball moving up and down at the end
of a rubber string), and, in the same way, the foot and the
shadow of the foot separating and rejoining, ceaselessly brought
back to each other, the shadow retracting into itself like the
arm of a squid and the hoof rising, the foot describing a natural
rounded curve while beneath and slightly behind it the shadow
retreats only a trifle, foreshortened, and then returns to join
the hoof – and because of the oblique slant of the sun's rays,
the speed with which the shadow returns to its goal increasing,
so that, starting slowly, it seems to rush at the end like an arrow
to the point of contact, of juncture) as though by a process of
osmosis, the double movement multiplied by four, the four
hoofs and the four telescoped shadows separating and rejoining in a kind of motionless oscillation, a monotonous trampling,
the dusty ground the cobble-stones or grass running underneath
like an ink-blot spreading and shrinking, leaving no trace on the
rubbish, the dead, the scar, the stain, the wake of wreckage
war leaves behind it, and that must have been where I saw it
for the first time, a little before or a little after we stopped to
drink, discovering it, staring at it through that kind of half-
sleep, that kind of brownish mud in which I was somehow
caught, and maybe because we had to make a detour to avoid
it, and actually sensing it more than seeing it: I mean (like
everything lying along the road: the trucks, the cars, the suitcases, the corpses) something unexpected, unreal, hybrid, so
that what had been a horse (that is, what you knew, what you
could recognize as having been a horse) was no longer anything

now but a vague heap of limbs, of dead meat, of skin and sticky hair, three-quarters covered with mud – Georges wondering without exactly finding an answer, in other words realizing with that kind of calm or rather deadened astonishment, exhausted and even almost completely atrophied by these last ten days during which he had gradually stopped being surprised, had abandoned once and for all that posture of the mind which consists of seeking a cause or a logical explanation for what you see or for what happens to you: so not wondering how, merely realizing that although it hadn't rained for a long time – at least so far as he knew – the horse or rather what had been a horse was almost completely covered – as if it had been dipped in café-au-lait and then taken out – with a liquid grey-brown mud already half absorbed apparently by the earth, as though the latter had stealthily begun to take back what had come from it, had lived only by its permission and its intermediaries (in other words the hay and the oats the horse had fed on) and was destined to return to it, to dissolve again in it, covering it, then, enveloping it (like those reptiles that begin by coating their prey with saliva or gastric juices before swallowing them) with that liquid mud secreted by it and which already seemed like a seal, a distinctive mark certifying its provenance, before slowly and definitely engulfing it in its breast probably with some kind of sucking noise: yet (though it seemed to have been there for ever, like one of those fossilized animals or plants that had returned to the mineral kingdom, with its two front feet bent into a foetal posture of prayer like the anterior limbs of a praying mantis, its neck stiff, its head stiff and thrown back so that the open jaw revealed the violet blob of the palate) it had been killed not long ago – perhaps only the last time the planes came over? – for the blood was still fresh: a large red spot, bright and clotted, shiny as varnish, spreading over or rather beyond the crust of mud and sticky hair as though it were gushing not from an animal, a mere murdered beast, but from some inexpiable and sacrilegious wound made by men (the way, in legends, water or wine springs out of the rock or gushes from a mountain struck with a rod) in the clayey flank of the earth; Georges looking at it while he mechanically made his horse describe a wide half-circle to avoid it (the horse obeying docilely without shying or hurrying or forcing its rider to hold it in, Georges thinking of the agitation, the kind of mysterious terror that gripped the horses when, leaving for exercise, they happened to follow the wall of the knacker's yard at the end of the field of manoeuvres, and then the whinnying, the rattling of bits, the swearing of the men clinging to the reins, thinking: 'And there it was only the smell. But now even the sight of one of their kind dead doesn't mean anything to them, and probably they'd even walk over it, just because it would save three steps,' thinking: 'And I would too . . .' He saw it slowly pivot beneath him, as if he had set it on a turntable (first showing its inner surface, the head thrown back, fixed, the neck stiff, then gradually, the bent feet coming in between, concealing the head, then the nearest flank, the wound, then the hind legs stretched out, pressed together as if they had been tied that way, the head reappearing then, everything else behind it seen in perspective, the outlines continually changing, in other words that kind of simultaneous destruction and reconstruction of lines and volumes (the bulges gradually collapsing while other protuberances seem to appear, rising then sinking and vanishing in their turn) as the angle of vision shifts, at the same time that the constellation all round it seems to move – and at first he saw only vague blurs – consisting of all kinds of objects (according also to the angle, the distances between them diminishing or increasing) scattered in confusion around the horse (probably the load of the cart it had been pulling but there was no cart in sight: maybe the people had harnessed themselves to it and had gone on that way?), Georges wondering how the war spread (then he saw the split suitcase spilling out like guts, intestines of cloth) that unimaginable quantity of rags, most often black and white (yet there was a faded pink one flung or hung on the hawthorn hedge, as if it had been put there to dry), as if what people regarded as most precious was rags, tatters, torn sheets scattered like ribbons, like lint over the green face of the earth . . .

Then he stopped wondering anything at all, and at the same time stopped seeing although he made himself keep his eyes open and sit as straight as possible on his saddle while the kind of dark slime in which he seemed to be moving grew still thicker, and it was completely dark and all he could make out now was the sound, the monotonous and multiple hammering of the hoofs on the road echoing, increasing (hundreds, thousands of hoofs now) until (like the pattering of the rain) it effaced, destroyed itself, engendering by its continuity, its uniformity, like a kind of silence to the second power, something majestic, something monumental: the progress of time itself, that is, invisible immaterial with neither beginning nor end nor point of reference and at the heart of which he had the sensation of remaining frozen, stiff on his horse that was also invisible in the darkness among the phantoms of cavalrymen whose invisible and tall figures slipped by horizontally swaying or rather slouching faintly as the horses jolted so that the squadron the whole regiment seemed to advance without progression, like those pantomimists whose legs imitate the movement of walking while behind them a trembling canvas backdrop unrolls on which are painted houses trees clouds, with this difference that here the canvas backdrop was only the night, blackness, and at one point the rain began falling, it too monotonous, infinite and black, and not falling but like the night itself uniting in its depths men and horses, adding mingling its imperceptible patter to that enormous patient and dangerous murmur of thousands of horses on the roads, like the nibbling sound thousands of insects would make gnawing away the world (besides, don't the horses, the old army horses, the ancient and immemorial hacks that walk through the rain at night along the roads, shaking their heavy heads, don't they have something crustacean, the stiffness of shellfish about them, that vaguely ridiculous vaguely frightening look of grasshoppers with their stiff legs their projecting bones their ringed flanks suggesting the image of some heraldic beast made not of flesh and muscles but instead like – animal and armour united, combined – those old rickety carriages with metal sides and rusty fittings, clattering, mended with a few pieces of wire, threatening to fall to pieces at any moment?) a murmur which in Georges's mind had finally become identified with the very notion of war, the monotonous trampling that filled the night like a clatter of bones, the black air harsh as metal against their faces, so that he seemed to feel (remembering those accounts of polar expeditions where the skin was described sticking to frozen iron) the cold solidified shadows sticking to his flesh, as if the air and time itself were only a single, solid mass of chilly steel (like those dead worlds extinct for billions of years and covered with ice) in whose density they were caught, immobilized for ever, their old walking horsemeat beneath them, their spurs, their sabres, their steel weapons: everything standing and intact, like the day when he would wake and discover them through the transparent, glaucous thickness appearing like an army on the march surprised by a cataclysm and which a slow invisibly advancing glacier would restore, would spit out a hundred or two hundred thousand years from now pell-mell with all the old lansquenets, reiters and cuirassiers of long ago tumbling down breaking in a faint tinkle of glass . . .

'Unless it all begins rotting and stinking right away,' he thought. 'Like those mastodons . . . ' Then he was wide awake (probably because of the horse's change of gait, that is, although it was still walking, a new jolt in the movement, forcing his body towards the pommel, which meant that the road had begun to slope down): but it was still as dark as ever, and even by squinting as hard as he could he could see nothing, thinking (at the sound of the hoofs that was different now, hollower and, for a moment, the sensation of a silence that was different too, of a different darkness, not wetter or cooler – for the same rain was still falling – but somehow liquid and moving beneath them) that they must have gone over a bridge; then under the hoofs the ground sounded hard and full again and the road began to slope up.

Where his riding-breeches rubbed against the saddle, between his knee and the saddlebags full of oats, the patient thread of water that seeped in had completely soaked the cloth and he could feel against his skin the cold of the wet stuff, and no doubt the road sloped up in zigzags for now the monotonous patter came from all sides: no longer only from ahead and behind but on the right, overhead, the left, below, and with his eyes wide open in the darkness, almost unconscious now (the stirrups kicked off, leaning over the pommel, his legs around the saddlebags to relieve his knees, letting himself bob up and down like a bundle) he thought he heard all the horses, the men, the carts tramping or rolling blindly in this same darkness, this same ink, without knowing where or why, the old and everlasting world itself trembling stirring and echoing in the shadows like a hollow ball of bronze with a catastrophic noise of clattering metal, thinking of his father sitting in the summerhouse with the different coloured glass in the windows at the end of the row of oaks where he used to spend his afternoons working, covering with his fine crossed-out and rewritten handwriting the eternal sheets of paper he carried around with him from one place to the other in an old dog-eared briefcase like a sort of inseparable complement of himself, a supplementary organ doubtless invented to remedy the inadequacies of the others (the muscles, the bones crushed under the monstrous weight of fat and distended flesh, of matter that had become unsuited to satisfy its own needs by itself so that it seemed to have invented, secreted like a kind of replacement by-product, an artificial sixth sense, an omnipotent prosthesis functioning by means of ink and wood pulp); but that evening, the morning newspapers still strewn messily on the rattan table on top of the briefcase, the precious papers which he had brought as on any other day but which were still in the same place where he had put them down when he came in, early in the afternoon, the newspapers in disorder and crumpled from having been read and reread and in the dimness of the summerhouse still keeping the light of the summer twilight through which the peaceful panting of the tractor reached them, the farmer almost through mowing the big field, the sound of the motor choking, struggling as it climbed up the hillside, furious, drowning out their voices, then, at the top, suddenly slackening, almost disappearing as it turned and passed behind the bamboo grove, came back down the slope, turned again following the base of the hill, then rushed forward again, the motor apparently bracing itself to attack the slope, and then Georges knew that he would see it gradually appear, rising, hoisting itself up with that irresistible slowness of everything which in whatever degree of immediacy and of whatever species – men, beasts, machines – has to do with the earth, the farmer's motionless body imperceptibly shaken by the vibrations gradually rising in the twilight against the background of the hills, passing above them, standing out at last, dark, against the pale sky, and his father in the rattan armchair that creaked under his weight at each of his movements, his eyes lost in the void behind the useless glasses where Georges could see the tiny figure silhouetted against the setting sun reflected twice as it crossed (or rather slowly slipped across) the convex surface of the glass undergoing the successive phases of distortion due to the curve of the lens – first drawn out lengthwise, then flattening, then extending lengthwise, threadlike again, as it gradually pivoted and disappeared – so that while he was listening to the old man's exhausted voice in the dimness he seemed to see the invincible image of the farmer not merely cross each of the two crescents of sky from one side to the other but (like those characters sitting on a merry-go-round) appear, grow larger, come closer, and diminish again as if it were following, eternal, quivering and imperturbable, the round and shining surface of the globe . . .

And his father still talking, as if to himself, talking about

what was his name that philosopher who said man knew only
two ways of taking what belongs to others, war and commerce,
and that he generally chose war first because it seemed easier
and quicker and then, but only after having discovered the
disadvantages and the dangers of the former, the latter, in other
words commerce which was a no less dishonest and brutal way
but more comfortable, and that moreover every nation had
necessarily passed through these two phases and had each in
its turn put Europe to fire and sword before being transformed
into incorporated joint-stock companies of commercial travellers
like the English but that war and commerce had always been –
one as much as the other – merely the expression of their rapacity
and that rapacity itself the consequence of the ancestral terror
of hunger and death, which meant that killing robbing pillaging
and selling were actually only one and the same thing a simple
need the need to reassure oneself, like children whistling or
singing loud to keep their courage up crossing through woods
at night, which explained why singing in chorus was also and
just as important a part of the military manual as handling firearms or target practice because nothing is worse than silence
when, and then Georges furious saying: 'Yes, that's it!', and
his father still staring blindly at the clump of aspens quivering
faintly in the twilight, the scarf of mist gradually rising from
the bottom of the valley, drowning the poplars, the hills darken-
ing, and saying: 'What's the matter with you?' and he: 'Nothing
nothing's the matter with me I just don't want to go on putting
words together and more words and still more words. Don't
you ever get tired of it yourself?' and his father: 'Of what?'
and he: 'Of making speeches Of wasting your time lecturing . . .'
then stopping, remembering he was leaving the next day, con-
trolling himself, his father looking at him now, silent, then
looking away (the tractor had finished now, passed noisily
behind the summerhouse, the farmer perched on the high seat,
the bright patch of his shirt alone visible in the deep shadows
under the trees, sliding, attached to nothing, ghostlike, moving

away, disappearing at the corner of the barn, the noise of the motor stopping soon afterwards, the silence flowing back then); he could no longer make out the old man's face, only a vague mask hanging over the enormous and confused mass collapsed in the chair, thinking: 'But he's suffering and trying to hide it to keep up his courage too That's why he's talking so much Because all he can manage is that ponderous stubborn and superstitious credulity – or rather faith – in the absolute pre-eminence of knowledge acquired by proxy, of what is written down, of those words which his own father who was only a peasant had never managed to decipher, lending them, charging them with a kind of mysterious magical power . . . ' ; his father's voice heavy with that sadness, that intractable and vacillating obstinacy in order to convince himself if not of the usefulness or the veracity of what it was saying at least of the usefulness of believing in the usefulness of saying it, persisting for itself alone – like a child whistling on his way through a wood in the dark he had said – , Georges still hearing it now, no longer through the dimness of the summerhouse in the stagnant heat of August, of the rotting summer where something was finally going completely bad, already stinking, swelling like a corpse full of worms and finally splitting open, leaving nothing behind but an insignificant residue, the pile of crumpled newspapers which had been illegible for a long time now (not even letters, recognizable signs, not even the headlines: only a blur, a darker shadow on the greyish blur of the paper), but (the voice, the words) rising now in the cold shadows where, invisible, the long line of horses that had apparently been walking for ever extended interminably: as if his father had never stopped talking, Georges catching one of the horses as it passed and leaping on its back as if he had merely got up from his chair, had mounted one of those shadows advancing since the night of time, the old man still talking to an empty chair while he went away, disappeared, the lonely voice continuing, speaking the useless and empty words, struggling step by step against that swarming thing which filled the autumn night, drowned it, submerged it finally beneath its majestic and indifferent trampling.

Or perhaps he had only closed his eyes and opened them immediately afterwards, his horse almost stumbling against the one in front of it, and then waking completely, realizing that the sound of hoofs had stopped now and that the whole column had come to a halt so that all that could be heard was the rain streaming around them, the night still as black, empty, a horse whinnying sometimes, snorting, then the sound of the rain drowning out everything again and a moment later orders shouted at the head of the squadron and then the platoon stirred and stood motionless again after a few yards, someone coming back down the column at a trot, the horse clanking faintly making a distinct metallic tinkle at each stride, and black against black a form rose up out of the nothingness, passed in a muscular rustle of a running animal, of harness and clanking metal, the man's dark body leaning forward against the horse's neck, faceless, helmeted, apocalyptic, like the spectre of war itself rising fully armed from the shadows and returning to them, after which a long while passed until finally the order came to start again and almost at once they made out the first houses, a little darker than the sky.

Then they were in the barn, with that girl holding up the lamp, like an apparition: something like one of those old paintings executed in gravy: brown (or rather blackish) and warm, and, so to speak, not so much the interior of a building as what it would have seemed if they had penetrated (penetrating at the same time into the acrid smell of the animals, the hay), into a kind of organic visceral space, Georges sitting there a little dazed, a little baffled, blinking, his eyelids burning, stupid, numb in his clothes that were stiff and heavy with rain, his stiff boots, his exhaustion, and that thin film of dirt and insomnia interposed between his face and the outer air like an impalpable and crackled layer of ice, so that he seemed to be able to feel at the same time the night's cold – or rather the dawn's – brought in, entering the place with him, still enclosing him (and, he thought, probably keeping him standing up, like a corset, still thinking that he would have to hurry up about unsaddling and lying down before he began to dissolve, to fall apart) and on the other hand that somehow ventral, womblike warmth at the heart of which she was standing, unreal and half naked, still half asleep, her eyes, her lips, all her flesh swollen by that tender languor of sleep, almost naked, her legs bare, her feet in heavy unlaced men's shoes, with some kind of knitted purple shawl that she pulled over her milky flesh, her milky, pure neck emerging from the coarse material in that pool of yellowish lamp light that seemed to flow over her from her raised arm like a phosphorescent layer of paint, until Wack managed to light the lantern and then she blew the lamp out, turned away and went out into the bluish dawn that was like a cataract on a blind eye, her figure silhouetted a moment while she was still in the darkness of the barn, then, once across the doorstep, seeming to vanish, although they continued to stare after her, not walking away but apparently dissolving, melting into what was really more grey than blue and was undoubtedly the day, since after all it had to come, but apparently without any of the powers, the virtues inherent in the day, although a little wall was discernible now on the other side of the road, the trunk of a big walnut tree and behind that the trees of the orchard, but everything flat, without colours or values, as if wall, walnut tree and apple trees (the girl had disappeared now) were somehow fossilized, had left only their imprint on this spongy and uniformly grey matter that now gradually crept into the barn, Blum's face like a grey mask when Georges turned round, like a sheet of paper with two holes torn for the eyes, the mouth grey too, Georges still saying the words he had started to speak or rather hearing his own voice saying them (probably something like: Say did you see that girl, she . . .), then his voice stopping, his lips still moving perhaps in the silence, then they stopping too while he looked at that paper face, and Blum (he had taken

33

off his helmet and now his narrow girl's face seemed still narrower between the unstuck ears, not much bigger than a fist, above the girl's neck coming out of the stiff wet coat collar as though from a carapace, miserable, mournful, feminine, stubborn), saying: 'What girl?', and Georges: 'What . . . What's the matter with you?', Blum's horse still saddled, not even tethered and Blum simply leaning against the wall as if he were afraid of falling, with his rifle still over his shoulder, without even the strength to take off his pack, and Georges saying for the second time: 'What's the matter with you? Are you sick?' and Blum shrugging, moving away from the wall, beginning to unbuckle the saddle girth, and Georges: 'For God's sake leave the horse alone. Go lie down. If I pushed you you'd fall over . . . ', he himself almost asleep on his feet, but Blum did not offer any resistance when he pushed him away: the hair on the horses' coppery rumps was pasted down by the rain, dark, flat and wet under the saddle blanket, giving off a harsh acrid odour, and while he set their two bundles of harness along the wall he still seemed to be seeing her, there where she had been standing a moment before, or rather still seemed to feel her, perceive her like a kind of persistent unreal imprint, stamped not so much on his retina (he had seen her so briefly, so little) as, somehow, on himself: a warm white thing like the milk she had come for at the moment they had arrived, a kind of apparition not lit by that lamp but luminescent, as if her skin were itself the source of the light, as if that interminable night ride had had no other reason, no other purpose than the discovery at its end of this diaphanous flesh modelled in the night's density: not a woman but the very idea, the symbol of all women which is to say . . . (but was he still standing, mechanically undoing straps and buckles or already lying down, sleeping, prone in the pungent hay, while the heavy sleep enveloped him, enshrouded him) . . . summarily sculptured in the tender clay two thighs a belly two breasts the round column of the neck and in the deepest recess as at the centre of those primitive and precise statues that hairy mouth that thing with an animal's name, a term of natural history – mussel sponge valve vulva – suggesting those deep-sea and blind carnivorous organisms still furnished with lips, with hair: the orifice of that matrix the original crucible that he seemed to see in the entrails of the world, like those moulds in which as a child he had stamped out soldiers and cavalrymen nothing but a bit of pulp pressed with his thumb, the innumerable spawn emerging armed and helmeted as in the legend and multiplying swarming spreading over the earth's surface murmuring with the innumerable rumour, the innumerable trampling of armies on the march, the innumerable black and lugubrious horses tossing sadly swaying their heads, following each other filing past endlessly in the monotonous crepitation of hoofs (he didn't sleep, lay perfectly still, and not a barn now, not the heavy and dusty smell of the drying hay, of the exhausted summer, but that impalpable, nostalgic and stubborn exhalation of time itself, of the dead years, and he floating in the shadows, listening to the silence, the night, the peace, the imperceptible breathing of a woman beside him, and after a while he made out the second rectangle of the wardrobe mirror reflecting the dim light from the window – the eternally empty wardrobe of hotel rooms with two or three hangers dangling inside, the wardrobe itself (with its triangular pediment framed by two pineapples) made of that urine-yellow wood with reddish veins which is apparently used only for this kind of furniture doomed never to hold anything except its own dusty void, the dusty coffin of the reflected ghosts of thousands of lovers, thousands of naked, furious and clammy bodies, thousands of embraces absorbed, mingled in the glaucous depths of the cold, unalterable and virginal mirror – , and he remembering: (' . . . Until I realized that it wasn't horses but the rain on the barn roof, opening my eyes then, discovering the light filtering in strips through the interstices between the planks of the wall: it must have been late and yet the light still had that dirty white colour into which she had disappeared which had absorbed her and

somehow sponged her away in the water-soaked or rather
drenched impregnated dawn like a cloth like our clothes smelling
of wet wool the blotter in which we had slept and now holding
us still half-asleep stunned staring into a piece of mirror fastened
over a tin basin full of icy water our faces dirty grey too drawn
sallow unshaved straw in our wild hair the rims of our eyes
red and that astonishment uneasiness repulsion (the kind you
feel when you see a corpse as if the swelling of putrefaction had
already set in had begun its work the day we had put on our
anonymous soldiers' uniforms, putting on at the same time,
like a kind of stigma, this uniform mask of fatigue of disgust
of filth) then I pushed away the mirror, my or rather that ghastly
face swaying spinning as though sucked up by the shadowy
brown depths of the barn vanishing with that lightning-like
rapidity which the slightest change of angle imposes on reflected
images and in its place I saw them at the other end of the stable,
palavering or rather saying nothing I mean exchanging silences
the way other people exchange words I mean a certain kind of
silence which they alone understood and which was undoubtedly
more eloquent to them than any speech, surrounding the horse
lying on its side: three men with peasant faces: three of those
taciturn suspicious close-mouthed types which made up the
larger share of the regiment's fighting force with that painful
expression in their precociously wrinkled faces stamped with
that nostalgia for their fields their solitude their animals for the
black and greedy earth, and I said What is it what's happening?
but they didn't even answer, undoubtedly thinking that it was
no use or that maybe we didn't speak the same language then
I went over and looked for myself for a moment the horse
breathing hard, Iglésia was there too but he didn't seem to have
heard me any more than the others although between us I thought
I hoped that there could at least be a possibility of contact, but
probably being a jockey is also a little like being a peasant
despite the appearances that would lead you to believe that he,
in other words since he had lived in cities or at least in contact

with cities it was understandable to suppose he was after all a little different from a peasant, I mean betting gambling and even somewhat enlightened the way jockeys often are, and having spent his childhood not tending geese or leading the cows to the watering trough but probably playing in the gutter and in the city's streets, but most likely it's not so much the country as the animals the company the contact of animals, for he was almost as close-mouthed as taciturn as uncommunicative as any of them and like them always occupied absorbed (as if he were incapable of remaining idle) in one of those intricate and slow tasks they have the secret of creating for themselves: from where I was (a little behind where he was sitting on an old wheel-barrow and with his back three-quarters to me, his shoulders moving slightly, probably already polishing his harness or de Reixach's, putting kaolin on the buckles and on the reins, that yellow wax of which he seemed to carry round a stockpile with him) I could see his big nose, his head bent as if it were dragged down by the weight of that beak, that artificial and carnival object that seemed to be stuck on to the front of his face like a knife blade, the kind that have probably not been made since the bravos of the Italian Renaissance wrapped in their assassins' capes, leaving only that protruding eagle's beak outside, giving him that terrible and at the same time woebegone expression of a bird suffering from . . . Where had I read that story in Kipling I think that tale or elsewhere, of some animal with a beak too big for it, a siskin, 'Go have your onion pared' he said, or 'you must have noodles up your ass' jockey slang for being lucky but there was no trace of vulgarity in his voice, instead a kind of candour, of naivety, of astonishment, and also of scandalized disapproval like when he had seen the way Blum had saddled his horse and that nevertheless it had not developed blisters after so long a day's ride, his broken hoarse and husky voice strangely mild, exactly the contrary of what anyone would have expected and even humble, with something childlike in it that seemed a paradoxical denial of that bony wrinkled carnival mask not to mention the fact that he was at least fifteen years older than most of us, it was as if he was surrounded by boys only because de Reixach had arranged matters, had probably pulled strings to get him assigned to our regiment so he could keep him as his orderly, and in fact it looked as if they couldn't do without each other, Iglésia needing de Reixach as much as the latter needed him, that arrogant attachment of the master to the dog and the humble one of the dog to his master without the question ever coming up of whether the master is worthy of it or not: merely admitting, recognizing, not discussing the state of things for a second, respecting it as indicated for instance by his manner or rather mania of patiently correcting, with that stubborn and obsequious loyalty, people who mispronounced his name by pronouncing it the way it was written: de Reixach, and he 'Reishak Good God haven't you learned that yet: shac the x like sh and the ch at the end like k God how stupid can you get that makes at least ten times I've explained it to you didn't you ever go to the races dumbbell the name comes up often enough . . . ' Proud of the name, of the colours, of the brilliant silk jacket he wore pink black braces black cap against the billiard green of the turf a livery and yet when de Reixach took that burst of machine-gun fire at point-blank range and when a moment later I proposed going back to see whether he was dead or not, looking at me (as when a little earlier de Reixach had forced that lost soldier to get off the led horse on which he had begged us to let him ride, saying to me a moment later: He was a spy, and I: Who?, and he, shrugging his shoulders: That fellow, and I: A . . . But how could you tell? and he looking at me then with those same bulging eyes that same astounded expression that was gentle but at the same time reproving faintly scandalized and taken aback as if he were trying to understand me, pitying my imbecility apparently as stupefied and shocked as when he heard someone cursing out the officers and consigning, sending to the Devil his de Reixach who now was undoubtedly there – with the Devil – for good), probably trying to penetrate that film that crust I could feel on my face like paraffin, cracking at the wrinkles, opaque, isolating me, consisting of fatigue of sleep of sweat and dust, his own face still stamped with the same incredulous mild and reproving expression, saying: 'See what?', and I: 'If he's dead. After all even like that at point-blank range the sniper might have missed him, might only have wounded him or only killed his horse since the horse fell when we saw him take out his sabre and . . . ', then I stopped talking realizing I was wasting my time, that the question of going back to see didn't even occur to him, not out of cowardice but probably merely wondering why in the name of what (and finding no answer) he should risk his skin to do something he had not been paid or specifically ordered to do, a problem that undoubtedly was beyond him: to clean de Reixach's boots to polish his harness to take care of his horses and make them win that was his work and he performed it with that scrupulous application of which he had given proof during the five years he had ridden for him, and not only his horses they said, also mounting climbing up his, but what didn't they say about him about them . . . '

And trying (Georges) to imagine it: scenes, fugitive spring or summer tableaux, as though glimpsed, always at a distance, through a hole in a hedge or between two bushes: something with lawns of an eternally brilliant green, white fences, and Corinne and he facing each other, he shorter than she, planted there on his short bow legs, with his soft top-boots, his white breeches and that brilliant silk jacket whose colour she had chosen herself and that looked (cut from that same gleaming satiny material out of which women's undergarments – brassières panties suspender belts – are made) like a comic, aggressive and voluptuous disguise: like those deformed dwarfs that used to be dressed up in the colours of queens and princesses, in precious and tender shades, he with his Italian carnival mask, his yellow skin, his bony ascetic face, his long sharp nose, his bulging eyes, his impassive (pensive) and uneasy expression (accentuated by that way of holding his head peculiar to jockeys, the jacket's high collar with a handkerchief knotted underneath, looking like a bandage wrapped round his neck, giving him that curious stiffness, his head thrust forward like someone suffering from an abscess on the neck or from boils), and she facing him (and apparently nothing but a deferential jockey listening patiently to his mistress's orders, mechanically turning the handle of his crop between his hands) in one of those dresses of many-coloured voile transparent against the light or else of that red apparently created to harmonize with the colour of her hair, her body silhouetted within it (the fork of her legs) by the sun's rays and as distinctly outlined as if she were naked, dark red within the vaporous cloud of veils, so that she made you think (but not think, any more than the dog thinks when he hears the bell that releases his reflexes: so not think, instead something like salivate) of something like one of those barley-sugar drops (and syrup, and orgeat, also words for her, for that), of sweets wrapped in bright-coloured cellophane (papers whose crystalline crackle, whose mere colour, whose very substance, with their folds where the paraffin appears in a fine network of crisscrossed lines, already provokes physiological reflexes), Georges able to see their lips moving, but not hear what they said (too far away, hidden behind his hedge, behind time, while he listened (later, when he and Blum had managed to win him over a little) to Iglésia telling them one of his countless stories about horses, for instance the one about that three-year-old suffering from lymphangitis and on which even so he had won several . . . Georges saying: 'But did she . . . ' and Iglésia: 'She came to watch when I administered that revulsive. It was a formula my first boss had given me, but you had to be careful to . . . ', and Georges: 'But when she came did you . . . I mean: did you both . . . ', and Iglésia still answering evasively); besides it didn't matter: he didn't need to know what the mouth was saying, the painted lips moving slightly, nor what the answer was from the heavy cracked, hard lips in the carnival mask, and for the good reason that they were, that they could only be, words of no importance, anodyne, banal (probably talking, he and she, about the revulsive or about the strained tendon, as he told the story with that kind of innocent naivety; and probably that was the truth: in other words not an idyll, an intrigue, verbose, concerted, orderly, starting, developing according to a harmonious and reasonable crescendo interrupted by the indispensable halts and false moves, and a culminating point and after that maybe a levelling off, and after that the obligatory decrescendo again: no, nothing organized, nothing coherent, no words, no preparatory phrases, no declarations or descriptions, only that: those few mute images hardly moving, seen from far away: she giving him his orders in the paddocks, or even he dirty and mired, streaks of earth or yellowish-green grass stains on his breeches, and maybe limping slightly, carrying over one arm his tiny doll's saddle with the stirrups dangling and making a silvery tinkle, walking beside her towards the scales behind the lathered and steaming horse whose bridle was being held by one of those little grooms with dirty hair that was too long, with ragged clothes and a pale delinquent face; or else a sunny morning in front of the stables, and he with his patched everyday breeches and his old cracked boots, and in his shirt sleeves, crouching, soaping and massaging the hocks of a horse, and suddenly, on the wet concrete floor, her shadow, in one of those light-coloured, simple, daytime dresses or even in riding clothes, she wearing boots too, tapping one of her legs with her crop and he still crouching, without turning around, still massaging the damaged tendon until she speaks to him, and standing up then, standing in front of her again, his body leaning forward slightly, his arms soapy to the elbow and, from the movements of their two heads, from the gesture he makes at one point with one of his arms, it is apparent they are talking about the horse, about the tendon, and that is all (except perhaps a suggestive wink exchanged between two grooms, the sly way one of them has of looking at her, one of those sickly ragged and vicious boys you see hanging from the sweating horse's bridle, with their wretched little starved faces, their nasty and woebegone expressions, in an electric blaze of manes muscles and brilliant blankets), and so not much question of love, unless it just happens that love – or rather passion – is what it was: that wordless thing, those impulses, those repulsions, those hatreds, all unformulated – and even unformed – , and then that simple series of actions, words, insignificant scenes, and, at the centre, without preamble or preparation that assault, that urgent swift, fierce grapple, anywhere, maybe in the stable itself, on a bale of straw, her skirts pulled up, with her stockings, her garters, the sudden flash of white skin at the top of her thighs, both of them panting, furious, and doubtless in terror of being surprised, she watching the stable door over his shoulder, her eyes wild, her neck twisted, and around them the ammonia smell of the stable litter and the noises of the horses in their stalls, and immediately afterwards he assuming again that mask of leather and bone, unchanged, impenetrable, sad, taciturn, and passive, and dejected, and servile . . .

That. And on top of that, in filigree so to speak, that insipid and obsessive chatter which, for Georges, had finally become something not inseparable from his mother although nevertheless distinct (like a wave escaping from her, a product she might have secreted), but somehow his mother herself, as if the elements that constituted her (the flaming orange hair, the diamond-encrusted fingers, the too-brilliant dresses she insisted on wearing not despite her age but apparently in direct proportion to it, the number, the brilliance, the violence of the colours increasing along with the years) had comprised only a brilliant and gaudy prop for that voluble and encyclopedic prattle through which, in the middle of stories about servants, dressmakers, hairdressers and innumerable relatives and acquaintances, the de Reixachs – that is, not only Corinne and her husband, but the line, the race, the caste, the dynasty of the de Reixachs – had appeared to him even before he had ever come near one of them, haloed with a kind of supernatural prestige, and inaccessibility all the more intangible because it did not derive merely from the possession of something (like simple wealth) which can be inherited and which, consequently, the (even theoretical) hope or possibility of acquiring largely strips of its prestige, but much more from (that is, in addition to or rather before the wealth, incomparably elevating that wealth) that particle, that title, that blood, which apparently represented for Sabine (Georges's mother) a value all the more glamorous because not only could it not be acquired (since it was in essence constituted by something which no power could give, could replace: antiquity, time) but even because she felt about them an agonizing, intolerable sense of a personal frustration because of the fact that she herself was a de Reixach (unfortunately, on her mother's side): which doubtless accounted for the stubbornness, the agonized and plaintive persistence with which she ceaselessly recalled (this – along with her endemic jealousy, her horror of growing old and household and kitchen matters – comprised the three or four themes round which her mind seemed to gravitate with the monotonous, stubborn and furious insistence of those insects suspended in the twilight, fluttering, endlessly circling around an invisible – and non-existent, save for themselves – epicentre), recalled the indisputable links of consanguinity that bound her to them, links recognized, moreover, as was attested by the presence in her wedding photographs of a de Reixach in the uniform of an officer of the dragoons before the First World War and corroborated in addition by the possession of the family mansion which, in the absence of the name and the title, she had inherited following a succession of divisions and legacies whose intricacies she was undoubtedly the only member of the family to decipher, just as she was probably also the only one to know by heart the endless list of past alliances and misalliances, telling in detail how some distant ancestor of de Reixach's had forfeited his rights as a member of the nobility by having betrayed the laws of his caste and 'going into trade', and how some other one whose portrait she pointed to . . . (for she had also inherited the portraits – at least several of them – from a numerous gallery or rather collection of ancestors, or rather of sires, 'Or rather stallions,' Blum said, 'because in a family like that I suppose that's what you should call them isn't it? Doesn't the army have a famous stable near there, a stud farm? Don't you call them Tarbais, all the various kinds . . . ' 'All right,' Georges said, 'stallions then, he . . . ' ' . . . thoroughbreds, half-bloods, stallions, geldings . . . ' 'All right, then,' Georges said, 'but he's a thoroughbred, he . . . ', and Blum: 'It shows. You didn't need to tell me that. Tarbo-Arab crossbreed, no doubt. Or Tarno-Arab. I'd just like to see him once without his boots on,' and Georges: 'Why?', and Blum: 'Just to make sure he doesn't have hoofs instead of feet, just to find out what kind of mare his grandmother was . . . ,' and Georges: 'All right, you win . . . '). And he seemed to see the sheets of notepaper, the yellowed papers Sabine had shown him one day, religiously preserved in one of those shaggy trunks you still find in attics and which he had spent a night looking through, forced to blow his nose every five minutes because of the dust that filled his sinuses (notarized documents in faded ink, marriage contracts, transfers of property, deeds of purchase, wills, royal patents, commissions, Convention decrees, letters with their wax seals broken, bundles of assignats, jewellers' bills, lists of feudal rents, military reports, instructions, baptismal certificates, death certificates, burial certificates: the wake of debris surviving, parchments like fragments of epidermis so that touching them was like touching – a little shrivelled, a little dried, like the speckled hands of old men, light, frail and immaterial, apparently about to fall into ashes when they were touched yet living nevertheless – beyond the years, time suspended, the very skin of dreams, of ambitions, of vanities, of futile and imperishable passions) and among which was a thick notebook with a worn blue cover tied shut by olive-green ribbons, in the pages of which one of the distant ancestors (or sires or stallions as Blum said they should be called) had accumulated a huge mass of poems, philosophic digressions, sketches for tragedies, travel narratives of which he could remember certain titles word for word ('Bouquet sent to an Old Lady who in her youth, without being pretty, had inspired passions'), or certain pages like this one, apparently transcribed from the Italian, judging by the translation of the words in the margin:

morbidezza
softnefs
delicacie
flection

The twenty-eighth Engraving and the three others like it are all equally beautiful and noble and seem to be from the same hand Everything in the Centaurefs is graceful and delicate and all deserves to be considered with an especiall attencion The node

candido
white
of a brilliant
whitenefs

and juncture where the human part ends and the equine part begins is indeed admirable The eye distinguishes the delicacie of the white flesh-tintes in the woman from the clarity of the brilliant fur in the animal of a light chestnut colour but one is

attegiamento
gesture
attitude

then confused in attempting to determine the confines The attitude of the left hand with which she is touching the strings of the lyre is agreeable as is that with which she appears to be striking a porcion

carnagione
carnacion
flesh-tinte

of the cymbal she holds in her right hand against the other porcion which the paynter by a truly noble idea of paynting (*these two words crossed out*)

ottimo
very fine

and pittoresque has placed in the right hand of the young man who is embraycing her close while pafsing under this woman's right arm his own left hand which emerges from under her shoulder The

otremodo
otherwise

young man's gown is violet and the habit hanging from the arm of the Centaurefs is yellow: it is suitable to remark as well the coifure, the bracellets

controverfia
dispute

and the Collar nottapoi l'attenza che hann o i centauri con Bacco equilimente, et con Venere . . .

Georges thinking: 'Yes, only a horse could have written that,' repeating: 'All right. Fine. Stallions,' thinking of all those enigmatic dead men, frozen and solemn in their gilded frames, staring at their descendants with a reflective, distant stare, and among which featured prominently that portrait which all during his childhood he had looked at with a kind of uneasiness, timidity, because he (that distant progenitor, sire) had in his forehead a red hole from which the blood ran down in a long undulating rivulet starting at the temple, following the curve of the cheek and dripping on to the lapel of the royal-blue hunting coat as if – to illustrate, perpetuate the stormy legend with which the character was surrounded – he had been portrayed bloodstained by the shot which ended his days, standing there, impassive, equine and decorous at the heart of a permanent aura of mystery and violent death (like others – the powdered marquis, the corpulent and bedizened generals of the Empire, the moire-ribboned wives – in a halo of fatuity, ambition, vainglory or futility) which had somehow forewarned Georges long before he had heard Sabine tell (undoubtedly impelled by the same ambiguous necessity which also made her emphasize the merchant's forfeiture, in other words animated by contradictory sentiments, probably uncertain herself if in narrating these scandalous, or ridiculous, or ignominious, or Cornelian stories she wanted to deprecate that nobility, that title she had not inherited, or on the contrary give it still more lustre, so as to further gorge her pride with the consanguinity and the glamour reflected from it) how that de Reixach had so to speak forfeited his noble status during the famous night of August fourth, how he had later held a seat in the Convention, voted for the king's death, then, probably because of his military learning, been assigned to the armies to get himself beaten at last by the Spanish and then, disavowing himself a second time, had blown his brains out with a pistol (and not a rifle as the hunting costume in which he had had himself painted, the weapon he was carelessly holding in the crook of his elbow had made the child imagine, just as the bloody streak that ran down his forehead in the portrait was actually only the reddish-brown preparation of the canvas revealed by a long crack in the paint's surface), standing beside the mantelpiece of the room that had now become Sabine's bedroom and where, for a long time, Georges had not been able to keep from instinctively glancing round the walls or at the ceiling for the trace of the enormous lead bullet that had shot away half the head.

Presenting themselves this way then, through a woman's exasperating prattle, and without Georges's even having to meet them, the de Reixachs, the de Reixach family, then de Reixach himself, alone, with that cohort of ancestors crowding behind him, the ghosts surrounded by legends, whispered rumours, after-dinner stories, pistol shots, notarized documents and clanking spurs that (the ghosts) melted into each other, superimposed in the smoky and shadowy depths of the old cracked paintings, then the couple, de Reixach and his wife, the girl twenty years younger than himself whom he had married four years before in a murmur of scandal and whispering over teacups, provoking that explosion of outrage, of uterine indignation, of jealousy and lubricity that comprises the inevitable accompaniment to this kind of event: haloed then (the middle-aged man, wry, dry, straight – and even stiff – , impenetrable, and the girl of eighteen in her brilliant shameless gowns with that hair, that body, that skin that seemed to be made of the same precious, almost unreal and also almost as untouchable materials as those – silks, perfumes – with which she was covered, he in his red cavalryman's jacket (she had made him resign his commission), at the annual horse show, or driving by, inaccessible, in that big black motor-car almost as big and impressive as a hearse (which, just as she had forced him to leave the army, she had forced him to buy instead of the anonymous ordinary car he had used till then), or again she alone at the wheel of the racing car he had given her (but that didn't last, probably bored her right away), and both of them as inaccessible, as unreal as if they already belonged to their (at least to his) collections of legendary sires immobilized for eternity in the tarnished gold frames), haloed then . . .

'But you don't even know her!' Blum said. 'You told me

they were never there, always in Paris or Deauville or Cannes, you told me you only saw her once, or rather glimpsed her between a horse's rump and one of those men dressed like a porter in a Viennese operetta, with a frock-coat, a grey hat and a monocle screwed into his eye, and an old general's moustache . . . And that's all you ever saw of her, you . . . ' Blum too had that blank half-asleep, half-dead face: he stopped talking and shrugged his shoulders. It had started raining again, or rather the landscape, the road, the orchard had begun to melt again, silently, slowly, decomposing, dissolving into a fine dust of water that slipped past without a sound, diluting the trees, the houses, as though behind a sheet of glass, and now Georges and Blum were standing on the doorstep of the barn, under the overhanging eaves, watching de Reixach dealing with a heated group of gesticulating men, the voices mingling in a kind of confused, incoherent chorus, a Babelesque wrangling, as though under the weight of a curse, a parody of that language which, with the inflexible perfidy of things created or enslaved by man, turn against him and take revenge all the more treacherously and effectively in that they seem to fulfil their function so docilely: a major obstacle, then, to any communication, any comprehension, the voices rising as if (the mere modulation of sounds revealing itself as impotent) their only hope was in their strength, swelling until they became shouts, struggling to dominate, to drown each other out . . . Then suddenly they all broke off at the same time, yielding to one among them that was vehement, declamatory, and then that one stopped too and they could hear de Reixach's alone, almost a murmur, speaking slowly, calmly, his pale face (rage or rather irritation or merely boredom expressed – as in his neutral, leaden, too-deep voice – by a lowering in tone, a negative alteration, his dull skin even paler – unless the pallor, the almost imperceptible voice were merely exhaustion, although he was still standing as stiff, as straight in his already gleaming boots which Iglésia had nevertheless not yet been able to polish that morning, which he must have polished himself, meticulous, impassive, with the same care he had given to shaving, to brushing his hair and tying his necktie, as if he were not in some forgotten village of the Ardennes, as if there were no war, as if he had not spent – he too – the whole night on horseback and in the rain), his pale face, then, not even pink with cold or animation, contrasting with the deep red, almost violet complexion of the short dark man standing in front of him on the doorstep of the house, wearing a leather-visored cap, patched rubber boots, and threateningly brandishing a hunting rifle, and when he took a step towards the door, Georges and Blum could see that he limped, Georges saying: 'But I saw enough of her to know she's like milk. That lamp was enough, for God's sake: it was just like cream, like spilt milk . . . ', and Blum: 'What?', and Georges: 'You weren't so bad off you didn't see her, were you? Even a dead man . . . All you could have wanted to do was begin crawling and licking, you . . . ', and just then the short dark man cried out: 'Don't take another step or I'll shoot!', and de Reixach: 'All right now, come on,' and the man: 'Captain: if he makes a move I'll shoot,' and de Reixach again: 'All right.' He stepped aside and found himself between the two men again, the one with the rifle and the other one who was standing behind his back now with the two officers and who seemed, in almost every detail, the exact replica of the lame man, wearing black, patched rubber boots too, not in overalls of course, but a shapeless grey uniform with something that looked like a necktie keeping his shirt collar closed, and a soft felt hat instead of a helmet, and holding an umbrella, a peasant but still with something different about him, and once he glanced up, quickly, and Georges looked too at what he had glanced at over the captain's head but probably not quickly enough for at one of the upstairs windows of the house he had only time to see the curtain falling back, one of those cheap net curtains the kind they sell in country fairs and whose pattern showed a peacock with a long flowing tail framed in a lozenge, the peacock's tail swaying once or twice, then hanging motionless while below (but Georges was no longer looking, merely staring greedily at the greyish-white netting motionless now where the ornamental and pretentious bird remained behind the impalpable drizzle that kept falling, silent, patient, eternal) the uproar, the cacophony, the imbroglio of voices rose again, vehement, incoherent, impassioned: ' . . . as sure as I'm standing here I'll shoot Come in if you want to Captain but that man will not walk through this door or I'll shoot I – Look my friend, Monsieur the assessor here only wants to make sure that room – And first of all why doesn't he stay home he's got a big house full of empty rooms he – Look I can't go into it now we – I can take your officers to the room myself I'm not refusing to take them in only there are some people in this village who have three or four rooms without a soul in them so I'd like to know why he And stop laughing you or I'll shoot you hear I'll shoot you right where you're standing you hear God damn it . . . ', putting the gun to his shoulder, aiming, the other man quickly slipping behind the two officers, but even then the peacock didn't move nor anything else, the housefront absolutely motionless, the whole house deathlike, except for a kind of rhythmic, monotonous, tragic moaning that rose inside, and certainly it was a woman's throat it came out of but not Hers: an old woman, and although they hadn't seen her they could imagine her sitting in an armchair, blind, black and stiff, groaning, swaying her body back and forth. He struggled but they managed to control him. 'All right,' de Reixach said, making an effort to keep his voice down. Or perhaps it was no effort at all, he merely stood outside, still at that remove (not height: there was nothing arrogant, nothing scornful: merely distant or rather absent), saying: 'Put down that gun, that's how accidents happen,' and the man: 'Accidents? You call that an accident? A bastard who waits till her husband isn't home and now in broad daylight he wants to come into the very house he . . . All right!' he shrieked, 'Get out of here!', and the other man: 'Captain! You're my witness that he . . . ' 'All right,' de Reixach said. 'Come on.' 'You're all witnesses that he . . . ' 'All right, come on,' de Reixach said. 'He's perfectly willing to take them in, he said so.'

But even though Georges waited for another long moment, she didn't reappear at the window, but only the peacock, greyish-white, motionless, and still audible from inside despite the door that was closed now, the old woman's voice that continued to raise its rhythmic, monotonous lamentation like an emphatic, endless declamation, like those mourners of antiquity, as if everything (those cries, that violence, that incomprehensible and uncontrollable explosion of rage, of passion) were not happening in the age of rifles, of rubber boots and mass-produced uniforms, but far back in time, or in any time, or outside of time, the rain still falling and perhaps having always fallen, the walnut trees the orchard endlessly dripping: to be seen it had to pass in front of something dark or a shadow, the edge of a roof, the quick drops making imperceptible stripes like hyphens over the dim depths criss-crossing grey, sometimes a larger drop bent a blade of grass that immediately rose again with a sudden shock the motionless meadow shaken here and there with tiny quivers; the houses and barns suggesting the three sides of an irregular rectangle round a pond and a kind of stone trough where Georges tried to wash a little laundry in the icy water his frozen fingers rubbing the soap against the worn rim where the wet material caught, the same grey as the sky with pockets of air imprisoned underneath making lighter grey blisters, as the soap went over them it pressed them out and they accum-ulated in parallel and sinuous folds, a bluish cloud spreading in the water when he rinsed them, bluish bubbles crowding, cluster-ing, drifting a little, meandering slowly, sliding across the black mud trampled by the horses where the water flowed from one hoofprint to the other, but when he was done the laundry was almost as grey as before, and Blum said: 'Why didn't you ask her to wash it for you? Were you afraid her husband would shoot you in the back?' 'That's not her husband,' Wack said, and then stopped as though he regretted having spoken, again lowering his taciturn, hostile Alsatian peasant's face towards the bucket in which he was rubbing his bit and spurs with wet sand, and Georges: 'How do you know?', and Wack still polishing his spurs without answering, Georges repeating: 'How do you know? What do you know about it?', Wack still not lifting his head, his face bent – hidden – over the bucket, at last saying reluctantly, furiously: 'I just know!', and Martin sniggering, saying: 'He helped them dig up their potatoes. The farm-hand told him: that's only her brother,' and Blum: 'And where's the husband? Walking round town?', and Wack turning his whole body round to answer: 'Walking round the way you are, you bastard, with a helmet on his head!', and Blum: 'You forgot to call me a filthy Jew. I'm not a bastard: I'm a Jew. You should remember that,' and Georges: 'All right now!', and Blum: 'Forget it. If you knew how much you . . . ', and Georges: 'So that's how it was, you helped them dig up their potatoes and the farm-hand told you the whole story?', their voices distinct against or rather through the grey continuous patient rain (like the manifold and secret nibbling of invisible insects gradually devouring the houses, the trees, the earth itself) the stirrups and the bits clanking sometimes: merely soldiers their voices tired monotonous too rising one after the other overlapping conflicting but the way soldiers talk, in other words as if they were sleeping or eating with that kind of patience, of passivity, of boredom as if they were forced to invent artificial reasons for arguing or merely reasons for talking, the barn still smelled of wet sheets of hay each time they opened their mouths a tiny puff of grey mist came out and almost immediately afterwards disappeared.

but why was he so eager to shoot someone

maybe because of the war, everyone

the hell everyone

but he limps they didn't want him

god damn lucky what wouldn't I give to limp too and not

probably he doesn't see it that way he seems to like guns to want to use them maybe he'd give anything to
and the other one
what other one
the one with the umbrella
you mean the mayor's assessor
don't tell me that in a dump with four houses like this there's a mayor and an assessor why not a bishop too
I didn't see any church
so she can't go to confession
maybe she
no curé no chemist no running water That makes things damn near permanent No wonder he watches over her with a rifle
what the hell kind of bull is that
well that woke Wack up I thought you were deaf I thought you didn't want to talk to a filthy Jew like me
all right
I don't give a damn see if I give a damn he can call me whatever he
for god's sake shut up Now what's the matter with that nag
They looked at the horse still lying on its side at the back of the stable: someone had thrown a blanket over it and only its stiff limbs stuck out, its terrible long neck at the end of which hung the head it didn't even have the strength to raise now, bony, too big, with its cheekbones, its wet hair, its long yellow teeth the rolled-back lips revealed. Only the eye still looked alive, enormous, melancholy, and inside it, on the shiny convex surface, they could see themselves, their silhouettes distorted like parentheses, outlined against the pale background of the open door like a kind of faintly bluish mist, like a veil, a film that was already forming apparently, fogging over the gentle cyclopean stare, accusing and moist.
the vet came he took blood
I know what's wrong

Wack always knows everything he
oh cut it
it's Martin he's always hitting her on the head with his helmet
during the halts he hit her all night long I saw him I'll bet he
broke something
no other way to keep her from jogging
you can't treat a horse that way
you can't treat a man that way either Sixty kilometres without stopping and bobbing up and down like a ball it's enough
to drive anyone crazy
still you can do something besides knocking your horse out
with your helmet Iglésia said
I'm no jockey I'm a trainer
since you're so damn smart and you like horses so much why
didn't you switch with him all you had to do was get on he would
have been glad to hand her over to you you know he
but what can the poor thing do if she jogs
nothing but Martin can't help it either and it's no fun for
him so all you had to do was offer to switch with him
I'm not switching horses I ride the horse I've been given
that's his horse
so shut your mouth
oh listen
you'd better shut your mouth
I'm no tell-tale
good for you
if you think you can scare me you've got another think
coming I may not have as much education as you but you don't
scare me all I have to do is give you a push and you'll fall
down
try it once
listen you can't even stand up you're half dead you wouldn't
only be
They went on arguing, their voices not even snarling, with
something plaintive instead, stamped with that kind of apathy

appropriate to peasants and to soldiers, and somehow impersonal, like their stiff uniforms still keeping (it was barely autumn, the autumn that had followed the last summer of peace, the dazzling and corrupted summer that they seemed to see now, already distant, like those old newsreels, badly shot and over-exposed, in which tight-laced high-booted ghosts gesticulated jerkily as if they had been moved not by their brutal old-soldiers' or idiots' brains but by some inexorable machinery that forced them to move about, make speeches, threaten and parade, feverishly carried by a blinding agitation of banners and faces that seemed both to engender and to transport them, as if the crowds possessed a kind of gift, an infallible instinct that made them distinguish and push forward by a kind of auto-selection – or expulsion, or rather defecation – the eternal idiot who will brandish the placard and whom they will follow in that kind of ecstasy and fascination into which, like children, the sight of their own excrement plunges them), their uniforms, then, still keeping the creases of newness and in which they had so to speak been stuffed: not the old outfits already worn, used in manoeuvres by generations of recruits, boiled in disinfectant every year and only good, probably for learning how to handle firearms, like those worn disguises, rented or bought on credit at a second-hand clothes-dealer's and handed out to the actors during rehearsals along with the tin swords and the cap-pistols, but (the outfits, the equipment they now had on their backs) brand new, virginal: everything (cloth, leather, steel) of top quality, like those undefiled sheets that families piously keep in reserve to wrap the dead in, as if the society (or the state of things, or fate, or the economic situation – since it seems that such matters are merely the consequence of economic laws) that was preparing to slaughter them had covered them (like those youths primitive tribes sacrificed to their gods) with the best of everything it had in the way of material and weapons, spending heedlessly, staging a barbarous display for what would one day be nothing more than pieces of twisted, rusted scrap and a few rags too big for the skeletons they fluttered over (dead or alive), and Georges lying now in the opaque and stinking darkness of the cattle car, thinking: 'But has it happened already? A business of bones counted, enumerated . . . ', thinking: 'Yes. That's it: they've numbered my bones . . . Anyhow, something like that.'

He tried to pull his leg out from under the body lying on top of it. He no longer felt it except as something inert, something that no longer really was a part of himself, and yet painfully clung to the inside of his hip like a beak, a bone beak. A series of bones strangely hooked together and connected to each other, a series of old clattering and grinding utensils, that's what a skeleton was, he thought, wide awake now (probably because the train had stopped – but for how long?), hearing them jostling each other and fighting in the corner where the air hole was, the narrow horizontal rectangle against which their skulls were outlined: blobs of fluid ink blurring and separating, and beyond which he could see the bits of the unalterable night sky of May, the distant and unalterable stars, stagnant, motionless, virginal, appearing and disappearing in the slits that opened and closed again between the heads, like an icy, crystalline and inviolable surface over which could slide without leaving either trace or taint that blackish, viscous matter, noisy and moist from which emanated the voices now complaining and furious in earnest, that is fighting now over real, important things like for instance a little air (the men further inside abusing the ones whose heads blocked the air hole) or a little water (those who were at the air hole trying to get the guard outside to fill their canteens for them), and finally Georges gave up trying to extract, disengage what he knew to be his leg from the inextricable swarm of limbs that weighed it down, lying there in the dark, trying to force into his lungs the air that was so thick and polluted that it seemed not to carry the odour, the suffocating mustiness of bodies, but to sweat and stink itself, and not transparent, impalpable as air usually is, but opaque, black, so that he seemed to be trying to breathe something like ink and which was nothing but the very substance from which the moving blobs were also made that filled the frame of the air hole and with which he had to try to fill his lungs (heads and tiny fragments of sky) as best he could in the hope of benefiting at the same time from one of the tiny metallic rays that sank in like sparkling, salutary and sudden sword thrusts springing from the stars, and starting all over again.

So that all he could do was resign himself to this so to speak filtering function, thinking: 'After all, I've read somewhere that prisoners drank their own urine . . . ', lying motionless in the dark feeling the black sweat penetrating his lungs and at the same time streaming over him, while he still seemed to see that stiff mannequin's torso, impassive and bony, advancing with a faint sway (that is the hips following the horse's movements, the upper part of the body – the shoulders, the head – as straight, as motionless as if he had been slid horizontally forward on a wire) against the luminous background of the war, the glaring sun that made the broken windows gleam, the thousands of brilliant triangular splinters strewing the endless empty street like a carpet winding slowly between the brick housefronts with their empty broken windows in the dazzling silence majestically punctuated by the slow duel of the two lonely cannons answering each other, the noises of firing (somewhere on his left, in the orchards) and of explosion (the shell falling anywhere on the dead and abandoned city where it demolished a patch of wall in a cloud of filthy dust that settled slowly) alternating, with a kind of brutal, futile and stupid punctuality, while the four cavalrymen still advanced (or rather seemed to sit motionless, like those cinema effects where you see only the upper parts of the characters, actually always at the same distance from the camera, while in front of them the long, winding street – one side in the sun, the other in shadow – seems to unfold, to come to meet them like one of those settings that you can make go past again and again, the (apparently) same patch of wall collapsing several times, the cloud of dust raised by the explosion growing closer, swelling, enlarging, reaching the top of the patch of wall still standing, rising above it, the sun touching its top then, the greyish-black mass topped by a yellow cap that swells, still rising, until the whole cloud disappears to the left of the last cavalryman, another housefront collapsing at the same moment over there, in the part of the street which the right-hand housefronts have just revealed as they turn, the new circling column of dust and debris (which seems to swell, enlarging a little like a snowball but actually drawing its substance from inside itself by a slow movement of spirals unwinding, shoving each other aside, superimposing) growing larger as it comes closer – or as the four cavalrymen draw closer to it – and so on); thinking: 'But even if twice as many had fallen he would still never have deigned to put his horse at a trot. Because it's doubtless not done. Or because he had perhaps already discovered a better solution, definitely solved the problem, made up his mind. Like the other centaur, the other vainglorious imbecile before him, a hundred and fifty years ago, but who at least used his own pistol to . . . But it's only pride, nothing else.' And panting weakly in the darkness, he went on insulting both of them under his breath: the deaf, blind and stiff back that went on advancing ahead of him among the war's smoking ruins, and the other one, facing him, just as motionless, solemn and stiff in his tarnished frame, the way he saw him all during his childhood, with this difference that the blob which spread, vertical and jagged, starting at the temple, ran down over the delicate, almost feminine neck in the opening of the shirt and stained the hunting jacket was no longer the reddish underpainting of the canvas revealed by the flaked paint now, but something dark and sticky flowing slowly, as if, through a hole made in the painting, some kind of thick dark jelly had been pressed against the canvas from behind which slid now, gradually spreading over the smooth surface of the painting, the pink cheeks, the lace, the velvet, while with that paradoxical

impassivity characteristic of martyrs in old paintings, the motionless face went on looking straight ahead with that slightly stupid,
surprised, incredulous and gentle expression people have when
they suffer a violent death, as if at the last minute something
had been revealed to them about which it had never in all their
lives occurred to them to think, in other words undoubtedly
something absolutely contrary to what thought could teach
them, something so astonishing, so . . .

But it was not his intention to philosophize or to tire himself
out trying to think of what thought was incapable of achieving
or learning, for the problem consisted more simply of trying to
get his leg free. Then, even before Blum asked him, he wondered
What time can it be, and even before beginning to answer
What difference does it make, he had already answered himself,
thinking that in any case the time could no longer be of any use
to them now, since they wouldn't get out of that wagon before
it had covered a certain distance, which was not a question of
time for those who controlled its progress, but of railway organ-
ization neither more nor less than if it had been carrying as
return freight empty crates or damaged material, things that in
wartime come after all other priorities: trying then to explain
to Blum that what time it was was merely a piece of information
making it possible to proceed according to the position of one's
shadow and not the means of knowing if the moment had come
(that is, when it was agreed that it was suitable) to eat or sleep,
since, as for sleeping, they could do plenty of that, had nothing
else to do, at least to the degree that several alien limbs, intertwined and superimposed, weren't crushing one of your own,
or at least something that you knew to be one of your limbs
although it had become virtually numb and somehow separated
from yourself, and as for the moment of eating it could easily
be determined – or rather decided – not by the fact of being
hungry as usually happens round noon or seven at night, but
when the critical point was reached where the mind (not the
body, which can endure much more than the mind) can no

longer stand for a minute more the idea – the torment – of possessing something that might be eaten: he groped then in the darkness slowly until he had managed to move from under his head where he was keeping it as a precaution (so that the awareness of the existence of the piece of bread was somehow permanently impressed on his mind) the flabby knapsack from which he removed, almost as if he were handling an explosive charge, what his fingers had identified (from a certain crumbly roughness, an approximately oval and flat shape – too flat) as being what they were looking for and which he made it his duty to evaluate (still by the sense of touch) as exactly as possible in regard to shape and dimensions until he decided he had a sufficient familiarity to begin breaking it into two equal parts by managing (still treating the bread as if it were something like dynamite) to receive its imponderable crumbs as they broke off whose fall he guessed at in his palm by a slight, almost imperceptible tickling and which he finally divided almost exactly in half in each of his hands, incapable too, when this was done, of going further, that is, of finding enough courage, abnegation or generosity to give Blum the piece that he supposed to be the larger, preferring to hold out to him in the dark both hands in search of which the other man held out one of his own, and after that trying then to forget as fast as possible (that is to say, to make his stomach forget, though at the very moment Blum had chosen, something in his stomach had twisted, rebelled, was roaring now with a kind of wild and whimpering fury) that he knew Blum had chosen the better share (that is, the one that must have weighed about five or six grammes more than the other), struggling then to stop thinking, at first, about everything except the crumbs he was slipping now from his palm into his mouth, then the sticky paste he was chewing as slowly as possible still trying to imagine that his mouth and his stomach were Blum's trying to make himself believe it was the sun's fault for disappearing at that moment, although, he decided, he had never really hoped that even with the sun they might have succeeded: 'Because I knew perfectly well that it was impossible that there was no other way out and that finally we would be caught: it all came to nothing yet we tried I tried went on to the end pretending to believe that it could come out right insisting not desperately but somehow hypocritically deceiving myself as if I hoped to succeed in making myself believe that I thought it was possible when I knew the contrary, wandering aimlessly along these lanes between these hedges identical to the one behind which his death had lain in ambush, where for a second I had seen the black gleam of a gun barrel before he fell, collapsed like an unbolted statue swaying to the right, and then we turned round galloped off leaning forward, flattened over the horse's neck to offer less of a target since he was aiming at us now, hearing the pitiful deadly and absurd explosions in the vast sunny countryside like fireworks, a child's popgun, and Iglésia said He got me, but we went on galloping I said Are you sure where, and he In the leg the bastard, I said Can you go on, the insignificant expectorations fading now then stopping completely: still galloping still leading that extra horse beside him he ran his fingers across his thigh then looked at them I looked too there was a little blood on them I said Does it hurt, but he didn't answer still running his fingers across his thigh that I couldn't see and staring at them, probably horses have a special sense because I don't remember having seen the road unless he had, still the fact of the matter was that they turned right still galloping all three together and Iglésia went Oh Ooooooooh . . . oooh laaaaa . . . and they began walking, and all we could hear now was the little birds, the horses breathing heavily, all three snorting I said Well? He looked at his hand again then twisted on his saddle but I couldn't see since he had been hit in the right leg, when he was beside me again he only looked preoccupied and sleepy really stupefied and above all irritated he rummaged in his pocket for a dirty handkerchief when he put it back still with that same dazed and ill-humoured look I said Is it bad? but he didn't answer only

shrugging his shoulders and putting the handkerchief back in
his pocket he looked disappointed as though furious not to be
really wounded furious that the bullet had only grazed him,
our shadows walking beside us to our left now following the
shape of the square-cut hedge: since it was spring the leaves
hadn't grown much and the countryside still looked like a well-
pruned garden, what do you call those bushes, shrubs or rather
conifers grass-plots geometrically shaped gardens à la française
making careful interlocking curves groves and nooks for marquis
and marquises disguised as shepherds and shepherdesses seeking
each other in disguise seeking finding love death disguised too
as a shepherdess in the labyrinth of lanes and then we might
have met him he could have been standing there where the path
turned, leaning against a hedge calm placid and stiff as death
in his blue velvet hunting suit with his powdered hair his rifle
the hole in the middle of his forehead out of which ceaselessly
flowed now like those images or those statues of saints whose
eyes or stigmata begin crying or bleeding once or twice a century on the occasion of great catastrophes earthquakes or rains
of fire, that kind of dark red jelly, as if war, violence, murder
had somehow resuscitated him in order to kill him a second
time as if the pistol bullet fired a century and a half before had
taken all these years to reach its second target to put the final
period to a new disaster . . . '

Then (still lying half asphyxiated in that suffocating darkness)
he really thought he saw him, as out of place, as unexpected
in the green countryside as those funerals you meet occasionally,
advancing through the fields like some sacrilegious and dissolute
masquerade and – like any masquerade – vagely pederastic, probably because (like the solitary old lady, discovering the boots
that stick out beneath the skirt and the thick hair with which
the cheeks are covered now, suddenly realizing with horror as
the soup is served that the elderly serving-woman she hired
that morning is actually a man, realizing then, and irremediably,
that she will be murdered in the night) you notice under the

immaculate surplice the priest's heavy boots and the dirty legs of the choirboy who walks ahead braying the responses without turning back and glancing at the blackberry bushes, the tall copper cross stuck in the leather socket of the belt hanging over his belly (so that he seems to be holding in both hands in a childish, equivocal and coarse gesture some enormous priapic symbol springing from between his thighs, black and topped with a cross) swaying above the corn fields like the mast of a ship adrift, the copper Christ, the heavy silver embroidery of the chasuble sparkling with hard metallic glints in the vaporous air where for a long time after there lingers like a funeral wake a macabre perfume of cellars and vaults: death, then, advancing overland in a heavy ceremonial robe and laces, shod with murderer's boots, and he (the other Reixach, the ancestor) standing there, like those apparitions on a stage, those characters rising from a trap door at the tap of a magician's wand, behind the screen of a smoke flare, as if the explosion of a bomb, a stray shell, had unearthed, exhumed him from the mysterious past in a mortal and stinking cloud not of gunpowder but of incense which as it settled would have gradually revealed him, anachronistically dressed (instead of the ubiquitous earth-coloured overcoat of all dead soldiers) in that aristocratic and supposedly casual quail-hunting outfit in which he had posed for that portrait in which time – deterioration – had afterwards remedied (like a facetious or, better still, a scrupulous corrector) the painter's forgetfulness – or rather his lack of foresight (and in the very way the bullet had been received, that is, by exploding away a piece of the forehead, so that it wasn't a rectification by addition, which would have been the result if a second painter had been assigned to make a later correction, but by also opening a hole in the face – or the layer of pigment imitating that face – so that what appeared was what was underneath), putting there that red and bloody spot like a stain that seemed a tragic denial of all the rest: that mildness – and even langour –, those doelike eyes, that bucolic and familiar carelessness about the clothes, and that rifle, it too like a prop from a masked ball or a cotillion.

For perhaps that virile hunter's outfit – the firearm, the wide red leather strap of a game bag postulating dead animals, something in which were confounded furs and spotted feathers as in a still life with a heap of hares, partridges and pheasants – was there only to provide him with an attitude, a pose as today people have themselves photographed at country fairs sticking their heads in those oval holes that replace the faces of characters (whimsical aviators, clowns, dancers) painted on a canvas backdrop, Georges staring with a kind of fascination at the rather fat, feminine and well-cared-for hand whose index finger, in the confusion of a far-off night, pressed the trigger of the weapon aimed at himself (he had seen it too, had touched it: one of the two long pistols with chased hexagonal barrels lying in opposite directions in the middle of the complicated paraphernalia, bullet moulds, powder horns and other accessories, each one set in its appropriate place hollowed into the moth-eaten billiard-green material inside the mahogany box that was still enthroned on the chest of drawers in the salon, wide open on days when company came, closed the rest of the time for fear of dust, and this: his own hand holding the weapon that was too heavy for his child's arm, cocking the trigger (but for that both hands were necessary, the curved butt pressed between his knees, his thumbs squeezing together to overcome the combined resistance of rust and the spring), setting the barrel against his temple and pressing, his tightened finger whitening under the effort, until the dry, insignificant (the flint had been replaced by a piece of wood wrapped in felt) and mortal click of the trigger came, falling in the room's silence, the same room – which was now the one where his parents slept – , and where nothing had been changed except perhaps the wallpaper and three or four of those objects – vases, frames for photographs, electric lamps – placed or rather introduced here, utilitarian and too new, like noisy and shiny supernumeraries picked up at the employment office to serve an assembly of ghosts: the same lacquered furniture, the same faded striped curtains, the same prints on the walls showing courtly or rural scenes, the same mantelpiece of white marble with pale grey veins against which Reixach had leaned to blow his brains out (they said, that is, Sabine said – or maybe she had invented it, embroidering in order to make the scene more effective – each time she told the story) and near which Georges had often imagined him, sitting there, his legs in muddy, steaming boots extended in a V towards the fire, one of his dogs at his feet, the little chubby and carefully manicured hand emerging from the lace cuff of one of those shirts with puffy pleats, this time holding not a pistol but something (for him, who had been taught only the exclusive and innocent handling of horses and dogs) just as dangerous, explosive (that is, to which the pistol shot had perhaps been only the ineluctable conclusion): a book, perhaps one of the twenty-three volumes that composed the complete works of Rousseau and across the flyleaf of which spread the same paraph, the proud, possessive Carolingian handwriting calligraphing with the goose-quill whose scratching he seemed to hear on the coarse and yellowed paper the invariable formula: *Hic liber* – the H disproportionate, emphatic, in the shape of two parentheses back to back and connected by a wavy line, the tips of the parentheses rolled up into a spiral like the ornaments of those rust-corroded gates that still guard the entrance to parks invaded by brambles – , then underneath: *pertinetadme*, all in one stroke, then, in diminishing characters, the latinized name without any capital letter: *henricum*, then the date, the millesimal: 1783.

Imagining him then, seeing him conscientiously reading one after the other each of the twenty-three volumes of sentimental, idyllic and confused prose, ingurgitating pell-mell the prolix and Genevese lessons in harmony and *solfège*, in education, silliness, effusions and genius, that incendiary chatter of a jack-of-all-trades vagabond, musician, exhibitionist and cry-baby which would ultimately make him press against his temple the

sinister icy mouth of that . . . (and then Blum's voice saying:
'All right! So he found, or rather he found the means of finding
what's called a glorious death. In the family tradition, you say.
Repeating, doing over what a hundred and fifty years before
another de Reixach (who called himself if I heard you correctly
just Reixach since, by an overmeasure of nobility, of stylish-
ness, of elegance, he had dropped that particle his descendants
have subsequently stopped to pick up and hang on to the front
of their name again after having it polished up by an army of
servants – or orderlies – in Restoration liveries – or uniforms),
what another Reixach, then, had already done by choosing to
put a bullet through his head (unless it happened quite clumsily
while he was cleaning his pistol, which happens all the time,
but in that case there would be no story, at least no story sensational enough for your mother to have filled your ears with it
and the ears of her guests, so let's admit, let's concede that's
the way it really happened) because he had so to speak cuckolded
himself, deceived himself: cuckolded then not by a faithless
feminine creature like his remote descendant but somehow by
his own mind, his ideas – or, in their absence, by other people's
ideas – which had played that nasty trick on him as if, lacking
a wife (but didn't you tell me that he had one into the bargain
and that she too . . .), so instead: as if not satisfied with having
a woman to support he had also burdened, encumbered himself
with ideas, with thoughts, which obviously for a gentleman-
farmer from the Tarn, constitutes, as for anyone, a much greater
risk than marriage . . . ', and Georges: 'Of course. Of course.
Of course. But how can you tell? . . . ')

Thinking at the same moment of that detail, that strange thing
that was spoken of only in hushed tones (and Sabine said that
she herself didn't believe it, that it wasn't true, that her grandmother had always told her it was a legend, a piece of slander,
scandal spread by the servants in the pay of political enemies –
the sans-culottes, her grandmother said, forgetting that he
happened to have been on their side, so that if slander had been

spread about him after and concerning the circumstances of his death it could only have been by the royalists, which, in a sense, confirmed at least in part the exactitude of the reports: since the source of these rumours was very likely from the servants, by virtue of the law that men linked to others by servile connections are fiercely loyal – like a sort of justification of their condition – to a strictly hierarchized society, so that if the adherents of the old régime had, as was in fact likely, sought allies against Reixach, they had probably found the best ones among his own servants), that circumstance which, true or false, gave the story a quality of ambiguity, of scandal: something in the style of one of those prints called The Surprised Lover or The Seduction that still decorated the walls of the room: the valet leaping up at the sound of the shot and running in, dressed haphazardly, his wide shirt half hanging outside his breeches pulled on as he jumped out of bed, and perhaps behind him, a servant girl in a night cap and almost naked, one hand in front of her mouth to stifle a scream and the other clumsily holding together the garment that in slipping off her shoulder reveals a breast (and perhaps it is not to stifle a scream that she raises her hand: instead, the fingers spread to shield the flame of a second candle (which explains why she is visible though she is placed in the background, not yet having stepped across the doorstep, still in the shadow of the hallway) which she is trying to protect from the draught caused by the bursting open of the door (the gleam of the flame passing between her fingers, so that it apparently produces in the centre of each the vague shadow of the bones enveloped by the transparent pink of the flesh): holding at the same time in one hand that shift that scarcely covers her breast and the candle she is protecting with the other, so that her young terrified face is lit from below, as though by the footlights of a stage, the shadows reversed, that is, placed not beneath the masses but above them, the parts in darkness being the lower lip, the ridge of the nose, the upper part of the cheeks, the upper eyelid and the forehead over the

67

eyebrows), the valet seen from the back, his right leg forward, half bent (in other words, his whole weight resting on the right leg: not a phase of walking or even of running, but instead the position of a dancer landing after a leap, the attitude eloquently expressing what has just happened: the rush of the body against the door, the straight leg bent again and raised, the last effort, the last impulse given by the left leg, then – at the third or fourth attempt – the door (or rather, the lock) yielding in a screech of nails torn out and wood bursting in splinters, and at that moment the valet's body catapulted, unbalanced, falling back on the bent right leg while he seems to draw his left leg behind him, the latter extended, its thigh, calf and foot in the same line, the heel raised, the foot (bare, for he – the valet – has only had time to pull on his breeches) touching the floor only with the tips of the toes, the right arm raising high the candle which is virtually in the centre of the scene, so that the valet is silhouetted against the light, the part of his body that can be seen – that is, his back – being almost completely in the shadow which the engraving needle indicated by fine cross-hatchings following the modelling of the masses, so that at close range the shapes and particularly his muscular forearm look as though they were wrapped in a kind of netting whose mesh grows finer where the shadow is deeper), all the light being so to speak concentrated, absorbed by the long body lying at the foot of the mantelpiece, pale and naked.

For that was the legend (or, according to Sabine, the scandal invented by his enemies): that he had been found entirely undressed, that he had first removed all his clothes before firing that bullet into his head beside that mantelpiece at the corner of which as a child and even later Georges had spent how many evenings instinctively searching in the walls or in the ceiling (although he knew perfectly well that the room had been re-papered and repainted several times since) for the trace of the bullet in the plaster, imagining, reliving it, thinking he could see him in that obscure, voluptuous and nocturnal disorder of a *scène galante*: perhaps an armchair, a table overturned, and the clothes, like those of an impatient lover, hastily, feverishly torn off, thrown aside, scattered here and there, and that body of a man whose complexion was delicate, almost feminine, lying there huge and incongruous, the candle's shifting shadows playing over the white and transparent skin, ivorine or rather bluish and in the centre that bush, that tuft, that dark blur, fluffy and dark, and the delicate sex of the reclining statue, lying across the groin, over the top of the thigh (the body in falling having slightly pitched to the left), the whole scene stamped with that element of the obscure, the equivocal, both clammy and frozen, fascinating and repugnant . . .

'And I wondered if he too had that astonished vaguely offended look that Wack had when he was pulled off his horse lying dead head down looking at me with his eyes wide open mouth wide open beside the road, but Wack had always had a fool's face and of course death hadn't exactly improved matters from that point of view, but probably on the contrary accentuated, in so far as it deprived the face of any mobility, the expression dazed, stupefied, as though astonished by the sudden revelation of death that is finally known no longer in the abstract form of that concept with which we have grown accustomed to live but rising up or rather striking in its physical reality, that violence that aggression, a blow of unheard-of unsuspected disproportionate unfair undeserved brutality the stupid and stupefying fury of things that have no need of reasons to strike like when you run headlong into a lamp-post you hadn't seen lost in your thoughts as they say then becoming acquainted with the idiotic revolting and fierce wickedness of cast iron, the bullet carrying off half the head, then perhaps his face expressed that kind of suprise of reprobation but only his face because I suppose that as far as his mind was concerned it must have long since crossed the threshold beyond which nothing could surprise or disappoint him after the loss of his last illusions in the rout of a disaster, and by then already hurled into that nothingness where the shot had only sent his carcass to join him: all I could see was his back so that I had no way of knowing if every faculty of astonishment or suffering and even of reason had not already abandoned or rather liberated him so that it was perhaps only his body not his mind that enforced the absurd and mocking gesture of unsheathing and brandishing that sabre for undoubtedly he was already quite dead at that moment if as is likely the other man behind his hedge had aimed for the highest-ranking officer first and it takes less time to put ten machine-gun bullets into a body than to accomplish the series of operations consisting of seizing the sabre handle over the left thigh with the right hand unsheathing it and raising the blade, but they say that corpses are sometimes capable of reflexes of muscular contractions strong enough and even co-ordinated enough to make them move like those ducks when you cut their heads off and they go on walking running away grotesquely covering several yards before falling down for good: a mere matter of throats cut after all since according to the tradition the version the flattering family legend it was to avoid the guillotine that the other one had done it had been forced to do it Then they should have changed their coat of arms after that replaced those three doves by a headless duck I suppose that would have been better a better symbol more explicit in any case since you could say that in any case neither one nor the other had his head any more: just a headless duck brandishing that sabre raising it glinting in the sunlight before falling to one side, horse and duck behind the burnt truck as if they had been cut down like in those farces where you suddenly pull on a rug on which someone is standing, the hedges here consisting of hawthorn or hornbeam I think it's called little crimped or rather fluted leaves like a flange on each side of the central vein, our long shadows sliding over breaking like the right-angles of a stair-case, horizontal, vertical, then horizontal again, my helmet moving over the flat part to the top of the hedge, the three horses (breathing less heavily now, the nostrils of the one Iglésia was riding dilated and contracting like pistons still quivering with red veins swollen branching like streaks of lightning) walking side by side taking up most of the lane's width, I leaned over to stroke the neck but where the reins had chafed it was all wet and covered with a greyish lather and I wiped my hand on my breeches he snorted and said The bastard, and I said Does it hurt? But he didn't answer still with that annoyed expression as if he were angry with me finally saying No I suppose it's nothing, saying The bastard you saw that, then I saw our shadows in front of us this time What rot he said who the hell are they? Standing at the crossroads watching us come towards them without moving they looked as if they were going to or leaving Mass in their Sunday clothes dressed as though for a ceremony a party the women in dark clothes and some in hats, holding a black umbrella or their bags black too and some carrying suitcases or those rectangular rattan baskets with a handle the lid attached by a ring with a lock, and when we were near them one of the men said Get away from here, their faces were expressionless, Did you see any cavalrymen come through here I said, but the same voice repeated Get away from here, the three horses had stopped the shadows of the helmets reached almost to their black Sunday shoes I said We're lost we fell into an ambush this morning our captain's just been killed we're looking, then one of the women began screaming then several voices cried out together They're everywhere get away from here if they find you with us they'll kill us all, Iglésia repeating Bastard but without raising his voice so I wondered if he meant them or the man who had shot at us but I couldn't tell and at that moment I remember that I heard the sound of the urine at the same time that she moved a little to separate her thighs and I leaned forward to relieve her back and I stayed that way flat on her neck looking at the ground, the yellow urine spattering everywhere and the nearest man moving away probably to keep his Sunday clothes from getting dirty, the urine winding across the recently paved road like a kind of

dragon covered with bubbles the head hesitating groping searching its way right and left while the body swelled but the earth
absorbed it quickly and there remained only a dark wet and
tentacular spot where tiny points shiny as pinheads vanished
one after the other, then I straightened up again saying All right
we can't stay here I dug my heels in and they moved aside to
let us pass solemn stiff and hostile in their Sunday clothes,
Those bastard peasants Iglésia said then we heard someone
shouting behind us and I turned round they hadn't moved it
was a woman shouting the others still had their same hostile
expressions they were looking at her now, with a kind of reprobation, What's she saying? I said, Iglésia had turned round
too, the hand holding the reins and the bridle of the third horse
resting on his thigh, she repeated the same gesture with her arm
several times Left he said she said you go left otherwise we'll
be surrounded, then they all began talking and gesticulating at
the same time I heard their furious and contradictory voices
Then which way I said then I found what I had been looking
for the last few minutes since I had seen them unexpected and
ceremonious dressed up not for a party but a funeral, I thought
that's why I had thought of those funerals you meet black and
measured in the green fields of the countryside (he went on
furiously shaking his umbrella to drive us away as if he were
still screaming Get away from here!) She said we should go
left, Iglésia said, but our shadows were ahead of us now I could
see them advancing before us as though on stilts. I said But that
way we'll be going back towards . . . , and Iglésia But she said
otherwise we'll be surrounded She may know more than you
do, the sun disappeared the shadows disappeared I looked behind
us again and they had disappeared hidden by the hedge, without
the sun the countryside looked even more dead abandoned
frightening because of its calm and familiar immobility hiding
death as calm as familiar as uneventful as the woods the trees
the flowery meadows . . . '

Then he realized it wasn't to Blum that he was explaining

all this (Blum who had been dead for more than three years now, that is, whom he knew was dead because all he had seen was this: the same face as on that rainy grey morning in the barn, but even further reduced, shrunken and woebegone between the huge prominent ears that seemed to have grown as the face shrank, melted, and the same feverish, silent, gleaming stare reflecting the greenish-yellow light of the bulbs illuminating the barracks at least lighting them enough for what they had to do: open their eyes, sit up on their cots and stay there for a minute or so, half numb until they managed to realize where they were and what they were, and then get up, simply to stand up without doing anything more than tying their shoes (since now they didn't know what it meant to undress, save on Sundays when they hunted for lice) and dusting off the night's straw, pulling on their overcoats and finally lining up outside in the darkness waiting for the dawn until they had been counted like a herd of cattle: light enough for that then, and for him to see the handkerchief Blum was holding in front of his mouth, and that the handkerchief was almost black, but not with dirt, that is, if the bulbs had been strong enough he would have been able to see that it was red, but in the dimness it was merely black, and Blum still not saying anything, with only that woebegone, desperate and resigned something in his too shiny eyes, and Georges: 'But it's only a little b ... Lucky bastard! You sure can pick your days: the infirmary, sheets, and they'll probably send you home disabled ... Lucky bastard!' and Blum still looking at him without answering, his eyes burning in the dimness, wide as a child's, and Georges saying, repeating: 'Lucky bastard, what I wouldn't give to be able to spit up a little like that myself: nothing but a little drop like that Good God then I could go too but I wouldn't be that luck ... ', and Blum still looking at him without answering, and he hadn't ever seen him again), realizing then that it wasn't to Blum that he was trying to explain all this, whispering in the darkness, and not the cattle car either, the narrow air-hole blocked by the heads or rather

73

the blobs jostling each other noisily, but a single head now that he could touch merely by raising his hand as a blind man recognizes and doesn't even need to bring his hand closer to know in the darkness, smelling the warmth, the breath, breathing the air coming out of the faint dark flower of the lips, the whole face like a kind of dark flower leaning over his as if it were trying to read to divine . . . But he seized her wrist before she reached him, grasping the other hand in the air, her breasts rolling over his chest: they struggled a moment, Georges thinking without even wanting to laugh Usually they're the ones who don't want the lights on but there was still too much light in the darkness she leaning over the side her head as it moved away from the window revealing the stars and he could feel the cold gleam reach him splashing like milk on his face thinking Good fine look, feeling her weight the weight of all that female flesh her hip crushing his leg the hip shining phosphorescent in the darkness he could see it gleaming in the mirror too and the two pineapples on each side of the wardrobe pediment and that was almost all and she: Go on talk to him some more, and he: Who? and she: Whoever it is, not me, and he: Then who? and she: But even if I had been only an old moth-eaten whore to you, and he: For God's sake all I've done is dream about you think about you for five years, and she: Not me, and he: Who then who, and she: Not who, you'd be smarter to say what, I think it's not hard to guess I think it's not hard to imagine what a bunch of men without women for five years can think about, the kind of things you see written on walls of telephone boxes or toilets in cafés I think it's natural I think it's the most natural thing in the world but in those drawings you see there they never show the faces it usually stops at the neck when it goes that far when whoever has used the pencil or the nail to scratch the plaster has taken the trouble to draw something else, to go higher than, and he: Oh for God's sake but then the first woman who comes along, and she: But back there you had me in the palm of your hand (and making a sound that was something like a laugh in the dark, something that shook her slightly, shook them both, the two bodies sealed together, the breasts, so that he seemed to hear it echoing in his own body, so that he laughed too, that is, not really a laugh, in the sense that it expressed no joy: only that sort of spasm, hard, like a cough, echoing together in their two bodies then stopping when she spoke again:) or rather all of you did since there were three of you, Iglésia you and what was his name . . . , and Georges: Blum, and she: . . . That little Jew who was with you the one you had found again . . .

Then Georges no longer listening to her, no longer hearing her, sealed again in the stifling darkness with that thing on his chest, that weight which wasn't the warm female flesh but merely air as if the air was lying there too lifeless with that tenfold hundredfold weight of corpses, the heavy corpse of the black air stretched out at full length on top of him its mouth pressed to his own, and he desperately trying to make that breath tasting of death of corruption penetrate his lungs, then suddenly the air came in: they had slid back the door again, the explosion of voices, of orders coming in with the air, Georges wide awake now, thinking: 'But it's not possible, it's not possible that they can get any more in, we . . . ' then something violent, jostling, swearing in the darkness, then the door sliding closed again, the iron bolt shooting to outside, and again it was the darkness populated only by breathing, the ones who had just come in probably pressed against the door and probably wondering how long they could stay inside without fainting or just waiting (probably thinking: it can only last a few minutes, which is all to the good) for the moment when they would lose consciousness, the continuous sound of breathing in the darkness like bellows, then (probably tired of waiting for it to happen) someone who had just come in talking, saying (but not angry, only with a kind of boredom): 'Could you maybe at least make room for us to sit down?', and Georges: 'Who just spoke?', and the voice: 'Georges?', and Georges: 'Yes, over here, over . . . God, so they got you too! So you . . . ', still talking while he was trying to crawl towards the door despite the swearing, without even feeling the blows they rained on him, then a hand grabbed his ankle and he fell, someone kicked him hard on the side of the face, at the same time that Blum's voice reached him, closer now, saying, 'Georges,' then the voice of the man from Marseilles saying: 'Stay where you are. You can't get through!', and Georges: 'Listen, it's an old pal . . . ', and the man from Marseilles: 'Go to hell!', and Georges charging, trying to stand up, then when he was half standing, feeling something like a ton of steel hit him in the chest, thinking in a kind of blinding flash: 'God it's not possible they put horses in here too, they . . . ', then hearing the iron door slam against his head (or his head ring against the iron door – unless there was no iron door, unless his head rang all by itself), Blum's voice right beside him now saying without sounding any louder: 'Bunch of bastards,' Georges able to hear him hitting out in the darkness, patiently somehow although as fast as he could, landing the greatest possible number of kicks and blows, Georges trying to fight too but not very well because his arm or his foot immediately met something he couldn't strike very hard, then there was probably too little air for them to continue fighting long, for gradually and by a kind of tacit agreement between them and their opponents (that is, between them and that darkness in which they were trying to land and from which blows landed on them) they stopped, the voice of the man from Marseilles saying that he'd take care of them later, and Blum saying: 'That's right,' and the man from Marseilles: 'I know what you look like', and Blum: 'That's right, you took my picture,' and the man from Marseilles: 'Go on show off, wait till it's daylight, wait till we get out of here,' and Blum: 'That's right: take my picture,' and probably there wasn't even enough air for them to go on insulting each other because that stopped too, and Blum said: 'Are you all right?' and Georges groping in the knapsack, and there was still the piece of bread and the bottle wasn't broken, saying: 'Yes I'm all right,' but his lip seemed to be made out of wood and then he felt something running down the inside of his mouth, feeling his lip with his fingers, exploring it carefully, thinking: 'Fine. I'll eventually wonder if I was really in the war. But at least I managed to get myself wounded, to shed at least a few drops of my precious blood so that afterwards at least I'll have something to tell and so I can say that all the money they've spent to make me into a soldier hasn't been completely wasted, although I'm afraid that that isn't in the regulations, that is, the right way, that is, hit by an enemy aiming at me, a crouching sniper, but only by a hobnail boot, although that's not ever sure although I'm not even sure I can boast later of anything as glorious as being wounded by one of my own kind because it probably was something like a mule or a horse that was stuffed into this wagon by mistake, unless we were the ones who were in this wagon by mistake since its original purpose was to carry animals, unless it's no mistake at all and they filled it with animals the way it was meant to be filled, so that we've become something like animals without realizing it, I think I remember reading somewhere a story like that, men changed with a tap of a wand into pigs or trees or stones all by reciting some Latin verses . . . ' then think-ing 'And so he's not completely wrong. And so after all words are at least good for something, so that in his summerhouse he can probably convince himself that by putting them together in every possible way you can at least sometimes manage with a little luck to tell the truth. I'll have to tell him that. It'll make him happy. I'll tell him that I've already read in Latin what's happened to me, so that I wasn't too surprised and even to a certain extent reassured to know that it had already been written down, so that all the money he's spent too to make me learn Latin wasn't completely wasted either. It'll probably make him happy, yes. It'll certainly be a . . . ' Then he stopped. It wasn't his father he wanted to talk to. And it wasn't even the woman lying invisible beside him, maybe it wasn't even Blum to whom he was explaining, whispering in the darkness, that if the sun hadn't disappeared they would have known which side their shadows were on: now they were no longer riding through the green countryside, or rather the green lane had suddenly stopped and they (Iglésia and he) stayed where they were, stupefied, sitting on their skeletal mounts in the middle of the road, while he thought with a kind of stupor, a despair, a calm disgust (like the convict letting go the rope that has allowed him to climb up the last wall, crouching, standing up, preparing himself to jump, and then discovering that he had just fallen at the very feet of his guard who is waiting for him): 'But I've already seen this somewhere. I know this. But when? And where was it? . .'

2

Who could have given God the notion of creating male and female beings and making them couple? Here is man, and lo! He gives him woman. She has two teats and a little slit between her legs. Put a drop of human semen there, and a regular human body will come out; that poor little drop becomes flesh, blood, nerves, skin! Job said it in Chapter ten: 'Hast thou not poured me out as milk, and curdled me like cheese?' In all his works, God has something comical. If he had asked my opinion of human procreation, I would have advised him to stop at the lump of clay. And I would have told him to put the sun in the middle of the earth, like a lamp. That way, there would have been daylight all the time.

MARTIN LUTHER

A<small>ND</small> after a moment or so he recognized it: what was not a rough mass of dried mud but (the bony legs joined and bent back in an attitude of prayer, the carcass half covered, absorbed by its matrix of clay – as if the earth had already begun digesting it – with, on the hard, crumbling crust, its aspect, its morphology of both insect and crustacean) a horse, or rather what had been a horse (whinnying, snorting in the green fields) and reverting now, or already reverted to the original earth without apparently having had to pass through the intermediate stage of putrefaction, that is, by a kind of transmutation or accelerated transubstantiation, as if the margin of time normally necessary for the passage from one kingdom to the other (from the animal to the mineral) had this time been crossed at once. 'But,' he thought, 'maybe it's tomorrow already, maybe there've even been days and days we've spent here without my knowing it. And he still less. Because how can you say how long a man is dead since for him yesterday tomorrow and just now have definitely ceased to exist, that is to preoccupy him, that is to bother him . . . ' Then he saw the flies. No longer the wide pool of clotted and shiny blood he had seen the first time, but a kind of dark swarm, thinking: 'Already,' thinking: 'But where do they all come from?' until he realized that there weren't so many (not enough to cover the pool of blood) but that the blood had begun to dry, had darkened now, more brown than red (apparently this was the only change that had occurred since the first time he had seen it, so that, he thought, only a few hours could have passed, or perhaps only one, or perhaps not even that, and just then he noticed that the shadow cast by the corner of the brick wall along the road covered the hindquarters of the horse that had been in full sunlight, the shadow cast by the part of the wall parallel to the road constantly widening, thinking: 'But then our shadows were on our right, so now

the sun has crossed the axis of the road, so . . . ', then no longer
thinking, or rather no longer trying to calculate, merely thinking: 'But what difference does that make? What difference can
it make to him now where he is . . . '), the big blue-black flies
crowding round the edge, the lips of what was more a hole, a
crater than a wound, and where the gashed skin was beginning
to look like paper, reminding him of those amputated or broken
children's toys that show the yawning cavernous insides of
what had been only a simple shape surrounding emptiness, as
if the flies and the worms having already finished their work,
that is having eaten all there was to eat, including the bones
and the skin, nothing was left (like the carapaces of those creatures
despoiled of their flesh or those objects whose insides are eaten
away by termites) except a fragile envelope of dried mud, no
thicker than a layer of paint, neither more nor less empty,
neither more nor less inconsistent than those bubbles rising to
break at the surface of the mud with an indecent noise, releasing,
as though ascending from unsoundable and visceral depths, a
faint exhalation of rottenness.

Then he saw the man. That is, from high on his horse, the
gesticulating shadow bursting out of a house, running crabwise
towards them along the road; Georges remembering having
first been struck by the shadow because, he said, it was stretched
out flat, while Iglésia and he saw the man from above, foreshortened, so that he was still staring at the shadow (like an
inkblot that slid along the road without leaving a trace, as
though on an oilcloth or some vitrified matter) incomprehensibly
waving its two claws while the voice reached him from another
point, the movements and the voice apparently separated, dissociated, until he raised his head, discovered the face raised
towards them, stamped with a kind of bewilderment, a furious
and suppliant exaltation, Georges only then managing to understand what the voice was screaming (that is, what it had screamed,
for it was already screaming something else, so that when he
answered it was with a lag, as if what the other man was scream-

ing took a moment to reach him, to penetrate the depths of his fatigue), hearing his own voice come out (or rather expelled with effort) hoarse, uneven, and screaming too, as if they all had to shout to manage to make themselves heard although they were only a few yards (and then not even that) from each other and there was no other noise then save for a distant cannonade (because probably the man had begun screaming as soon as he had seen them, screaming while he ran down the front steps of the house, still screaming without realizing that it was less and less necessary the closer he came to them, his thinking that he had to scream probably explained too by the fact that he didn't stop running, even when he stood motionless for a second beneath Georges, pointing at the place where the sniper was concealed, still running probably in his mind, not even realizing that he had stopped, so that it was probably impossible for him to express himself except by screaming, the way a man does when he's running) and Georges screaming too then: 'Hospital men? No. Why hospital men? Do we look like hospital men? Do we have armban . . . ', the furious dialogue exchanged at the top of their lungs on the sunny, empty road (except, on each side, that double streak of rubbish, of wrecks, as if some flood, some unleashed stream, inundating and immediately drying up, had passed along here, rejecting, leaving on its slopes these confused, filthy and motionless heaps – things, animals, dead men – quivering slightly in the layer of warm air that vibrated just above the ground in the May sunshine), between the cavalryman on his motionless horse and the man running, screaming again: 'Bandages . . . You've got to . . . There are two men who've just been shot. You don't have, you aren't . . . ', and Georges: 'Bandages? Good God, where do you . . . ', and the man beginning to turn round to start back towards the house, now slowing down, screaming again, in a kind of desperate rage: 'Then what the hell are you doing there on your horses in the middle of the road Don't you know they're firing at anything that goes by?', and waving his arms again, turning round but still running, pointing at something, screaming: 'There's one over there, just behind the corner of that brick house!', and Georges: 'Where?', and the man already moving, starting back, turning round, screaming furiously: 'Good God . . . : the brick house over there!', and Georges: 'But they're all brick,' and the man: 'Damn fool!', and Georges: 'But he didn't shoot,' and the man (farther away now, running, his face turned towards them to answer, so that his whole body is twisted like a corkscrew, the head looking the opposite way from the direction he is running, his body – that is, the plane of his chest – in the axis of his trajectory and his hips (the plane of his hips) oblique in relation to the latter, so that he is running crosswise, again, rather like a crab, seeming to drag his feet after him clumsily, his legs threatening to get tangled at any moment, while his outspread arms continue to gesticulate) screaming: 'Damn fool! He won't shoot at you from over there. He's waiting until you're close and then he'll shoot!', and Georges: 'But where . . . ', and the man over his shoulder: 'Damn fool!', and Georges shouting: 'But Good God where's the front, where . . . ', and the man stopping this time, puzzled for a second, outraged, standing there, his arms outstretched, screaming with rage now: 'The front? Damn fool! The front? . . . There *is* no more front, you fool, there's nothing left!', and Georges (his voice raised now because the other man has turned his back, started running again, and has almost reached the steps of the house he had come out of and would disappear into): 'But what shall we do? What can we do? Where can we . . . ', and the man: 'Do what I did!', his arms falling, his wrists turned in so that his fingers pointing towards himself seem to invite the two cavalrymen to examine his clothes, screaming: 'Get out of those! Get into civilian clothes! Look for some clothes in some house and lie low. Lie low!', raising his arms again and suddenly lowering them towards them in the gesture of pushing them away, warding them off, cursing them, and disappearing inside the house, and now nothing again except Georges and

Iglésia perched on their horses in the middle of the sunny road bordered here and there with houses and absolutely deserted except for the dead animals, the dead men, the enigmatic and motionless heaps in the distance, slowly beginning to rot in the sun, and Georges looking at the corner of the brick house, then the house where the man has just disappeared, then again the mysterious corner of the house, then hearing hoofbeats behind him, turning back, Iglésia already trotting, the extra horse trotting beside him, the two horses turning down a side road, this time to the left, and Georges spurring his horse to a trot too, catching up with Iglésia, saying: 'Where are you going?', and Iglésia, without looking at him, snorting, his expression still sulky, resentful: 'To do what he said. Look for some clothes and lie low,' and Georges: 'Lie low where? And then what?', and Iglésia not answering, and a moment later the horses tethered in an empty stable and Iglésia furiously knocking his rifle-butt against the door until Georges merely turns the handle, the door opening by itself, and then walls, darkness around them, in other words an enclosed, finite space (not that they hadn't learned enough in a week to know the worth, the solidity of walls and the trust they could put in them, that is, about as much as a soap bubble — with this difference that once it bursts nothing is left of the soap bubble but the imperceptible droplets instead of an inextricable, greyish, dusty and deadly mass of bricks and beams: but it didn't matter, that wasn't it, the point was not to be outside now, to have four walls around them and a roof over their heads); and this: four urine-yellow rods of imitation bamboo, their bevelled ends sticking out beyond the corners of the mirror whose four sides framed a face he had never seen, wan, the features haggard, the eyes red-rimmed and the cheeks covered with an eight days' beard, then he thought: 'But that's me,' standing there looking at that stranger's face, frozen where he stood not by surprise or interest but merely by fatigue, leaning so to speak against his own image, standing stiff in his stiff clothes (remembering that scornful slang expression he had heard one day: 'You're only standing up because your pants are starched'), holding his rifle by the barrel, the butt on the floor, his arm dangling slightly, as though he were holding something he was dragging behind him, for instance a leash from which some practical joker had removed the dog, or the way a drunkard holds an empty bottle while he leans his forehead against a plate-glass window, hoping to find a little coolness, hearing Iglésia behind him opening the wardrobe and rummaging through it, throwing the men's and women's clothes on the floor, then his face vanished and the mirror with it, the rectangle in front of his eyes now that of the door framing an emaciated man with a yellow death's head and a mole the size of a pea on his right cheek, near the corner of his mouth.

Later he would remember that exactly: the yellow skin and the mole he kept staring at, and then the stumps of teeth, yellow too, growing crosswise and irregularly in the mouth, that he saw when it opened, the cadaver-like figure saying: 'Hey there! . . . ', then putting out his hand, calmly shoving aside the rifle-barrel aimed at his stomach, Georges's eyes now following the fleshless hand, watching his rifle describe a half circle, in other words lowering his eyes at the same moment that his arms felt the pressure transmitted to his own body by the weapon, discovering the latter then, with that same astonishment, that same blasé surprise he had felt discovering his unknown face a moment earlier in the mirror, trying unsuccessfully to remember how he had turned around, cocked and aimed the rifle, while now his muscles were contracted, trying to resist the push and to turn the barrel towards the man again, then suddenly no longer struggling, turning away, looking for the chair he knew he had seen a moment before and sitting down, the rifle-butt again resting on the floor, his right hand holding it by the barrel again, not quite at the end, the way an old man sitting down holds a stick or a cane, that is, the rifle serving as a support, a prop, for the arm, the left forearm and hand lying flat on the left thigh, exactly like an old man, and not even feeling like laughing as he thought: 'And that would have been my first dead man. And that would have been the first shot I fired in this war that was almost what it took to . . . ', then too tired even to finish the sentence, to go on to the end, hearing as in a dream the cadaver and the jockey quarrelling now, the man shouting in front of the open wardrobe, the clothes thrown on the floor, saying: 'And first of all who let you come in here anyway, who . . . ', and the voice calm, low, not irritated, not aggressive, not even impatient, but merely full of that patient and inexhaustible faculty of astonishment Iglésia seemed to possess: 'There's a war on dad Don't you read the papers?', the man (the cadaver) not seeming to hear, picking up the clothes now and examining them one by one the way an old-clothes vender would do in order to make a price for the lot, an estimate before throwing them one after the other on to the bed, still insulting them and calling them thieves, until he (Georges, and probably the cadaver too, for he suddenly stopped fuming, stood perfectly still, half bent over, a woman's dress – or at least something soft, shapeless and limp that, compared to a man's clothes, could not lie in any one direction, look like anything except on a woman's body, even if it too were limp or shapeless – in his hand) heard the noise, the double and abrupt click in both directions of a breech locked, Iglésia now holding his own rifle aimed at the man's chest, still saying in the same plaintive (and almost whining and bored rather than irritated, and resigned rather than threatening) voice: 'And what if I shot you down? Would you call the police? I could kill you without making any more fuss than if you were a fly All I have to do is pull this trigger and we'll have one more body around And with all that are out there rotting on the road already one more or less won't make much difference you know,' the man motionless now, still holding the limp piece of cloth in his hands, saying: 'All right boy All right We're not going to,' Georges still sitting in his chair like an old man taking the sun on the bench of an old-age home, thinking 'He's perfectly capable of doing it,' but still not moving, not even finding the strength to open his mouth, merely thinking with dejection: 'It's still going to make a terrible noise,' preparing himself, stiffening in anticipation of the shot, the explosion, then hearing Iglésia's plaintive voice saying: 'All right stop whining We haven't broken anything All we want are some clothes to wear.'

Then they (all three: the fleshless cadaver, Iglésia and Georges – they dressed now like farm-hands, that is, vaguely uncomfortable, vaguely embarrassed, as if – abandoning their heavy carapace of cloth and leather – they felt almost naked, weightless in the weightless air) were outside again, floating in that kind of enormous emptiness, that cottony void surrounded on all sides by the sound or rather the somehow calm murmur of the battle, and then the three planes appeared, grey, low, fishlike and not very fast, flying parallel and horizontally with slight variations in altitude which made them waver, rise and sink imperceptibly in relation to each other, exactly like fish undulating in the current, strafing the road behind them (Iglésia, Georges and the cadaverous man motionless now but not trying to hide, standing in the lane the hedge up to their chests, staring, Georges thinking: 'But there's nothing left but corpses It's silly they're firing on They can't expect to kill them twice'), the machine-guns making a faint noise like sewing-machines, absurd, without conviction, quite slow, not even as loud as the sound of a two-cylinder pump, like this: tap . . . tap . . . tap . . . tap . . . lost, absorbed, drowned in the enormous motionless countryside (from where they were nothing moved on the road), under the enormous motionless sky, then everything grew still again: the houses, the orchards, the hedges, the sunny fields, the woods that formed the horizon to the south, the calm sound of the cannon, a little stronger on the left, carried by the warm calm air, not very loud and not very insistent, merely there, patient, like workmen somewhere demolishing a house without hurrying, and nothing else.

And a little later, walls around them again, something enclosing in any case, and Georges sitting down obediently, his mouth, his tongue, his lips trying to say: 'I'd rather eat something If you have something to eat I . . . ', but not managing to, looking with impotent despair at the man with the cadaverous face talking to the woman standing beside their table, then the woman going away, coming back, setting down the glass in front of him and filling it (the glass a tiny reversed cone very wide above the thin stem) with something transparent and colourless like water but which he felt like spitting out when it was in his mouth, harsh, burning. Still he didn't spit it out, swallowed it, as he docilely swallowed the contents – also colourless, transparent, harsh and burning – of the second glass she poured out, still trying (or rather struggling to try) to say that he would rather eat a piece of but realizing with the same mute despair that such a thing (asking for something to eat) was completely beyond his strength, contenting himself, then, with listening (trying to listen) to what they were saying and emptying the little cones filled with the colourless and burning liquid, wondering if the flies had already begun to buzz round him as over the dead horse, thinking of the planes, thinking again: 'But they couldn't have killed him twice So?' until he realized that he was drunk, saying: 'I don't know what it was. I mean: I didn't know where I was or when or what was happening if I was thinking about him (beginning to rot in the sun wondering when he would begin stinking for good still brandishing his sabre in the black buzzing of the flies) or about Wack head down on the slope looking at me with that ridiculous expression his mouth wide open and on which by now the flies must also have had plenty of time to gather probably the pièce de résistance so to speak since he had been dead since morning when that other sabre-wielding idiot had ridden head first into that ambush, thinking fools fools fools, thinking that after all idiocy or intelligence didn't have much to do with it, I mean with us, I mean with what we think is us and makes us talk act hate love since once it's gone our body our face goes on expressing what we thought was appropriate to our mind, then maybe those things, I mean intelligence idiocy or being in love or being brave or cowardly or murderous the virtues the passions exist outside of us taking up residence without asking our permission in this clumsy carcass which they possess because even idiocy was apparently something too fine too subtle and somehow too intelligent to belong to Wack, then maybe he had existed only to be Wack-the-idiot, in any case he didn't have to worry about it any more, poor Wack poor idiot poor fool: I remembered that day that rainy afternoon when we had ourselves a time making him mad arguing to pass the time round that sick horse, it wasn't the way it is now the sun the heat and I suppose that if they had died then they would have been dissolved and not rotting like carrion, it was raining all the time and now I thought that we were something like virgins, puppies despite the blasphemies, the swearwords we used, virgins because the war death I mean everything . . . ' (Georges's arm making a half circle, his hand leaving his chest, pointing to the swarming interior of the barracks, and on the other side of the dirty windows the tarred wooden partition of another identical barracks, and behind – they couldn't see them but they knew they were there – the monotonous repetition of the same barracks set approximately every ten yards on the bare plain, aligned, parallel, identical, on each side of what was supposed to be a street, streets intersecting at right-angles, making a gridiron, all the barracks facing in the same direction, low, grim, long, and the nauseating smell of rotten potatoes and latrines permanently floating in the air, probably forming – Georges supposed – over the huge square that exhaled it, excremental, stubborn, nasty, a kind of hermetic lid, so that they were – he said – doubly prisoners: first of that barrier of barbed wire stretched between the raw pine poles with the bark still on them, and second of their own infection (or abjection: that of conquered armies, fallen warriors), and both of them (Georges and Blum) sitting with their legs dangling over the edges of their cots, trying to pretend they weren't hungry (which was still quite easy, because a man can manage to make himself believe almost anything provided it makes life easier for him: but much harder, and even impossible, to convince the rat that ceaselessly gnawed at their stomachs, until, Blum said, it seemed as though there were only two alternatives: get yourself eaten dead by the worms or alive by a starving rat), groping in their pockets in the hope of finding there some forgotten grains of tobacco, taking out the nasty mixture of breadcrumbs dust and lint that lay in the seams, so that they had every reason to wonder if such a thing was supposed to be smoked or eaten, that is, arguing (Georges and Blum) if the rat would deign to swallow it, and finally deciding they would try to smoke it; and around them the incessant murmur, the confused and muddy racket – discussions, bargaining, arguments, bets, obscenities, boasting, recriminations – like, somehow, the breathing (it never stopped, even at night, merely muffled as if under the sleep itself you could still perceive that kind of constant discomfort, that sterile and vain agitation of caged animals) that filled the barracks, and there was music too, an orchestra, a screeching fiddle, bursts of rhythm, strings scraped in time on instruments made from empty tins, pieces of wood and bits of wire (and even real banjoes, real guitars brought here and kept God knows how) rising sporadically over the racket (then submerged again, stifled, melting, disappearing into the other sounds – or perhaps they forgot about it, simply forgot to be aware of it?), the same tune, the same measures repeated over and over again, the same refrain rising, repeating itself, monotonous, plaintive, with its nonsensical words, its gay and nostalgic cadence:

Granpèr! Granpèr!
Vouzou blié vo! tre! che! val!

and then immediately afterwards, two notes higher:

Granpèr! Granpèr!

like a suppliant and clownish invocation, an ironic and clownish reproach, or reminder, or warning, or something, probably nothing, except the meaningless words, the light, carefree notes in tireless repetition, time somehow motionless too, like a kind of mud, of mire, stagnant as though caught under the weight of the suffocating lid of stench exhaled from thousands and thousands of men stagnating in their own abjection, excluded from the world of the living but not yet in the world of the dead: between the two, so to speak, dragging like ironic stigmata their absurd debris of uniforms that made them look like a race of ghosts, of souls left on account, that is, forgotten, or rejected, or refused, or vomited up, both by death and by life, as if neither one nor the other had wanted them, so that they seemed now to be moving not in time but in a kind of greyish glue without dimensions, a glue of nothingness, of uncertain duration sporadically pierced by the nostalgic, gay and stubborn repetition of the same refrain, the same meaningless, melancholy words:

> Granpèr! Granpèr!
> Vouzou blié vo! tre! che! val!
> Granpèr! Granpèr!

and Georges, and Blum, finally stuffing between their lips a thin, flat, shapeless twist of paper surrounding more lint and rubbish of every kind than tobacco, and flatter and thinner than a toothpick, and sucking in the harsh, revolting smoke, and Georges: ' . . . all that rot still hadn't ruptured broken inside of us what must be like the hymen of young men opening that wound rending something that we'd never get back that virginity those fresh virginal desires lying in wait for the girl glimpsed you remember we were watching we kept looking up towards that window that net curtain we thought we had seen moving I said Look you saw her she just looked out now she's gone again, and you Where? and I For God's sake at that window, and you Where? and I Over there that brick house, and you I don't see anything, and I The peacock's still moving, there was a peacock woven into the net curtain with its long tail covered with eyes and we were ruining our own eyes watching still teasing Wack trying to imagine to divine that hidden seething of passions: we weren't in the autumn mud we weren't anywhere a thousand years or two thousand years earlier or later in the middle of madness murder the Atrides, riding across time the night streaming with rain over our exhausted horses to reach her discover her find her warm half naked and milky in that stable by the light of that lantern: I remember that at first she held it up at arm's length then while we were beginning to unsaddle she lowered it gradually probably tired so that the shadows ran across her face, and finally she vanished, disappeared as if she had only waited for us there to be snatched away from us at once us in our stiff soldiers' disguise soaked through listening in the spongy grey morning to the cries the voices the incomprehensible anger, those tragedians dressed in blue overalls sheltered under umbrellas swimming in their uniforms black rubber boots speckled with red patches, the limping man, the *disgraciado* holding that rifle I always thought he had killed himself with, an accident the gun going off by itself making him bloody streaming down his temple (the days when rifles fire of their own accord, went off in your face just like that without your ever knowing why) but maybe he merely wanted to fire his shot too like everyone else and Wack said You think you're awfully smart I'm only a peasant I'm not a Yid but, and I Oh you poor fool poor fool poor fool, and he: But it's not because I'm from the country that a city Yid like, and I: Oh you poor fool Good God you poor fool, and Wack: I'm not afraid of you you know, and I: Oh for God's sake, and later we had walked as far as that café in the village square I mean the rectangle of black mud around the watering trough trampled by horses and cattle that was supposed to be the square, we sat down and she filled the glasses in front of us again and I said No no not for me thanks, because my head was going round I remember that it was a big tiled room with a low ceiling the walls painted blue with streaks of saltpetre there were about ten tables a player-piano a bar and on the walls the inevitable fly-specked Statute Relative to the Suppression of Public Drunkenness aperitif and beer posters with girls with red lips and affected mincing gestures or else huge breweries drawn in free perspective as though seen from a plane their chimneys smoking their roofs bright red and two coloured prints one of marquises in pastel dresses in an evanescent park the other a group of people in Empire costumes in a green and gold salon the men leaning over the women's shoulders elbows on the backs of their chairs probably whispering sweet nothings in their ears, and also one of those racks for newspapers made out of rusty wire and on the bar a vase with a chipped rim, but it wasn't to drink that we had come it was that girl that disturbance it was those cries that tumult around that momentarily glimpsed flesh the incomprehensible story divined suspected that furious and obscure unleashing of violence at the heart of violence, that lame man and the other one both in the same kind of patched boots confronting each other with something savage excessive and probably as alien incomprehensible to them as to us, what was happening to them beyond them, forcing them to defy each other at the risk of their lives, that is, one ready to (or rather burning devoured by the desire or rather the need or rather the necessity to) commit a crime and the other also prepared to be its victim and this despite his cowardice the visible fear that made him hide behind another man's back, and de Reixach the arbiter or rather trying to calm them down, with his bored patient absent impenetrable expression, between them, he for whom passion or rather suffering took the form not of one of his kind of his equals but of a jockey with a clown's head against whom we had never heard him even raise his voice and whom he made follow him like his shadow like those ancient what were they Assyrians wasn't it? on whose funeral pyre they killed the houri the horse and the favourite slave so that they would still lack for nothing and be served properly in the other world where undoubtedly Iglésia and he would have gone on exchanging taciturn and occasional remarks about the only subject perhaps the only thing that really interested both of them which is to say the suitability of a ration of hay or the warming of a tendon, and if that was the case then he had managed to bring off one part of the programme I mean getting that horse killed beneath him at the same time as himself but zero for the second part, the one he was counting on, to discuss pastern swellings or the best horseshoes until the end of time, turning back at the last moment leaving him abandoning him to the flies under the dazzling May sunshine where for a second the steel of the brandished sabre had glinted, and she filled that little cone they used for a glass once again up to the brim with what do they call gin I think there they say *g'nievr'*, serving me with that way of showing off that they're giving you good measure so that a little always overflows, the surface of the liquid bulging over the rim of the glass forming by capillary action or whatever you call it that phenomenon a slight convexity like a lens above the rim of the glass a meniscus that's it trembling when I raised it cautiously to my lips my hand trembling the silvery light sparkling trembling with the colourless liquid running down my fingers burning when it went down my throat . . . '

And Blum: 'But what are you talking about? That's the first time I ever heard of anyone taking two weeks getting over a binge . . . '

And Georges suddenly breaking off, looking at him with a kind of incredulous perplexity, and both sitting there among the incessant racket they no longer even heard (any more than people living on the seashore hear the sound of the sea), and Blum saying: 'It wasn't gin, not that time,' their terrible wisps consumed now, that is reduced to a fraction of an inch of an empty flattened tube of paper, still white or rather grey where their lips had pressed it, then shading into yellow, then brown, then jagged, crumpled and black, and although he knew there was nothing left to inhale, Georges mechanically trying, sucking in two or three times with no other result except a nauseating valvelike sound, and finally resigning himself to removing his lips from the tiny shapeless butt but still not throwing it away, sitting there looking at it with perplexity, still calculating the chances of getting another draw or two at the risk of a precious match, saying: 'Hmmm? What?', and Blum: 'It wasn't gin. Hot rum: I was feeling sick and you used that as an excuse to get to the tavern . . . I mean: you couldn't have cared less whether I was sick or not, or rather I suppose you thought it was an ideal way to get around the proprietor, looking for a room for your poor sick pal that you couldn't leave in a draughty barn when all you cared about was picking up some gossip about that girl, that man with a limp, and as for your poor pal . . . ', and Georges: 'Oh all right all right all right all right . . . ' (leaving the café, the darkness falling, the little puffs of smoke coming out of their mouths at each word almost invisible now except against the light, when they walked through the light from a lighted window, and yellowish then), and Blum saying: 'If I got it right that lame riflery champion's in love?', Georges saying nothing now, his hands in his pockets, careful to keep from slipping in the invisible mud, and Blum: 'That assessor with his umbrella and his patched boots! The village Romeo? Who would have believed it? Him and that bowl of milk . . . ', and Georges: 'You're getting it all mixed up: not with her: with his sister,' and Blum: 'His sis . . . ', then suppressing an oath, catching hold of Georges's shoulder, and both of them swaying a second like two drunkards, then walking on in the streaming icy darkness that grew even blacker as they moved away from the square, from the few lighted doors or windows, until they couldn't even see each other, until only their voices represented them, answering each other, alternating in the darkness with that false carelessness, that false gaiety, that false cynicism of young men:

I don't get it

then you're even stupider than Wack I bet he got it a long time ago

all right stupider than Wack But say it again He (I mean the assessor the man who went this morning armed with an umbrella his cowardice and the rampart of an officer and deliberately provoked defied the other man who was armed with a rifle) slept with his own sister who was the wife of the lame man is that it?

yes

nothing like country people is there?

yes

their sisters and their goats hmm? So that if they don't have a sister they can always do it with the goat At least that's what people say Maybe they can't tell the difference

that man in the tavern didn't look as if he could tell the difference between his wife and his dog

maybe it was a dog changed into a woman

maybe

know how to tell fortunes Traditions forgotten now Easy though

so he changed his goat into a girl or his sister into a goat and Vulcan I mean that lame man married the goatfoot and that billygoat brother came and did it to her in his house is that it?

that's what he said

so it was goat's milk?

what?

the girl who was in the stable that morning the one hiding behind that mythological peacock the one who put you in such a stupid poetic trance and expensive too since you had to pay for two pints in that filthy tavern to

Good God you really are stupider than Wack I told you ten times it was his brother's wife

(they couldn't see the rain, only hear it, divine it murmuring, silent, patient, insidious in the dark night of the war, streaming all around them, over them, under them, as if the invisible trees, the invisible valley, the invisible hills, the whole invisible world were gradually dissolving, vanishing in pieces, in water, in nothing, in icy liquid darkness, the two falsely assured, falsely sarcastic voices rising, as if they were trying to cling to them, hoping to use them to ward off that spell, that liquefaction, that disaster, that blind patient endless debacle, the voices shouting now, like the voices of two boastful children trying to keep their courage up:)

Christ What brother? Christ now What is this business So they're all brothers and sisters I mean brothers and goats I mean billygoats and nannies So billygoat and his nanny and that damn lame man who married the nannygoat who serviced her billygoat of a brother who

but he'd had enough he kicked her out Or rather repudiated her

re . . . What did you say

repudiated

no fooling Like in the theatre then Like

yes

all right fine So he (that Vulcan) probably surprised them and caught them both in his net and

no he said she was heavy

heav . . .

he said heavy Like a cow do I have to draw pictures

I said it was a nannygoat Didn't he need any little billygoats to sell at the fair?

probably preferred selling little limpers

probably And then the other one began again?

who?

the billygoat

yes but this time with the wife of the one who's a soldier

probably he likes the nannygoats in the family

probably That's why the other one kept a rifle around To keep watch

that's why that rifle could feel like going off by itself God it's dark

we're almost there there's the light

(finding the rest still sitting together round the dying horse, lit by a lantern set on the ground, they turned round when Georges and Blum came in and their voices stopped, looking at the newcomers for a minute, Georges realizing then that they had almost forgotten about the horse, that they were sitting up with it like old women sit up with the dead in the country, sitting in a half circle on wheelbarrows or buckets, telling each other in their monotonous plaintive and clumsy voices their habitual stories of harvests that the bad weather spoiled before they could be brought in, the price of wheat or beets recipes for making cows calve or of Herculean exploits calculated in the number of bales of straw, of sacks of grain carried and of fields tilled, while in the lantern's glimmer the head of the horse lying on its side seemed to grow longer, assuming an apocalyptic, terrifying look, the bony flanks rising and falling, filling the silence with their wheezing, the huge velvety eye still reflecting the circle of soldiers but as if it were unaware of them now, as if it were looking through them at something they couldn't see, their reduced silhouettes outlined on the moist sphere as on the surface of those bronze balls that seem to seize, to suck up in a dizzying, distorting perspective engulfing the whole of the visible world, as if the horse had already ceased to be there, as if it had abandoned, renounced the spectacle of this world to turn its gaze inward, concentrating on an interior vision more restful than the incessant agitation of life, a reality more real than the real, and Blum said then that except for the certainty of dying what is more real? (he crossed the group without speaking, heading straight for the ladder to the loft and groped, grumbling, in the hay arranging his blankets) and Georges said: 'The certainty that you have to eat. Aren't you waiting for soup?', and Blum still grumbling between his teeth, saying 'Pretend I'm sick. That was good enough for you to get round the man in the café. And all for a farm girl you saw five minutes by the light of a lantern. So I think you could at least remember it, can't you?' and Georges: 'If you have to die, wait a little while. Let it be worth while. Wait till they can give you a medal at least,' and Blum: 'Which is better: dying of cold or dying decorated?', and Georges: 'Wait till I think that over. How about dying of love?', and Blum: 'It doesn't exist. Only in books. You've read too many books,' and in the shadows, the darkness, their two voices answering each other again:)

Do you think the horse has read too many books too

Why

Because he knows he's going to die

He doesn't know anything Not a thing

Yes he does it's instinct

How many things do you know instinctively

Well one at least: you bore the hell out of me

Fine In your opinion which is worth more the skin of a horse or the skin of a soldier

Well you know how things are on the Stock Exchange It's all a question of circumstances

Still there are always signs

I have the impression that at this moment a kilogram of horse is worth more than a kilogram of soldier

That's what I thought

There's nothing like war to teach you to think like these peasants: they always think by weight

That's it A kilogram of lead is heavier than a kilogram of feathers everyone knows that

I thought you were sick

I am Let me sleep now Get the hell out

then (Georges) going down the ladder, gradually entering, feet first, the yellowish light of the lantern that mounted his legs to his chest, finally standing in it, blinking a little, feeling their eyes on him (there were only two now, Iglésia and Wack), and a moment later Iglésia saying: 'What's the matter with him Is he sick?' their two heads raised towards him, their eyes questioning and sullen, the two faces in the theatrical lighting of the lantern on the floor reminding him of scarecrows, Iglésia's almost like a lobster claw (nose, chin, papery skin) if a lobster claw had eyes, and that look of permanent and incurable misery all the more incurable since he probably never knew what it was to be either miserable or happy, Wack with his long stupid face, his body frozen in his crouching monkey pose, his two enormous hands crackled and encrusted with earth, like split wood, like bark, like worn tools, hanging lifeless between his knees, and Georges shrugging, and finally Wack saying in his stupid voice: 'Damn this war! . . . ' without it's being possible to know whether he was thinking of Blum being sick, or of the harvests, the hay lost, or of the furious lame man brandishing his rifle, or of the horse, or of the girl without a husband, or perhaps merely of the three of them there, in the night, round that lantern, round that dying animal with its terribly fixed gaze, full of a terrifying patience, and whose neck seemed to grow still longer, stretching the muscles, the tendons, as if the weight of the enormous head dragged it out of the litter in the dark kingdom where dead horses gallop tirelessly, the huge black herd of old nags sent into a blind charge, struggling to pass each other, thrusting ahead their empty-eyed skulls, in a thunder of bones and clashing hoofs: some ghostly cavalcade of bloodless and extinct horses ridden by their bloodless and defunct horsemen with their fleshless tibias rattling in their oversize boots with their rusty and useless spurs, and leaving behind them a wake of whitening skeletons that Iglésia seemed to be staring at now, fallen back into his eternal silence, his huge fishy eyes stamped with that dismayed, patient and outraged expression, apparently the only one he had, or at least the only one life had taught him, probably during the time he went from one country race to another, riding in challenge meets on vicious or wild horses for one man or another, on racetracks that were usually just fields with half-rotten symbols of wooden grandstands, and sometimes no grandstand at all, just a mound of earth, or even the hillside up which people climbed, and only three or four plank barracks like bathhouses with a window sawed through to take the bets, and a ring of policemen to keep the horse buyers, the butchers with their pockets full of bills and the farmers that composed the public from lynching the defeated jockeys, and usually racing in the rain, getting off the soaked horse muddy up to the eyes and feeling satisfied if he merely got out with his breeches dirty but intact which he washed himself that night in the wash-basin of a hotel room, unless it was in the trough of a stable where they let him have an empty stall with a bale of straw to sleep on (which saved the hotel money) – or sometimes merely the hay-loft – , and if he had only a wrist or an ankle sprained, and only the insults of the betters and not their blows, dressing in one of the rotten wood shacks or when there was no shack then in just a van, wrapping an old strip of friction tape almost as black as a furnace wall and about as elastic around his wrist, a thread of blood trickling out of the corner of his mouth without his paying any more attention than he had to the (nor perhaps even felt the) fist that had managed to pass over or between the shoulders of the policemen without his (Iglésia) or their (the police) and probably still less the man the fist belonged to caring about the reasons or rather the validity of the reasons the aggressor might have, the only real and always valid one being that Iglésia had ridden a losing horse, and nothing else:

'Because,' he said, 'they couldn't care less about all the rest. . . . ' (he was sitting on the edge of his cot too, his legs dangling, head down, completely absorbed by one of those mysterious and minute tasks that apparently seemed as necessary to his hands as food to a stomach, supporting them in time of need when he had, as now, no bridle to saddlesoap or no stirrup to polish (Georges vainly trying to remember a single occasion when he had seen him idle, that is without rubbing one of those harness accessories or a boot or something of the kind), and now it was a thread and a needle and a button he was carefully sewing on to his jacket in the middle of that slovenly and tattered group where the last of their problems was a missing button or a ripped seam, and saying, still bent over his work:) ' . . . Be-cause you've never seen someone who plays the races think he's lost his money just because of bad luck or because he chose a bad horse, instead of supposing he's been robbed by a trick . . . ' (Georges realizing then that he was still staring at the same fraction of an inch of butt, or rather of twisted yellowed paper, and then shaking his head like someone who has just fallen asleep, at the same time that his ears suddenly filled again (as if he had suddenly pulled his hands away from them) with the foul and cacophonous racket of the barracks, and finally resigning himself to throwing away what certainly could not even give the illusion of a butt any longer, and saying: 'Lucky for you she liked horse-racing too. Otherwise one of those butcher boys would have eventually managed to hit as hard as he wanted, wouldn't he?' Iglésia turning his face towards him then, but without raising his head, glancing out of the corner of his eyes with that same expression of baffled, outraged perplexity still on his face (not suspicious or hostile: merely perplexed, morose), then looking away, sniffling, examining the button he had sewn back on, pulling at it, then patting the jacket with the flat of his hand while he folded it up, saying: 'Yeah, Probably. A still better chance if all she had wanted to do was watch them run . . . ', then folding his jacket twice, carefully rolling it up, using it as a pillow, taking off his shoes, setting them down against the edge of his cot, pivoting on his buttocks and stretching out, saying as he pulled his coat over him: 'If those bastards only stopped their racket for a while we could get some sleep!', turning over on to his side then, pulling up his knees and closing his eyes, his yellow face expressionless, completely blank then, as if it were made of paper, some lifeless, dead material, and probably by virtue of the faculty he possessed of not thinking (or of not talk-ing) more than was strictly necessary, and when he had made up his mind to sleep (probably deciding that the best thing to do on an empty stomach once the chores of maintenance – buttons, mending, cleaning – were finished was to sleep) no longer thinking at all; his ruffian's face completely neutral, absent, like one of those mortuary Aztec or Inca masks set motionless, impenetrable and empty on the surface of time, that is to say that kind of glue, of greyness without dimensions in which they were sleeping, waking, moving, falling asleep and waking again without, from one day to the next, any variation whatever to make them think it was the next day and not the day before or even the same day so that it wasn't day after day but somehow from place to place (like the surface of a painting darkened by varnish and filth and that a restorer might reveal in sections – testing, experimenting here and there on different areas with different cleaning solutions) that Georges and Blum gradually reconstituted, piece by piece or more accurately ono-matopoeia by onomatopoeia wrung one by one by ruse and guile (the strategy consisting of forcing his tongue in some way, that is by advancing all kinds of hints or suppositions until he made up his mind to emit a sullen grumble, negative or resigned) the whole story, from that day when in one of those improvised dressing-rooms, in the shelter of which, with a black eye or a split lip, he was dressing when that trainer hired by de Reixach had offered him a few mounts (for apparently he wasn't a bad jockey: probably he had only lacked luck till then, and the trainer knew it) including the one where he found he had replaced the man who had hired him, and all this because a woman or rather a girl had one fine day decided she would like to own a racing stable, the notion doubtless suggested by one of those magazines, those monthlies where women on slick paper look like species of birds, long-legged waders, not embellished but merely de-stroyed as women, a conversion or reduction by man to a simple yardage of silk: creating an angular silhouette, bristling with nails, talons, sharp gestures, and furnished too with that long-legged bird's stomach, that ostrich belly that allows her not only to digest but to make her own the misogynist and malignant inventions of the designer, and also to reconvert them, somehow in the opposite direction: no longer sophisticated, flat and slick, but that assimilation of silk, leather, jewels to the tender and downy skin so that the leather, the cold silk, the hard stones themselves seem to become something warm, tender, alive . . . – having probably read somewhere, then, that really fashionable people owed it to themselves to own a racing stable, for from all appearances she had never seen a horse before then in her life, Iglésia telling how once she had even taken it into her head to learn to ride too: de Reixach having bought her a half-blood for that purpose, and Iglésia saw them come five or six mornings in a row, she in one (or rather several – each time a different one) of those outfits, he said, that must have cost just for itself as much as the animal on which she tried to sit, and he who could have been her father trying to explain with that same impenetrable, patient and neutral expression that a horse wasn't exactly a convertible (nor a servant) and wasn't driven (didn't obey) in exactly the same way; but that didn't last (probably, Iglésia said, because no animal has ever enjoyed getting up on the back of another animal, and no animal has ever enjoyed feeling another animal on its back, except in circuses, because after the horse had thrown her once or twice, she didn't insist), any more, in fact, than the infatuation for the Italian sports car had lasted, and the half-blood stayed in the stable after that, which only made one horse more to groom and exercise, and if she reappeared after that in those riding breeches and those boots that cost as much as the horse on which they were supposed to permit her to mount, it was probably just for the pleasure of exhibiting herself in them, the saddled half-blood waiting an hour or two (that was usually the average delay after the telephone call notifying him to have the horse ready) before she arrived, lingering a moment in the stables and leaving again (usually not in the sports car which already didn't amuse her much any more, but in that kind of chauffeur-driven hearse as big as a room and on the back seat of which she looked something like the host (that is, something unreal, melting, something that can be known, tasted and possessed only by the tongue, the mouth, by deglutition) in the centre of one of those enormous luxurious monstrances) after distributing a few lumps of sugar and asking to watch – with a massive gold chronometer in her hand which fortunately she didn't know much about using – the horse that was to run the following Sunday.

And Iglésia told how the first time he had seen her he had taken her from a distance for a child, a girl de Reixach might have taken out of boarding school on Sundays and dressed up as a woman out of fatherly weakness (which would have explained that indefinable sensation of uneasiness you felt at first, he explained in his own way, as at the sight of something vaguely, indefinably monstrous, embarrassing, like those children dressed up, travestied in clothes copied from grown-ups', like sacrilegious and disturbing parodies of adults, prejudicial both to childhood and to the human condition), and he said that that was what had struck him first: that childish, innocent, fresh, somehow pre-virginal quality, so that it had taken him a minute to notice, to realize – seized then by a kind of stupor, feeling a wave of something furious, scandalized and fierce rising in him – that she was not only a woman but the most Woman of all the women he had ever seen, even in fantasy: 'Even in films,' he said. 'Fantastic!' (speaking of her not the way a man talks about a woman he has possessed, penetrated, held in his arms moaning and beside herself, but like some kind of alien creature, and alien not so much to himself, Iglésia (that is – although he had pushed her back, thrown her down, held her beneath him – above him by her situation, by money, by social position) as to the whole human race (including other women), therefore speaking of her in virtually the same words, the same intonations as if she were one of those objects among which he included probably film stars (deprived of all reality, save an imaginary one), horses, or even those things (mountains, boats, planes) to which the man who perceives through them the manifestations of the natural forces he is struggling against, attributes human reactions (anger, malignancy, treachery): beings (the horses, the celluloid goddesses, the motor-cars) of a hybrid, ambiguous nature, not quite human, not quite object, inspiring both respect and irreverence by the combination, the compromise in them of disparate constitutive elements (real or supposed) – human and inhuman – , which was doubtless why he talked about her the way horse dealers talk about their animals or mountain climbers about mountains, his manner both coarse and deferential, crude and delicate, his voice when he described her expressing a kind of vaguely scandalized stupefaction, but vaguely admiring and reproving at the same time, exactly like the time he had come up to examine Blum's horse during a halt without managing to discover the blisters which should normally have been produced by the abominable way Blum saddled and rode, his big round incredulous, pensive, slightly bewildered eyes staring into nothingness while he was talking, staring, probably seeing again – with the same incredulous astonishment, the same disarmed reprobation with which he had looked at the horse's back without discovering on it the sores that should have been there – the woman he was describing, or rather of whom he let the image, the memory be wrenched from him, which his reticence natural to men of the people, combined with the respect (not servile, since it hadn't even occurred to him to turn back and look at the place where de Reixach had fallen, but merely timid) for his employers, would have prevented him from discussing if he hadn't apparently been convinced of Corinne's inhuman or nonhuman character, saying:) 'I had to get close to her. Fantastic! Only then I realized why he couldn't have cared less about what people might or might not think or say, and about looking like her father, and letting her ruin the horses just for the pleasure of pressing the chronometer button and moving her buttocks around in those jodhpurs he could only pay for with money when he would probably have preferred to have had them made out of gold if there had been a way to make jodhpurs out of . . . ' And Blum: 'Oh yes, and I suppose if he'd been able to find a couturier capable of shutting it up for him in a safe, and with a lock, one of those combination locks whose combination no one else would have known, when as it was the first comer, the first number to come along, the first key to come along did the trick just as . . . ', and Georges: 'Oh shut your mouth, that's enough!', and to Iglésia: 'And then it must have been after that story with the filly, I bet, that's what decided her, that was when she . . . ', and Iglésia: 'No, before, She . . . I mean we . . . I mean I think that's why he was so eager to race her. Because I think he had suspected something. We had done it only once and no one could have seen us, but I think he had smelled something funny. Or maybe she had even arranged it so that he would half guess it, short of throwing me out, because in those days I don't think that would have made any difference to her. Or perhaps she hadn't been able to keep one word, one remark from slipping out. And then he wanted to ride her . . . ' And with no transition he began talking to them about the filly, the chestnut, with the same words he had used to describe the woman, saying: 'That bastard' (and though he meant de Reixach there was nothing insulting in it, on the contrary: something like a promotion, raising him, doing him the honour of raising him to the rank of a jockey, that is, admitting he possessed a jockey's qualities and consequently able to forget that he was his employer, using about him a word not pejorative but familiar, only tinged with a faint but affectionate nuance of blame, that he would have used for one of his own kind, that is, for one of his equals, saying then – in that nasal, plaintive and almost whining, almost childish voice which contrasted with his hard and caricatural ruffian's face, his knife-blade nose, his skin or rather his yellowed leather, pitted with smallpox scars:) 'That bastard, I told him he shouldn't try to force her, to let her go, all he had to do was let her alone, let her forget as much as possible that he was on her back, and then she'd go all by herself. I told him: "It's not my business to tell you how to ride, but you're driving her too hard. A steeplechase isn't a horse show: in the bunch she'll take all the jumps she'd never be willing to take any other way. So it's not worth driving her so hard. It doesn't matter so much for the others, but she can't stand it . . . " '

And this time Georges could see them, exactly as if he had been there himself: all three (by then the trainer – the former

adjutant – had been gone a long time, without their being able
to tell from the few words they had been able to get out of
Iglésia if it was he, the trainer, who had watched Corinne spoil
his horses for him and refused to go on taking care of them or
if it was Corinne who had had him sacked, for after he left,
according to what Iglésia said, and when he himself had taken
over the training, she stopped coming to make them gallop for
the mere pleasure of pressing the chronometer button), seeing
the three of them in or rather in front of that stall where the
hydrocephalic groom with the doll's limbs, the face precociously
aged (puffy, with pouches under his eyes, his eyes themselves
with something stale, prurient in them, that is, containing, filled,
at fourteen, with the experience of a man of sixty, or almost, or
maybe even worse), trying to hold the filly still while Iglésia,
crouching, adjusted her gaiters, she and de Reixach standing,
watching him, and she saying almost without opening her lips,
without looking away from Iglésia, speaking in a furious, imperceptible voice: 'You're still bent on this nonsense, you're
really going to ride her?' and de Reixach: 'Yes,' the sweat (not
fear, apprehension: merely the suffocating heavy atmosphere of
the stifling stormy June afternoon that was also making the
chestnut restive) standing in tiny gleaming drops on his forehead, also answering without turning his head, without raising
his voice, not casual or provocative, not even stubborn, merely
saying yes, watching Iglésia's movements below him, saying
without transition, but aloud now: 'Don't wrap them too tight,'
and she stamping her foot furiously, repeating: 'What's the good
of it? What good can it do you?' and he: 'None, I just want
to . . . ', and she: 'Listen: let him ride her, he . . . ', and he:
'Why?', and she: 'What good can it do you?' and he: 'Why?'
and she: 'No reason. Because it's his job to be a jockey, isn't it?
Isn't that why you pay him?', and he: 'But it's not a question of
money,' and she: 'But it's his job, isn't it?' and he loudly: 'Why
don't you cool her off a little? She . . . ', and Iglésia standing up:
'She'll be all right, Monsieur. Do what I told you and she'll be

all right. She's a little nervous from the weather, but she'll be all right,' and she talking to Iglésia now, but somehow more with her eyes than with her mouth, her eyes hard, furious, fixed on Iglésia's, or rather planted in them like nails, while underneath, her lips moved without either of them needing to hear what they were saying: 'Don't you think that with this storm coming she'll be, I mean wouldn't it be better if you . . . ' and de Reixach: 'There: put the sponge on . . . There, yes, like that, yes, that's right, there . . . ', and she: 'Ooohh! . . . ', and Iglésia: 'Don't worry, she'll be all right. Just let her go and she'll be all right, she only wants . . . ', and she suddenly opening her bag (a sudden, unforeseeable gesture, with that lightning-like rapidity of animal movements, the execution not following but apparently preceding the intention or, so to speak, the thought, rummaging furiously in it, her hand immediately coming out again, the two men having just time to glimpse the sparkle – the flash – of diamonds, a bracelet, the dry click of the clasp snapped back in place), the hand with the polished nails, the fragile porcelain fingers now holding out a crumpled mass of loose bills, or rather stuffing them under Iglésia's nose, the furious voice saying: 'Here. Go bet for me. For us. Half and half. Go do it yourself. Take your choice. I don't want to see the tickets. You don't even need to take them if you think it isn't worth it, if you think he wouldn't know the . . . ', and de Reixach: 'Now what the . . . ', and she: 'I don't want to see the tickets, Iglésia, I . . . ', and de Reixach (a little pale now, the muscles of his jaw bulging, shifting under the skin, the sweat streaming down over his temples, saying, still without raising his voice – still impersonal, calm, but now maybe a little drier, shorter): 'Now look. Stop that,' suddenly ordering her or else perhaps addressing Iglésia as well, or perhaps the groom, the toad-faced apprentice pressing the sponge on the filly's head, for he stepped forward, took the sponge out of his hands, wrung it out and began wiping it, scarcely moist now, over the neck several times without turning round, speaking gently to the groom – the toad – , the

latter saying: 'Yes Monsieur – No Monsieur – Yes Monsieur . . . '
while behind them Iglésia and Corinne went on staring at each
other, Corinne talking very fast, in that voice she was trying to
control now, to keep down, but still a shade too loud without
revealing if it was anger, anxiety or what, as if it were merely
the transparency of the cerise picture-hat that reddened her face,
her neck, the upper parts of her arms bared to the armpits
(showing, where the shoulders and the breasts met, those two
delicate, fan-shaped folds of the impetuous, hard, swollen flesh)
by one of those violent, not antagonistic but antagonized dresses,
that is, whose fragility, insubstantiality, meagre dimensions gave
the impression that half of it had already been torn away and
that the little still remaining only held by something like a thread,
and more indecent than a nightgown (or rather which would
have been indecent on any other woman but which on her was
something beyond indecency, that is, suppressing, making senseless any notion of decency or indecency), Corinne saying:
'Halves, Iglésia. On her. To win. You can choose: bet on her,
make him let you ride her, and win about six months' salary.
Or if you think he can make her win, it's the same thing. Or if
you think he can't make her win, keep the money. I don't want
to see the tickets. Now are you going to keep on saying she'll
go by herself?', and Iglésia: 'I don't have time to bet, I have to
take ca . . . ', and she: 'It only takes two minutes to go over to
those windows and get back here. You have plenty of time,' and
then Iglésia said that it was like the opposite of what he had
felt that day when he had seen her for the first time walking
beside de Reixach, that is, it seemed to him that he had in front
of him not a child or a young woman or an old woman but an
ageless woman, like an accumulation of all women, old or young,
something that was just as much fifteen, thirty or sixty as thousands of years old, animated by or exhaling a fury, a resentment,
a hostility, a guile that were not the result of a certain experience
or a certain accumulation of time, but of something else, thinking (later telling what he had thought): 'Old whore! Old bitch!',

and looking up seeing only the angelic face, the transparent halo of blonde hair, the young impetuous unpolluted unpollutable flesh, and then quickly looking down, staring at the crumpled bills in his hand, calculating that he was holding virtually the equivalent of what it took him two months to earn, and how many months' salary that would make if he bet as he should have bet, then looking at Corinne again, thinking: 'But what does she want Does she even know It doesn't make sense It doesn't make sense,' and finally lowering his eyes for good, saying: 'Yes, Madame,' and Corinne: 'Yes what?', and de Reixach still with his back to them, crouching now, checking the buckles of the gaiters, calling: 'Iglésia!', and she: 'Yes what?', and de Reixach still without turning round: 'Listen we have other things to do besides . . . ', and she stamping: 'Then you're going to let him ride? Are you . . . Are you . . . ', and Iglésia: 'Don't worry Madame, She'll go by herself, I'm telling you. You'll see,' and she: 'Which means you're going to bet on her all the same or are you just keeping the money?', and before he had opened his mouth to answer: 'But I don't want to know. Do whatever you want. Go on and help him play the fool. He pays you for that too, after all . . . ' Then she and Iglésia standing beside each other in the grandstand, Iglésia (he had ridden a horse in the first race) with a frayed jacket over his brilliant silk, his face streaming with sweat now, and a little winded from having run to catch up with her, – having trotted round the whole track beside the filly, carrying that bucket full of water (which he could have had the groom carry, but which he had taken, or rather torn from his hands), running then, as though crushed by the weight of the bucket, on his short and twisted jockey's legs, his head raised towards de Reixach who occasionally handed him the sponge which he dipped in the bucket, wrung out, letting it swell up again without stopping for a minute as he trotted beside him, without interrupting the voluble flood – advice, recommendations, objections? – of words that came out of his mouth, excited, passionate, panting, de Reixach merely nodding now and then, trying to make the filly walk straight when she shied, advanced diagonally, constantly dancing, taking (de Reixach) the sponge held out to him, pressing it on the filly's head between the ears and tossing it back to Iglésia who caught it in the air. Then they reached the gate, he tossed the sponge behind him without looking, and the chestnut leaped ahead like a spring, starting at a gallop, pulling as hard as she could at the bridle, neck turned slightly to one side, one shoulder forward, her long tail whipping the air, bounding as if she had been a rubber ball, de Reixach inseparable from her, almost standing in the stirrups, his chest forward, the pink spot of the silk quickly diminishing from bound to bound, silently, Iglésia standing there against the white barrier, watching them diminish disappear scarcely rising as they took the little hedge before the turn, after which he saw nothing but the black cap and the silk no longer diminishing, moving now – rising and falling – above the hedge and to the right, and disappearing behind the little woods: then leaving the bucket and sponge there and as fast as his legs allowed (that is, the way a jockey can run, that is, almost the way a horse runs if you've cut off its legs at the knees) heading towards the grandstand, butting into people, head raised, looking for Corinne, passing the place, finally discovering her, turning back, climbing the stairs and as soon as he was beside her suddenly motionless, turned towards the little woods, the pair of enormous binoculars (the ones de Reixach habitually used) already trained, as if, like a magician, he had had them ready in the palm of his hand – although they were about a foot long – or up his sleeve: appearing, extracted, one might have said, from nowhere and not from their case, because it was impossible for him to have had time to open the case and then get them out of it so quickly, that is, between the moment when he had appeared, panting, beside Corinne, and the one when he had them, holding them in both hands, glued to his eyes above that eagle (or clown) nose like a natural part of his body, a kind of functional organ (like those little black tubes screwed into jewellers' eyes), protuberant, abnormally developed, enormous, shiny, and covered with a black, grainy leather – like those bulging, carbuncular and faceted eyes that can be seen on the heads of flies or certain other insects in microphotographs.

And then as motionless as a statue. And then Corinne, too, as motionless as a statue, trying with the same eagerness to see what was happening behind the little wood, saying without opening her mouth or turning her head or raising her voice, exactly the way she had argued with de Reixach a little earlier: 'Damn flunkey.' And he so to speak totally absorbed in the huge binoculars and probably not even hearing her, or perhaps realizing that she was talking to him but not even bothering to listen, to try to understand, saying: 'Yes, that was a nice break, yes, that's it, that's it, you have to . . . Yes: she's, she's going . . .', and around them the calm uproar of the crowd, the last betters flowing back towards the rail or climbing into the grandstands like a slow black tide, although most of them were running, but already not looking in front of them, all with their heads turned towards the little wood, the heads of the ones who were running facing the same way as the heads of the ones already sitting in the stands or standing on chairs dragged out into the paddock: the painted porcelain heads of mannequins surrounded by photographers, the wrinkled and papery heads of old colonels under their grey bowlers, the heads of millionaires with their horse-dealer's look, merchants or distillers or money salesmen from father to son, usurers, owners of horses, of women, of mines, of whole districts of houses, of slums, of villas with swimming pools, of chateaux, of yachts, of skeletal Negroes or Indians, of big or little slot machines (from the ones six storeys high made out of stone, concrete and steel to the trash made out of painted tin and reflectors the colour of gumdrops): a species or class or race whose fathers or grandfathers or great-grandfathers or great-great-grandfathers had one day found a means, by violence, trickery or constraint exercised in a more or less legal fashion (and probably more than less, considering that right, law is always only the consecration of a state of force) of amassing the fortunes they were now spending but which, by a sort of consequence, a curse attached to the violence and the trickery, condemned them to find growing round them only that fauna which is also trying to acquire (or to profit by) those very fortunes (or merely fortune) by violence or trickery, and whom the former managed to jostle (breathing the same air, trampling the same dusty gravel, as if they had been assembled in the same salon) without even seeming to notice their presence, nor even – perhaps – to see them: the heads of the betters with dubious occupations, with dubious collars, with dubious faces, with hawks' eyes, with hardened, pitiless, frustrated faces gnawed, corroded by passion: the North-African workers who paid almost the equivalent of a half-day's work for merely the fond privilege of seeing up close the horse on which they had bet their week's pay, the pimps, the pedlars, the tipsters, the grooms, the chauffeurs, the con-cessionaires, the old baronesses, and the ones who had come only because it was a beautiful day, and those who would have come anyway, trampling in the mud and shivering in the draughts, if it had rained spears, all huddled now in the stands with the sculptured gingerbread floating in the sky with the whipped-cream clouds, motionless, like meringues, that is, swollen, puffed up on top and flattened underneath as if they had been set on an invisible sheet of glass, neatly aligned in successive rows which the perspective brought closer together in the distance (like the trunks of trees along a road) to form, far away, towards the misty horizon, above the tree tops and the delicate factory chimneys, a suspended, motionless ceiling, until when you looked more carefully you realized that the whole drifting archipelago was imperceptibly sliding, sailing over the houses, the incredibly green turf, the little wood to the right of which the horses appeared at last, heading now towards the gate: no longer one, three or ten but, with the varicoloured and motley patches of the silks, the undulating tails, the arrogant gait of the animals on their tiny legs no thicker than twigs, a medieval apparition,

a brilliant group in the distance (and not only in the distance, at
the end of the turn, but as though advancing so to speak from
the depth of time, across the brilliant fields of battle where, in
the space of a sparkling afternoon, of a charge, of a gallop,
kingdoms and the hands of princesses were lost or won): then
Iglésia saw him, he told them later, separate, dissociated by the
binoculars from the anonymous motley of the colours, on that
filly like a streak of pale bronze, and wearing the black cap and
that bright pink silk bordering on mauve that she had somehow
imposed on both of them (Iglésia and de Reixach) like a kind
of voluptuous and lascivious symbol) like the colours of an order
or rather the emblems of functions so to speak seminal and
turgescent), able to make out between the two (between the
silk and the cap) that perfectly inexpressive face, apparently
empty of emotions and of thoughts, not even concentrated or
attentive: merely impassive (Iglésia thinking, saying later: 'Well
Good God he could have let me ride. If it was to prove something, hell! What did he expect? That after that she wouldn't
sleep with anyone but him, that she'd go without being screwed
by the first man to come along simply because she's seen him
on her back? But if it hadn't been me it would have been the
same. Because she was in heat. And the weather didn't make it
any better. So even before she started she was soaked to the
skin! . . . ') able to see as if he had been only a few yards away
the filly's neck covered with a grey lather at the place where
the reins rubbed it, the group, the hieratic and medieval group
still heading for the stone wall, having crossed the centre of the
figure eight now, the horses hidden again up to the belly by the
border hedges, half disappearing so that they seemed cut off half
way up, only their backs still visible, seeming to slide along the
field of green corn like ducks on the motionless surface of a
pond, I could see them as they were turning right he at the head
of the bunch as if it had been July 14th one then two then
three then the whole first group then the second the horses
calmly following each other like those petticoat horses children

116

used to play with those aquatic animals floating on their bellies propelled by invisible webbed feet slipping slowly one after the other with their identical arched chess-piece necks their identical riders with their identical arched bodies swaying half falling asleep probably although it had been daylight for some time the sky pink with dawn the countryside still half asleep too, there was a kind of vaporous moistness there must have been dewdrops clinging to the blades of grass which the sun would evaporate I could easily recognize him in the distance out ahead by the way he had of sitting straight up on his saddle contrasting with the other limp figures as if for him fatigue simply didn't exist, about half the squadron caught when they flowed back towards the crossroads like an accordion as though under the pressure of an invisible piston pushing them back, the last ones still advancing while the head of the column somehow seemed to retract the noise coming only afterwards so that there was a moment (perhaps a fraction of a second but seeming longer) when in the complete silence there was only this: the little petticoat horses and their riders thrown back in disorder, one against the other, exactly like chess pieces collapsing in a row the sound when it came with that slight delay in time with the image itself exactly like the hollow sound of the ivory pieces drumming falling one after the other on the chessboard like this: tac-tac-tac-tac-tac the bursts of gunfire superimposed accumulating apparently then on top of us the invisible plucked guitar strings weaving the invisible chain of deadly silky torn air also I never heard the order shouted seeing only the bodies in front of me collapse closer and closer while the right legs moved one after the other over the rumps like the pages of a book flipped backward and once on the ground I looked for Wack to hand him the bridle at the same time that my right hand was struggling behind my back with that damn rifle hook then it came on us from behind the thunder of hoofs the galloping of wild horses riderless now eyes huge ears flat stirrups empty the reins whipping the air twisting like serpents and two or three covered with blood and one with his rider still on his back screaming They're behind us too they let us get through and then they, the rest of his words carried away with him leaning over the neck his mouth wide open like a hole and now it was no longer with the rifle hook that I was struggling but against that nag trying to break away head high neck stiff as a mast the pupil entirely blank as though she were trying to look behind her ears stepping back not by fits and starts but so to speak methodically one foot after the other and me pulling at her hard enough to tear off her jaw saying All right All right as if she could even hear me in that racket gradually shortening the reins until I could reach her neck with one hand patting her repeating All right All right Theeeeeere . . . until she stopped, standing motionless but tense strained trembling in every limb her hoofs stiff and wide apart like stilts and probably there had been another order shouted while I was struggling with her because I realized (not seeing because I was too busy watching her but sensing, divining) in that disorder that uproar that they were all remounting getting close to her then (still as stiff as strained as if she had been made out of wood) as gently as possible watching carefully in case she kicked or reared or broke into a gallop just when I would have a foot in the stirrup but she still didn't move just trembling where she stood like a motor idling and she let me get my foot in the stirrup without doing a thing, only when I seized the pommel and the cantle to lift myself up the saddle turned over, I was expecting that too for three days I had been trying to find a girth to exchange for this one that was too long for her after I had had to leave Edgar behind but you can't get a thing out of those peasants it was as if asking them to switch girths was trying to rob them and Blum's was too long too so it was really the perfect moment for a thing like that to happen to me when there was shooting on all sides at once but I didn't even have time to swear not even enough breath not even enough time to get out a word just enough to think of it while I was trying to get that damn saddle on her back again in the middle of all those men who were passing round me at a gallop now and then I saw that my hands were trembling but I couldn't stop them any more than I could stop her body from trembling I stopped trying I began running alongside her holding her by the bridle she starting to canter with the saddle now almost directly under her belly among the horses – with riders or riderless – that were passing us the deadly network of plucked guitar strings stretched like a ceiling over our heads but it was only when I saw two or three fall that I realized that I was in the ditch of the road while they were too high on horseback so they got shot down like ninepins then I saw Wack (things happening paradoxically enough in a kind of silence a void in other words the sound of the bullets and the explosions – they must have been using mortars now or those little tank cannons – once accepted admitted and somehow forgotten neutralizing themselves somehow you heard absolutely nothing no shouts no voices probably because no one had time to shout so that it reminded me of when I was running the 1,500 metres: only the whistling noise of the breathing the swearing itself choked before it came out and then came a jostling as if the lungs were seizing all the available air to distribute it through the body and use it only for useful things: looking deciding running, things consequently happening a little as though in a film without its sound track), I saw Wack who had just passed me leaning over the neck of his horse his face turned back towards me his mouth open too probably trying to shout something which he didn't have air enough to make heard and suddenly lifted off his saddle as if a hook an invisible hand had grabbed him by his coat collar and slowly raised him I mean almost motionless in relation to (I mean animated by almost the same speed as) his horse that kept on galloping and me still running although a little slower now so that Wack his horse and I comprised a group of objects among which the distances were modified only gradually he being now exactly over the horse from which he had just been lifted wrenched slowly rising in the air his legs still arched as though he were still riding some invisible Pegasus who had bucked and made him fall slowing then and somehow making a kind of double *salto mortale* on the spot so that I saw him next head down mouth still open on the same shout (or advice he had tried to give me) silent then lying in the air on his back like a man stretched out in a hammock and letting his legs hang down to the right and left then again head up body vertical his legs beginning to come together hanging parallel then on his stomach arms stretched forward hands open grabbing snatching something like one of those circus acrobats during the seconds when he is attached to nothing and liberated of all weight between the two trapezes then finally the head down again legs apart arms outstretched as though to bar the way but motionless now flat against the roadside slope and no longer moving staring at me his face stamped with a surprised and idiot expression I thought Poor Wack he always looked like a fool but now more than ever he, then I no longer thought, something like a mountain or a horse falling on me throwing me to the ground trampling me while I felt the reins wrenched out of my hands then everything went black while thousands of galloping horses went on passing over my body then I no longer even felt the horses only something like a smell of ether and the dark my ears buzzing and when I opened my eyes again I was lying on the road and not one horse and only Wack still on the slope head down still looking at me his eyes wide open with that shocked look but I was careful not to move waiting for the moment when I would begin to suffer having heard somewhere that the worst wounds create a kind of anaesthesia at first but still feeling nothing and after a moment I tried to move but nothing happened managing to get on to my hands and knees my face towards the ground I could see the earth of the road the stones looking like triangles or irregular polygons of a slightly bluish white in their matrix of pale ochre earth there was something like a carpet of grass in the centre of the path then to the right and the left where the wheels of the cars and carts passed two bare ruts then the grass growing on the

sides and raising my head I saw my shadow still very pale and
fantastically elongated thinking Then the sun's up, and at that
moment I was aware of the silence and I saw that just beyond
Wack there was a man sitting on the roadside: he was holding
his arm a little above the elbow his hand hanging all red between
his legs but it wasn't a man from the squadron he said They've
got us, I didn't answer he stopped paying any attention to me
and went on looking at his hand, in the distance there were still
a few bursts of gunfire I looked at the road behind us in the
direction of the crossroads I saw brownish-yellow heaps on the
ground that didn't move and horses and near us a horse lying
on its side in a pool of blood its legs still twitching feebly, spas-
modically then I sat down on the slope beside the man thinking
But it was only just dawn, I said What time is it, but he didn't
answer then there was a burst of gunfire very close this time I
threw myself down into the ditch I heard the man say They've
got us again, but I didn't turn round I crawled down the ditch
to where the slope stopped and after that I began running bent
double to a grove of trees but no one fired and no one fired
when I ran from the grove of trees to a hedge I crawled through
the hedge on my belly pulling myself out the other side by my
hands lying flat until I managed to catch my breath again there
wasn't any more firing now I heard a bird singing the shadows
of the trees grew longer ahead of me across the meadow I crept
on all fours along the hedge perpendicular to the shadows of
the trees until the corner of the field then I began climbing up
the hill on the other side of the meadow still on all fours against
the hedge my shadow in front of me again now and when I was
in the forest walking among the flakes of sunlight I was careful
to keep the sun in front of me calculating as the time passed that
I would have to keep it in front of me and slightly to the right
at first later on to the right but still ahead of me, there were
cuckoos in the forest other birds too I didn't know their names
but especially cuckoos or maybe it was because I knew their
name that I noticed them maybe too because of their more

characteristic cry the sun through the leaves cast my leafy shadow that moved on ahead of me then slightly to the right, walking a long time without hearing anything except the cuckoos and those birds whose names I didn't know, finally I got tired of walking through the woods all the time and followed a path but my shadow was on my left then, a moment later I found a path that crossed it I took that one and my shadow was ahead of me again and to the right but I calculated I should follow it longer than the first one to compensate for the digression I had had to make and then I was hungry and I remembered the piece of sausage I was carrying round in my coat pocket I ate it while I was walking I ate the skin too down to the stub knotted by the thread I threw that away then the forest stopped collided so to speak with the empty sky opening on a pool and when I lay down to drink the little frogs jumped in they didn't make any more noise than big raindrops: near the edge where they had jumped in a tiny cloud of grey mud hung in the water then dissolved between the reeds they were green and no bigger around than my little finger the surface of the water was covered with little round pale-green leaves about the size of confetti that was why it took me a moment to realize they were coming back I saw one then two then three breaking the pale-green confetti letting just the tips of their heads stick out with their tiny bulging eyes like pinheads staring at me there was a faint current and I saw one drifting slowly letting itself be carried between the archipelagos of agglutinated confetti the same colour as it was it looked like a drowned man its arms outstretched the head half out of the water the delicate little webbed hands open then it moved and I didn't see it any more I mean I didn't even see it move, it simply wasn't there any more except for the tiny cloud of mud it had stirred up, the water was viscous with a viscous fishy taste I pushed aside the little confetti when I drank being careful not to drink the mud my face raised among the reeds and the broad lance-shaped leaves then I stayed there sitting at the edge of the woods behind the thickets listening to the cuckoos

calling to each other among the silent tree trunks in the spring
green air looking at the road that followed the pond and then
skirted the trees from time to time a fish jumped with a plop I
never saw one, only the concentric circles growing wider and
wider round the place where it had jumped once some planes
passed over but very high in the sky I saw one or rather something a silver point hanging motionless sparkling a fraction of
a second in a blue hole between the branches then disappearing
their noise seemed to be suspended too vibrating in the light air
then it gradually faded and again I could hear the delicate rustling
of the leaves and again the song of a cuckoo and a little after at
the turn of the road two officers came out walking their horses
but maybe they didn't know there was a war on they were
walking calmly in step chatting when I saw they were wearing
khaki and not green I stood up thinking of the face they would
make when they saw me and when I told them that the panzers
were strolling up the road six or seven kilometres from here
probably someone had forgotten to warn them I stood up in
the middle of the road in the woodland peace where I could still
hear the cuckoos and occasionally the sudden invisible and lazy
leap of a fish out of the unalterable mirror of the pond then I
thought Good God Good God Good God Good God, recognizing him recognizing the voice that reached me now or rather that
fell on me arrogant distant calm with something playful almost
gay in it saying So you managed to get out of it too? saying as
he turned towards the short second-lieutenant You see they're
not all dead There are still some who got out, saying again in
my direction Iglésia's leading two horses You take one, I could
hear the water murmuring where the pond made a little waterfall
the rustling of the leaves stirred by the imperceptible breeze, on
a level with my eyes I saw the knees press almost imperceptibly
and the horse start forward passing in front of me the boots
sparkling the mahogany flanks covered with dried sweat the
rump the tail then again the calm pond across which the breeze
stirred the broad lance-shaped leaves with a papery rustle, his

voice as he moved away reaching me again (but it was not me he was talking to now he had resumed his conversation with the short second-lieutenant and I could hear him slightly bored distinguished nonchalant) saying: . . . bad business. Apparently they use those tanks as . . . , then he was too far away I had forgotten that such things are merely called a 'business' the way you say 'that business' when you mean 'fighting a duel' a delicate euphemism a discreeter more elegant formula well so much the better not all was lost since we were still among well-bred people say don't say, example don't say 'the squadron has been massacred in an ambush,' but 'we had a bad business outside the village of,' then Iglésia's voice and his clown's face looking at me with his round eyes his offended impatient and vaguely reproving expression saying Then you're riding yes or no? All the time I've been dragging these two nags behind me, it isn't funny I can tell you! I got in the saddle and followed them I had to trot to catch up with Iglésia then I slowed the horse down to a walk I could see him from the back now with that little second-lieutenant beside him walking calmly the horses moving with that tremendous slowness, that complete absence of haste that you find only in those beings or things (boxers, serpents, planes) capable of striking, moving or changing position with lightning-like speed, the sky, the calm cottony clouds still drifting by at a speed that was also almost imperceptible in the opposite direction (so that between the graceful, medieval and elegant silhouettes that kept advancing towards the right where, with his whip in his hand, the starter was waiting for them, and the clouds, one of those infuriating slowness contests seemed to be in progress, a demonstration in which each entrant vied with the rest for majesty, unconcerned with that feverish and futile impatience that made the crowd seethe: the stiff, delicate and foolish thoroughbreds, capable not of reaching but of becoming in the wink of an eye something not released at a tremendous speed but which would be speed itself, the slow clouds like those proud armadas apparently resting motionless on the sea and which seem to move by leaps and bounds at a fantastic speed, the eye exhausted by their apparent immobility abandoning them, discovering them a moment later, still apparently motionless, at the other end of the horizon, thus covering fabulous distances while beneath them, tiny and ridiculous, parade cities, hills, woods, and under which, without their ever seeming to have moved, still majestic, puffy and imponderable, still other cities, other woods, other absurd hills would parade, long after the horses, the public had abandoned the racetrack, the grandstands, the green turf speckled and soiled by the thousands of betting tickets lost like so many tiny stillborn corpses of dreams and hopes (the marriage not of heaven and earth but of earth and man, leaving it soiled by the persistence of that residue, of that kind of giant and foetal pollution of tiny furiously torn scraps of paper), long after the last horse had kicked up the last clod of the turf and had left, surrounded by more servants, more attentions, precautions and care for its nerves than a film star, and the echo of the last and furious cries had fallen over the silent stands abandoned to the clean-up crews, no longer echoing save to the faint and prosaic rustle of the brooms), Corinne no longer watching what was happening at the end of the turn, stamping furiously again, saying: 'Couldn't you stop watching for a second? Do you hear me? There's nothing to see now. They're going back to the gate. They . . . Do you hear me, or don't you?', and he reluctantly taking the binoculars away from his face, turning his great fish eyes towards her, the lids blinking, the pupils cloudy, a little blurred from the effort he was making to focus at this proximity, saying in his frail, timid, whining voice: 'You . . . You shouldn't have. He . . . ', his voice dying away, swallowed up, submerged (beneath the brutal and piercing ringing of the bell) by the kind of long sigh rising from the relieved crowd, swooning and voracious (not exactly an orgasm, but somehow a pre-orgasm, something like the moment when the man penetrates the woman), while far in the distance, they could see now a kind of elongated and motley blur moving quickly across the turf, at the level of the ground, the horses shifting without transition from their casual semi-immobility to movement, the bunch running fast without fits and starts, as though it were mounted on a wire or on rollers, like those children's toys, all the horses soldered together in a single block cut out of a piece of cardboard or painted tin that was being slid along the slot arranged for this purpose in a *trompe-l'oeil* painted and varnished landscape, the jockeys all leaning forward at the same angle, the horses hidden up to the belly by the border hedges: then they came out on to the junction of the track and for a moment you could see their legs coming and going fast, like compasses opening and closing, but always to the same mechanical, regular and abstract rhythm of a spring-operated toy; then again there was nothing else to see, behind the little wood, except for the silks passing behind the tree trunks the branches like a handful of confetti and which seemed – perhaps because of their material, their brilliant colours – to gather up, to concentrate in themselves all the sparkling light of the dazzling afternoon, the tiny pink spot (and yet under which there was a man's body, the flesh, the tense muscles, the tumultuous afflux of blood, the organs abused and forced) in fourth position:

'Because after all he knew how to ride. Have to give him his due: he knew what he was doing. Because he had got off to a damn good start,' Iglésia told them later; now they were crouching all three of them (Georges, Blum and he: the two young men and that Italian (or Spaniard) with olive skin and who himself had almost as many years behind him as the first two together, and probably something like ten times their experience, which must have made about thirty times that of Georges because despite the fact that he and Blum were both apparently of the same age Blum possessed by heredity a knowledge (intelligence Georges had said, but it wasn't only that: still more: the intimate atavistic experience, which had passed to the reflex stage, of human stupidity and wickedness) of things that was worth a good three times what a young man of good family could have gained from the study of the classical French Latin and Greek authors, and ten days of combat, or rather of retreat, or rather of a chase, where he – the young man of good family – had played the role of the game), all three, then, as different in age as in origin collected here from the four corners of the world ('All we need is a Negro,' Georges said. 'What have we got already? Shem, Ham and Japhet, but we needed a fourth; we should have invited him: after all, it was harder to find this mess and bring it all here than to take off a wrist-watch!') crouching in that corner of the still unfinished camp behind piles of bricks and Iglésia cooking over a fire something they had stolen or bartered for (this time a part of the contents of a sack of flour Georges had received in exchange for his watch – the one that had been given to him by his two old aunts Marie and Eugénie when he had been awarded his first diploma – from, as it happened, a Negro – a Senegalese from the Colonial Regiment – who himself had pinched it God knows where (as had been pinched God knows where and brought into the camp God knows why – to what end? probably on the off chance, for the superstitious pleasure of stealing, possessing and keeping – everything that could be found to sell, to buy or to barter, that is almost anything, the whole stock – and even more – of a departmental store, notions counter, antiques and staples included: not only useful or edible things – like the sack of flour – but even things without utility and even bothersome, and even incongruous things, like women's stockings or books on philosophy, false jewels, tourist guidebooks, obscene photographs, parasols, tennis rackets, agricultural pamphlets, loudspeakers, tulip bulbs, accordions, bird-cages – sometimes with the bird inside – , bronze Eiffel towers, clocks, preservatives, not to mention of course thousands of watches, chronometers, pigskin, crocodile or vulgar leather wallets that constituted the common coin of this realm, objects, relics, spoils painfully lugged kilometre after kilometre by hordes of exhausted and famished men, and hidden, concealed from searches, preserved despite prohibitions and threats, reappearing incoercibly for furtive, clandestine, feverish and hard bargainings whose object was most often not so much to acquire as to have something to sell or to buy), which, given the value of the watch, set on the pancake (for that was what Iglésia was making, pouring out on a piece of rusted iron the paste made of water, flour and a little of that coal-oil margarine distributed to the prisoners in tiny slices), a price which no proprietor of a three-star restaurant would have dared ask for a serving of caviare, – so all three of them (one crouching, the other two keeping watch), like three famished vagabonds in one of those empty lots on the outskirts of cities, and nothing soldierly left (or rather, wearing those absurd rags that are the lot of defeated warriors, and not even their own but, as if the facetious conqueror, to make fun of them at their expense, had thrust them still deeper into their condition of victims, rubbish, debris, but probably it wasn't even that: only the logical conclusion of orders, of arrangements perhaps rational in their origin, but lunatic at the stage of execution, as happens whenever an executive machinery sufficiently rigid, like the army, or sufficiently rapid, like revolutions, reflects to man without those retouches, that softening-up process provided by either an untrustworthy application or by time, the exact image of his naked thought), all three wearing, then, instead of their cavalrymen coats that had been taken away from them, overcoats of Czech or Polish soldiers received in exchange (soldiers dead perhaps, or perhaps – the coats – the spoils of war seized from untouched stockpiles in the Warsaw or Prague quartermaster stores), and of course not fitting, Georges's with sleeves that came just below the elbow and Iglésia, more of a scarecrow, a clown than ever, swimming (his delicate jockey's skeleton vanishing in a huge overcoat from which the carnival nose and the fingertips were all that emerged:) three ghosts three grotesque and unreal shadows with their fleshless faces, their eyes burning with hunger, their shaved skulls, their absurd clothes, leaning over a wretched clandestine fire in that ghostly setting of the barracks aligned on that sandy plain, with here and there on the horizon groves of pines and a motionless reddish sun, and other vague silhouettes wandering, approaching, circling angrily (abjectly) round them with envious, vulpine and feverish glances (and they too wearing those cast-off rags the colour of bile, of mud, as if a kind of corruption were covering them, corroding them, attacking them even as they stood, first their clothes, then spreading insidiously like the very colour of war, of earth, gradually taking possession, their faces ashen, their rags muddy, their eyes muddy too, with that filthy, vague tinge that already seemed to assimilate them to this clay, this mud, this dust from which they had sprung and to which, wandering, abject, dazed and sad, they returned a little more each day), and not even vulpine, that is, famished and emaciated and surly and threatening, but afflicted with that weakness only men betray, afflicted with reason, then, contrary to what would have happened if they had been real wolves, prevented from attacking by the very consciousness of what would have encouraged wolves to attack (their number), discouraged in advance by the calculation of what the wretched pancakes they lusted after would have represented once they were divided among a thousand, remaining there, then, merely prowling, with those murderous gleams in their eyes, – and once a brick flew through the air, hit Iglésia's shoulder and knocked over the iron plate and the half-cooked dough spilled into the fire, and Georges tossed the brick he was holding ready in the direction of the man running away (and probably it had not even been thrown with the intention of murder or aggression, but despair, and that unendurable rat of hunger gnawing at his belly, and the gesture then – the brick thrown – uncontrolled, uncontrollable, and immediately afterwards the miserable flight, not because of the reprisal, out of fear, but because of his own shame, his own failure), Iglésia scraping up the dough as well as he could, replacing the iron plate and starting the pancake over again, and now there were black pieces of coal in it that they tried to take out later, but some still remained, and when they ate the pan-

cake these grated against their teeth but they swallowed everything all the same, down to the last crumb, sitting like monkeys
on their heels, burning their fingers pulling the pancakes off the
stove – or rather off the piece of rusty iron that served as a
stove – , Iglésia (once he had started, talking incessantly, slowly
but continuously, patient and, apparently, for himself, not for
them, his huge eyes staring at nothing, astonished, grave and at
the same time admiring) saying between two mouthfuls: 'And with
the other bastards riding in that race it couldn't have been easy,
I tell you, because any owner who rides in a race with professional
jockeys can't expect them to make him any presents. Only he
had started off damn well: he was in fourth position now, and all
he had to do for the moment was to keep her there, and he
would have his hands full with that, I can tell you, because that
animal could pull worse than anything, the bitch . . . '

They appeared finally after the last tree, still in the same order,
the pink lozenge still in the same position as they rounded the
last section of the turn, the bunch moving gradually in a confused
mass (the last seeming to catch up with the first) which, at the
end of the straight stretch, was nothing more than a surge, a
billowing of heads rising and falling in one place, the horses
clustered, no longer seeming to advance (merely the jockey's
caps rising and sinking) until suddenly the first horse didn't
cross but burst over the hedge, in other words suddenly it was
there, its forelegs stuck straight ahead, stiff, together, or rather
one slightly ahead of the other, the two hoofs not quite at the
same height, the horse caught for half the width of its body
between the brown faggots that topped the barrier, apparently
resting on its belly as though balanced, motionless for a fraction
of a second, until it collapsed forward while a second, then a
third, then several together, all frozen successively in equilibrium,
in that rocking-horse position, appear, stay motionless, then
collapse forward, recovering movement simultaneously with
contact with the earth, the bunch galloping now, massed again,
towards the grandstands, growing larger, clearing the next

obstacle, and then it was there: the silent thunder, the muffled pounding of the earth under the hoofs, the clods of turf flying far behind, the rumpled silks flapping in the wind and the jockeys' bodies leaning over the necks, not motionless as they seemed to be on the opposite side but swaying slightly to the rhythm of the strides, with their identical mouths open, gasping for breath, their identical look of fish out of water, half asphyxiated, passing in front of the grandstands surrounded or rather enveloped by that attentive cape of dizzying silence that seemed to isolate them (the few shouts rising out of the crowd seeming – and not to the jockeys' ears but to those of the spectators themselves – to come from far away, futile, vain, incongruous and as weak as the inarticulate stammering of infants), to accompany them, leaving behind them, long after their passage, a persistent wake of silence within which the hammering of the hoofs faded, broken only sporadically by the dry clack (like the sound of a branch snapping) of a whiplash, tiny explosions fading too, diminishing, the last horse crossing the live hedge crowning the slight rise, exactly like a rabbit, the image of its hindquarters in kicking position remaining for a second immobilized on the retina and finally vanishing, jockeys and horses invisible now, re-descending the slope on the other side of the hedge, as if it had all never existed, as if the lightning-like apparition of the dozen animals and their riders had suddenly been whisked away, leaving behind, like those clouds of smoke in which goblins and magicians vanish, only a bank of reddish fog, of dust in suspension in front of the hedge, in the place where the horses had taken their leap, clearing, diluting, slowly sinking in the waning afternoon light, and Iglésia turning towards Corinne that carnival mask both terrible and pathetic, but for the moment stamped with a kind of childish excitement, boyish delight, saying: 'Did you see that? He . . . I said she . . . she'd go all by herself, that all he had to . . . ', Corinne looking at him without a word and still with that kind of fury, that silent, icy rage, Iglésia stammering, stuttering, saying: 'He's going . . . she's going . . . You . . . ', then finally falling silent, Corinne staring at him a moment longer, still without saying a word, with that same implacable contempt, and finally shrugging her shoulders suddenly, her breasts moving, trembling beneath the light stuff of her dress, all her young, firm and insolent flesh exhaling something pitiless, violent, and also childish, that is, that total lack of moral sense or charity of which only children are capable, that candid cruelty inherent in the very nature of childhood (the proud, the impetuous and irrepressible seething of life), saying coldly: 'If he's as capable of making her win as you are, I wonder why you get paid?', both of them staring at each other (she in that symbol of a dress that left her three-quarters naked, he in that old, stained jacket that matched the brilliant silk it revealed underneath about as well as the sickly and pockmarked face above it, the (baffled, dazed) expression, as if she had thrust her fist or her bag or the binoculars into his stomach) for an interval of perhaps a fraction of a second, and not interminable as he thought it was, said it was when he told about it later, saying that what wakened them, wrenched them both out of their mutual fascination, that furious and mute confrontation, wasn't a shout – or a thousand shouts – , or an exclamation – or a thousand – , but something like a murmur, a sigh, a rustling, something unexpected running, rising so to speak from the surface of the crowd, and when they looked, they saw the pink blur no longer in third but in about seventh position, the bunch that had just crossed the rise no longer welded together but spreading now over some twenty yards along the diagonal track, Corinne saying: 'I told you so. I was sure of it. The fool. The Goddamn fool. And you . . . you . . . ', but Iglésia no longer listening, looking through his binoculars at de Reixach's streaming face that was agitated only by brief tremors each time the arm holding the crop fell back, the filly extending her stride, passing one by one, with long thrusts of her loins, the horses that had passed her, so that she was once again almost in third position when they approached the stream, the chestnut, the long pale streak of bronze then seeming to stretch out even further, light now, tearing herself not from the ground but from gravity itself, for she seemed not to fall back but merely to float on, slightly above the earth's surface, in second position now, while they were crossing the intersection of the figure eight, the pale blur undulating horizontally, de Reixach not using the crop now, Corinne repeating: 'The fool, the fool, the fool . . . ', until without looking away from his binoculars Iglésia said harshly: 'For God's sake shut up! I told you to shut up, now shut up!', Corinne standing there with her mouth open, stupefied, while to their left now the bunch stretched out in the golden dust with the sun behind it beneath the immutable archipelago of clouds suspended or perhaps merely painted in the sky, the horses now distinctly divided into two groups: first four, then a space of some fifteen yards, then the second group in compact mass dragging behind it like a train the slowest runners strung out down to the last one, far back, whose jockey was using his crop at each stride, the lead group turning right, disappearing again behind the little wood, the motley silks appearing and disappearing between the trees as they had a moment before, but in the opposite direction, that is from left to right, at the same time that the crowd on the turf moved away (first a black dot, then two, then three, then ten, then in huge clusters) from the rail along which the bunch had just passed, running (the specks like flies, like a handful of marbles) in the same direction as the horses in order to cluster along the transverse track, the pink silk reappearing this time in first position, but virtually glued to the next jockey, de Reixach on the outside, swerving, carried to his left at the moment when the two horses, almost neck and neck, went into the straight stretch, so that he was almost in the middle of the track and alone, slowly passing the second horse, the next two about five yards behind, all four heading towards the bullfinch at a gallop that was less even now, jerkier, so that at first it looked as though the chestnut were only getting tired, only shortening her strides a little, Iglésia desperately pressing the enormous binoculars against his eyes, while she continued to gallop not straight towards the jump but diagonally, de Reixach pulling on the opposite rein with all his strength and using the crop, managing to pull her to the left, the filly still slowing, seeming somehow to hunch under him and taking the tremendous obstacle (for he succeeded, managed to impose his will on her), not the way she had crossed the stream but practically stopping raising her four legs at once, straight up in the air, and falling back so hard that de Reixach almost fell off over her neck at the same time that he gave her a terrible blow with the crop and she sprang ahead again, now two yards behind the two horses that had been behind her before approaching the bullfinch, Corinne and Iglésia able to see the arm holding the crop falling tirelessly, their ears buzzing, full of the crowd's wild, disappointed clamour, and once again the four horses leaped, crossed the last hedge, de Reixach close on the heels of the third horse now, then there was no longer anything in front of them but the huge and luxuriant green carpet against which they seemed (jockeys and horses) tiny and absurd, as though out of place, frantically struggling, separate, swaying slowly forward and back, jerky, pathetic, absurd, the four horses exhausted, the four riders with their fish faces, mouths open and gasping for breath, three-quarters asphyxiated now, the cries of the crowd surrounding them like a solid, dense substance through which they were vainly trying to advance (the impression of immobility accentuated still further by the effect of the binoculars cancelling out the perspective) as though through an invisible and hostile layer of passion as dense as water – or a vacuum – , then the shouting stopped, died away, and letting his binoculars fall back, Iglésia realized that she was no longer there, discovering the aggressive dress far beneath him now already at the bottom of the stand, then leaping down the steps four by four after her, running, catching up with her, then Corinne turning her head without stopping (Iglésia thinking quickly: 'But where's she going, what does she want?'), looking at him as if he had been a fly, or even nothing at all, then not looking at him any longer,

and he: 'At least he came in second, at least he found a way to
pass the other two . . . ', and she not answering, not even seeming to hear him, and he still trotting along beside her on his short
legs, saying: 'She finished very strong, you saw it, she . . . ',
and she still walking: 'Second! Fine. Bravo. Second! He should
have won by ten lengths. You think that's . . . ', then suddenly
stopping, turning towards him with a movement so sudden, so
unanticipated, that he almost bumped into her, screaming now
(although she didn't raise her voice, but, he said, it was much
worse than if she had shouted at the top of her lungs): 'Did you
bet on him to win or place? Tell me! Or did you even bet on
him at all?', then even before he had time to open his mouth,
still screaming in that scarcely audible tone which was worse
than the worst shrieking: 'No, I'm not asking to see them! I told
you I wouldn't even ask you to show them to me, you could
have kept the money for yourself . . . As a tip, as . . . ', and then,
he said, he realized with a kind of stupefaction that she was
crying, 'Perhaps just from rage,' he said later, 'perhaps just from
irritation, perhaps from something else. Can you ever tell with
women? But in any case she was crying, she couldn't even make
herself stop. Right there in the middle of all those people . . . ',
and he told how they stood there facing each other, motionless
among the crowd that was slowly flowing back round them,
she repeating No I tell you no you hear no I don't want to I
don't want to see them all I want is for you to tell me I only
want to hear you say it I . . . then saying: 'My God, Oh my
God, you did it anyway, you . . . you did . . . ', stupidly staring
at the handful of tickets he was slowly taking out of his pocket,
holding out to her, she avoided taking them as if they had been
on fire or something like that, Iglésia standing there that way
for a minute, arm outstretched, then, still slowly, still looking
at her, his arm moving, his hands coming together, the fingers
calmly tearing up the bunch of tickets and not throwing them
furiously to the ground, but simply letting them fall between
them, between the old cracked boots that were apparently as

thin as cigarette paper from frequent polishings and the tender apricot-coloured feet with their blood-red nails and those incredible shoes that looked like a wager, a bet born in the mind of a mad cobbler who swore to make a woman stand up and walk (that is, after all, a human being, a plantigrade), balanced on (for you couldn't really say in) something made as much for walking as an acrobat's props: a challenge not only to balance, to good sense, but even to the simple laws of economics, a piece of merchandise whose value was inversely proportional to the amount of material used, as if the rule of the game had been to sell a minimum of leather at a maximum price, and . . .

And Blum: 'Because you mean you had bet on the horse to win? Good God, you had bet all that money to win on a man who . . . '

And Iglésia, still in that low, reflective, stubborn voice: 'Not on him. On her. On that horse . . . And then he didn't ride so badly. Only he was too nervous, and she felt it. Horses are funny that way. They can guess things. If he hadn't been so nervous he would have come in first without even needing to use his stick.'

And Blum: 'And so then after that she didn't want to use any but yours? Hell, you're no prize package, you know!' And Iglésia not answering, carefully stamping out the last embers of the fire and covering them with dirt, looking more than ever (in that ridiculous costume, that huge dirt-coloured bile-coloured coat from which his tiny hands and his bilious, muddy aquiline face emerged) like some Punch-and-Judy character saying: 'If those damn Germans see we've eaten our mess here we'll never hear the end of it . . . And tomorrow we should try to get to the head of the line at the tool-shed, because they give out the shovels first and by the time we get there there's nothing left but picks and then you've got a sore arm all day because with a shovel all you have to do is fake your work but if you have to lift one of those pickaxes each time instead of . . . '

And Blum: 'And then . . . ' (but this time Iglésia wasn't there
any more: that whole summer they spent with a pick (or a shovel,
when they were lucky) in their hands, working on embankments,
then at the beginning of the fall they were sent to a farm to dig
potatoes and beets, then Georges tried to escape, was caught (by
accident, and not by soldiers or police sent after him but – it
was a Sunday morning – in a wood where he had fallen asleep,
by civilians out hunting grouse), then he was brought back to
the camp and put in a cell, then Blum reported sick and went
back to the camp too, and both of them stayed there, working
during the winter unloading the coal wagons, wielding the huge
pitchforks, straightening up when the sentry walked away,
shabby and grotesque figures with their caps pulled down over
their ears, their coat collars turned up, their backs to the wind
the rain the snow and blowing on their fingers while trying to
transfer themselves by proxy (that is, by means of their imagination, that is, by assembling and combining all they could find
in their memory by way of things seen, heard or read, so that –
here, among the wet and gleaming rails, the black wagons, the
black and soaking tree trunks in the cold pale daylight of a Saxon
winter – summoning up the iridescent and luminous images by
means of the ephemeral, incantatory magic of language, words
invented in the hope of making palatable – like those vaguely
sugared pellets disguising a bitter medicine for children – the
unmentionable reality) in that futile, mysterious and violent
universe in which, in the absence of their bodies, their minds
moved: something without any more reality than a dream, than
the words that came out of their lips: sounds, noises to conjure
away the cold, the rails, the livid sky, the sombre pines:) 'And
then he – I mean de Reixach . . . (and Georges 'Reishak', and
Blum: 'What? Oh, yes . . . ') . . . wanted to ride that chestnut
too, that is, to tame her, because he probably also thought that
she . . . (this time I mean the woman-chestnut, the blonde female
he couldn't or wouldn't . . . and who had eyes – and apparently
other things besides eyes – only for that . . .) In short: perhaps

he thought that he would kill, so to speak, two birds with one stone, and that if he managed to mount the one he could control the other, or vice versa, that is, that if he controlled the one he would also mount the other victoriously, that is that he would lead her to the stake too, that is, that his own stake would lead her victoriously to where he had probably never managed to lead her, would make her lose the taste or the desire for another stake (am I expressing myself clearly?) or if you prefer of another stick, that is if he managed to use his own stick as well as that jockey who . . . ', and Georges: 'All right, stop! Are you going on like that until . . . ', and Blum: 'Fine, sorry. I thought you enjoyed it: you're always sifting, supposing, embroidering, inventing fairy tales where I bet no one except you has never seen anything but an everyday piece of sex between a whore and two fools, and when I say . . . ', and Georges: 'A whore and two fools, and here we are looking like corpses, and about as deprived as corpses, and maybe tomorrow corpses for good in case one of these lice swarming all over us carries typhus or some general feels like bombing this depot, so what can I, what can we do, what else can I think of except . . . ', and Blum: 'Fine, fine, nice speech. Bravo. So go on. So he – I'm still talking about de Reixach – so he . . . ', and Georges: 'Reishak: x like sh, ch like k. For God's sake, how long are you . . . ', and Blum: 'Fine, fine: de Reishak. Fine. If you insist on being as boring as Iglésia . . . ', and Georges: 'I don't . . . ', and Blum: 'But you weren't wearing his livery after all. You weren't working for him, were you? He never paid you to take care of the people who were giving him a bad name? Unless you think you were offended, wronged too? Unless out of deference for your common progenitors, in memory of that other cuckold who . . . ', and Georges: 'Cuckold?', and Blum: ' . . . theatrically put a bullet through his head with a revolver . . . ', and Georges: 'Not a revolver: a pistol. The revolver hadn't even been invented yet. But cuckold?', and Blum: 'All right: pistol. Which doesn't make it any the less theatrical, doesn't keep the scene from being any the less picturesque: didn't you say he had called in a painter for the occasion? In order to perpetuate for the use of his descendants, and in particular to supplement the conversation of your lady mother when she receiv . . .', and Georges: 'A painter? What painter? I told you the only picture that exists of him had been made long before . . .', and Blum: 'I know. And completed, bloodied later by time, rot, the erosion of the years, as if the bullet that went through his head and whose traces you spent your childhood looking for on the walls had then struck the painted and eternally calm face, I know: and then there was that engraving too . . .', and Georges: 'But . . .', and Blum: ' . . . representing the scene that you interpret according to your mother, that is, according to the version most flattering to your familial pride, and probably by virtue of the law that states that History . . .', and Georges (unless it was still Blum, interrupting himself, clowning, unless he (Georges) wasn't having this dialogue under the cold Saxon rain with a little sickly Jew – or the shadow of a little Jew, and who was not much more than a corpse – one more corpse – of a little Jew – but with himself, that is, his double, all alone under the grey rain, among the rails, the coal wagons, or perhaps years later, still alone (although he was lying now beside a woman's warm flesh), still having a dialogue with that double, or with Blum, or with no one): 'There we are: History. I've been waiting for it the last few minutes. I was waiting for the word. It's an odd thing if it doesn't put in an appearance now and again. Like Providence in the sermon of a Dominican priest. Like the Immaculate Conception: a shimmering, exalted vision traditionally reserved to simple hearts and strong minds, the good conscience of the informer and the philosopher, the incorruptible fable – or farce – thanks to which the executioner feels he has a sister-of-charity's vocation and the victim the boy-scout cheerfulness of the first Christians, torturers and martyrs reconciled, sprawling together in a pathetic debauchery that we could call the vacuum cleaner or rather the "dispose-all" of the intelligence ceaselessly adding to that enormous

mountain of rubbish, that public drain in which figure prominently – along with the oak-leaf kepis and the police hand-
cuffs – the dressing-gowns, the pipes and slippers of our thinkers,
but on the crest of which the *gorillus sapiens* nevertheless hopes
some day to attain a height which will prevent his soul from
following him, so that he can finally savour a happiness guaran-
teed to be uncorruptible, thanks to the mass production of
frigidaires, motor-cars and F.M. radios. But go on: after all there's
no law against imagining that the air expelled by the bowels full
of the good German beer fermenting in the guts of that sentry
produces, in the general concert a minuet by Mozart . . . ', and
Blum (or Georges): 'Are you through?', and Georges (or Blum):
'I could go on,' and Blum (or Georges): 'So go on,' and Georges
(or Blum): 'But I must also bring my contribution, participate,
add to the heap, augment it by some of those coal bricks), and
Blum: 'Fine. So that law that says that History . . . ', and Georges:
'Eat!', and Blum: ' . . . that History leaves behind it only a
residue excessively confiscated, disinfected and finally edible, for
the use of official school manuals and pedigreed families . . .
But actually what do you know? What else besides the prattle
of a woman more concerned to protect the reputation of one of
her own kind than to polish up – a job usually reserved for
servants like Iglésia – and escutcheon and a name somewhat
tarnished and that . . . ', and Georges: 'Oh, do you suppose that
pile of coal will begin walking all by itself if we don't at least
pretend to look like we're helping it before that Mozartian bundle
of guts over there begins looking at us and starts . . . ', and Blum:
' . . . so that that pathetic and noble suicide might well be . . .
Yes: that's it, that's it!' (the pathetic and absurd figure beginning
to move, wriggling, struggling, racked with sudden jolts, until
it managed to load the fork with four or five soaking lumps, then
the fork describing a rapid arc, the lumps in the air for a moment,
weightless, circling slowly then falling back with a muffled noise
on the back of the truck, then the fork vertical again, the tines
down, Blum's hands together at the top of the handle and his

chin leaning on it so that when he speaks again it isn't his –
fixed – lower jaw but his whole head that rises and sinks in a
movement of sententious approval at each word:) ' . . . Because
you say that that half-naked girl glimpsed at an open door, the
breast and the face lit from underneath by a candle, so that she
looked like one of those plaster Mariannes in a schoolroom or
a town hall where the dust that no feather duster ever disturbs
accumulates in grey layers on every projection, reversing the
relief or rather the light and even the expression since, with the
eyeballs in shadow, darkened on their upper part, they seem to
be sending their eternal blind stare towards the sky – you say
then that that woman would run in behind the man you've called
the valet or the servant wakened by the shot, and who's maybe
only her lover – not the servant girl's, for she's no such thing
but actually the wife, the spouse, that is your common great-
great-great-grandmother, the man – the lover – belonging moreover to the race of domestics as you call it, if only she had also
shared in sexual matters those plebeian or rather equine tastes,
I mean the same dispositions, I mean the same tendency to choose
her lovers from the stable side . . . ', and Georges: 'But . . . ',
and Blum: 'Besides didn't you tell me that there existed as a
pendant to the other bloody portrait a painting executed at the
same period and representing her in the costume not of a huntress
matching her husband's but stamped (the dress, the pose, the
style, the way of staring boldly at the painter who reproduced
her features and later at whoever was questioning them) with a
kind of insolence, of defiance, of controlled violence (particularly
since she was holding in her hand something much more dangerous than a weapon, a mere hunting rifle: a mask, one of those
Venetian Carnival faces both grotesque and terrifying, with a
black velvet screen around the eyes and an enormous nose that
made people look like monstrous birds still further accentuated
by those capes whose pleats fluttered around them or, in repose,
enveloped them like folded wings), and sticking out of the
opening of the blouse something impalpable, a foam, the delicate

and complicated lace escaping as if it were the very perfume of her flesh, of her breasts hidden further down in the silken darkness, exhaling the secret flowery breath of her flesh . . . ', and suddenly the voice changed, discordant, two tones higher, breaking, saying: 'So that Dejanira . . . ', and Georges: 'Virginia,' and Blum: 'What?', and Georges: 'Name was Virginia,' and Blum: 'Good name for a whore. So that virginal Virginia panting and naked, or more than naked, that is, dressed – or rather undressed – in one of those nightgowns that were probably only invented to let the hands imprisoned underneath slip across the liquid warmth of the belly, folding up, raising above the breasts, accumulating in folds a silky foam above the hips so as to denude, present – like those displays of boutique shops where the precious, delicate and fantastically expensive objects are shown in a seethe of satin – that hidden, secret mouth – : a woman not only stretched out but overthrown in the true sense of the word, that is, as if her body had made a half turn starting from that ancestral position in which she crouched to satisfy her needs – because she has only one position to satisfy them all, this creature: legs folded back, thighs pressed against her sides, the knees rising to touch the shadowy armpits – but now as if the ground had shifted, tipping her back, presenting now not to the earth but to the sky (as though expecting one of those legendary fecundations, some tinkling shower of gold) her twin buttocks, that mother-of-pearl, that bush, that eternal wound already streaming even before being forced open and so shamelessly offered that she seemed to be waiting for an act of a precision and a nakedness if not surgical (as is suggested by the notion of something that pierces, penetrates, thrusts into the firm flesh) at least almost medical inasmuch as it (the act itself physical, naked, without emotional significance) derives of course from the physiological domain: hence the abundance, the variety of that equivocal imagery in which the enema serves as a pretext for countless variations on the theme of the introduction of an object that is not only hard but capable of spraying shedding projecting violently outside itself and as a liquid extension of itself that impetuous milt, that spurt, that . . . '

And Georges: 'No that's . . . '

And Blum: 'And while you were so busy staring at the walls for the traces of a bullet that (if not glorious) at least was honourable, romantic, didn't you ever see that: projected by the candle set down beside the bed, the bulging, complicated and leaping shadow of a muscular back around the loins of which are knotted – like those of a shipwreck victim clinging to a mast – the milky legs, the feet with their apricot-coloured heels, swelling (the shadow) like a mountain, monstrous, rising to the ceiling and shaken with tempestuous jolts by that furious tide that racks beneath it the species of creature with two heads, four arms, four legs and two bodies welded at the stomach by means of that common organ (or if you prefer equally alien, for doesn't the man's member seem to plunge into his own body as it plunges into the woman's, to extend itself into the deepest cavern of her entrails by an equal and symmetrical member?), that muscle, that awl, that dark-red ram, gleaming and furious, appearing and vanishing between two bushy and tawny fleeces, and he (de Reixach, or rather just Reixach) suddenly appearing . . . '

And Georges: 'No that . . . '

And Blum: ' . . . coming in unexpectedly (or else tell me why he should come back at all if not for her? Because it seems to me that as far as hurrying yourself into the next world is concerned, you could just as well do it anywhere, the way you leave rubbish behind the first bush you come to, because I don't think it's very necessary at such moments to insist on special comfort . . .), so leaving his defeated troops, the infantrymen, the runaways probably screaming too at the top of their lungs, a prey to that panic, that kind of moral diarrhoea (have you noticed that it's also called the runs?) impossible to hold back, unreasoning – but isn't all that's asked of a soldier, isn't all the training he undergoes precisely in order to make him accomplish as

though by second nature actions in one way or another contrary
to reason, so that in running away he probably merely surrenders
to the same force or, if you prefer, to the same despair that in
other circumstances has impelled or will impel him to an act
which his reason can only disavow, as for instance to throw
himself shouting in front of a machine-gun firing at him: hence
probably the facility with which a squadron can turn in a few
seconds into a runaway and panic-stricken herd . . . And twice
a traitor, – first to the caste into which he was born and which
he had renounced, disavowed, destroying himself, virtually
committing suicide a first time for the sake (so to speak) of a
sentimental Swiss ethic of which he would never have been able
to have any knowledge if his fortune, his rank hadn't given him
the means, in other words the leisure and the power to read, –
then a traitor to the cause he had embraced, but this time by
incapacity, in other words guilty (he, the nobleman by birth
and whose speciality was war – that is, in a certain sense, self-
forgetfulness, that is, a certain casualness or futility, that is, in
a sense, the inner emptiness) of having tried to mix (or conciliate)
courage and thought, a disregarded and irreducible antagonism
that opposes all reflection to all action, so that now he had
nothing left but to watch or rather avoid watching (suffering
something like a terrible nausea, I suppose) that rabble leaving
the ranks on all sides (what else, what other word besides rabble,
since they knew too much now – or not enough – to go on
living as cobblers or bakers, and on the other hand not enough –
or too much – to be capable of behaving like soldiers) which in
his imagination or his dreams he probably already saw promoted
to that superior state to which, he supposed, you could accede
by the undigested reading of twenty-five volumes . . . ', and
Georges: 'Twenty-three,' and Blum: 'Twenty-three tomes printed
by a bookseller in The Hague for export and bound in full calf
with the arms . . . You said three ducks without heads, didn't
you? . . . ', and Georges: 'Doves, not du . . . ', and Blum: 'The
three pigeons then, symbolically decapitated . . . ', and Georges:

'No that . . .', and Blum: ' . . . that constituted the somehow prophetic blazon of his family: because he had merely forgotten to use his brain, if he ever had had one inside his well-brought-up thoroughbred's skull,' and Georges: 'Oh yes. Unfortunately this coal heap, this historical coal heap . . .', and Blum suddenly seized with frenzied agitation, leaping in the blackish puddles, waving his arms, saying: 'All right, all right: let's work at History too, let's write our daily little page of History too! After all, I suppose there's nothing more dishonourable or stupid about shovelling a mountain of coal than dying gratis for the King of Prussia, so let's give that Brandenburg Mozart his money's worth . . .', the fork coming and going several times, sending a total of about three and a half lumps into the air, two falling outside the truck, then stopping, winded, saying: 'But I wasn't through! I haven't told you everything. Where was I, oh yes, here: he came back then unexpectedly, he left his cobblers in chaos, his illusions, his idyllic dreams, in order to seek refuge with what still remained to him – at least that's what he thought – that is, with what he could still consider a certainty: not perhaps the heart (for probably he had after all managed to lose some of his naivety) but in any case the flesh, the warm and palpable body of that Agnes . . . (didn't you tell me she was twenty years younger than he was so that,' and Georges: 'No. You're mixing it all up. You're confusing him with . . . ' and Blum: ' . . . his great-grandson. That's right. But I think you can still imagine it: they used to marry off thirteen-year-old girls to old men in those days, and even if in those two portraits they look about the same age that's undoubtedly because the artist's *savoir-faire* (I mean his *savoir-vivre*, I mean his *savoir-flatter*) had made the bride look somewhat younger. No, I'm not making any mistake, I said the bride – I mean attenuate, temper what showed of her real experience, which in lies and duplicity would have made her about a thousand years older than he was.) . . . That philan-thropic, Jacobinical and soldierly Arnolphe, then, definitively renouncing the perfection of the human race (which doubtless explains why, reinforced by his memory and a wiser man, his remote descendant exclusively dedicated himself to the improvement of the equine race), and covering at full gallop the two hundred kilometres that separated him from her . . . ', and Georges: 'Three hundred,' and Blum: 'Three hundred kilometres, which in the measurement of the period makes almost eighty leagues, which by killing a horse represents at least four days (let's say five), finally arriving late on the fifth night, exhausted and covered with mud . . . ', and Georges: 'Not mud: dust. It almost never rains there,' and Blum: 'Good God, what does it do then?', and Georges: 'The wind blows. So to speak. Because it's about as much like the wind as a cannonball is like a popgun. But what do you . . . ', and Blum: 'All dusty, then, as if he had carried on himself an impalpable and tenacious dust of rubbish, the pulverized remains of his disappointed hopes: whitened precociously by the ashes of the stake where doubtless, during four days and five nights, on the roads of defeat, he had pondered, reviewed and burned all that he had adored, no longer adoring anything now but the woman he was burning to see again, and this: in the night's silence, noises, a trampling of hoofs, for probably he wasn't alone, also had with him, had been followed by a faithful valet, just as the other one had brought along to the war – to take care of his horse and polish his boots – the faithful jockey or rather stud his unfaithful Agnes had provided him with, or rather who had, as they say, lit up the young . . . ', and Georges: 'Oh for God's sake! . . . ', and Blum: 'But you can imagine it: the vague trampling of hoofs on the cobblestones, the exhausted animals whinnying, the night – or rather the beginning of dawn – bluish, the lantern the porter was holding sculpturing the muscles of the red and smoking horses' chests, and a swirl of cloaks as they dismounted, and he throwing the reins to the jockey, giving a brief order or not even that, no orders, not even making a sound with his voice, nothing but his footsteps, the clatter of spurs as he quickly reached the doorstep, stepped over it: all this she heard, wakening with a start, still in that soft languor of sleep and pleasure but already thinking – perhaps not her mind since she was still half asleep, but something in her that neither sleep nor pleasure could blunt, and which had no need to wait until she was wide awake to begin functioning at top speed and infallibly: instinct, the cunning that has no need to be learned, so that with her head, her brain itself still asleep, the agile body started up (pushing away the sheet, the legs showing for a second, kicking free, revealing in a flash the swift thighs, that shadow, that flame – but didn't you say she had blonde hair? then: – that honey, that golden fleece that had already vanished when she pivoted, the pushed-up nightgown revealing now the flow of her legs close together and parallel, the dazzling pearly flesh, the feet tinged with pink groping for the slippers) thinking all the time (the body), calculating, organizing, planning with lightning-like speed at the same time that her ears followed the noise of the boots climbing the stairs by fours, crossing the landing, coming closer (the legs out of sight now, the nightgown having fallen back), and she – the virginal Agnes – standing up, pushing the lover by the shoulders – the coachman, the groom, the dazed bumpkin – towards the inevitable and providential closet or cabinet of farces and tragedies that is always opportunely where it should be like those enigmatic boxes in vaudeville tricks whose opening could eventually release an explosion of laughter just as well as a shudder of horror because vaudeville is always only an abortive tragedy and tragedy a farce without humour, the hands (still the body, the muscles, not the brain which at this moment was only beginning to tear itself from the viscous mist of sleep, the hands alone then) picking up in passing the articles of masculine clothing scattered here and there and throwing them pell-mell into the closet too, the sound of the boots having stopped, standing (the boots, or rather the absence, the sudden and alarming cessation of sound) just outside the door, the handle shaken, then the fist pounding, and she screaming: 'Coming!', shutting the closet, turning round, heading for the door, then noticing a vest or a

147

man's shoe, picking it up, shouting: 'Coming!' at the door and running back to the closet, opening it, savagely throwing inside what she had just picked up without even looking, the door echoing now under the terrible blows of his shoulder (the door you heard burst into splinters under the furious assaults of a man – but it wasn't the valet!), then she standing there, childish, innocent, disarming, rubbing her eyes, smiling, holding out her arms, explaining that she locked herself in for fear of thieves pressing herself against him, enlacing him, enveloping him, the nightgown accidentally slipping off her shoulder, revealing her breasts whose bruised tender points she presses, crushes against the dusty tunic she is already beginning to unfasten with her feverish hands, talking to him with her mouth on his so he cannot see her lips swollen with another man's kisses, and he standing there in that disorder of spirit, that disarray, that despair: confused, disoriented, disconcerted, dispossessed of everything and perhaps already detached and perhaps already half destroyed . . . Wasn't it like that?', and Georges: 'No!', and Blum: 'No? But what do you know about it?', and Georges: 'No!', and Blum: 'He who had wanted to act out the fable of the two pigeons, only he was the pigeon, that is, returning to the dovecot with his wing broken, his dreams limping, realizing his wreck, and not only because he had the inopportune notion of going off, he the gentleman farmer, to fornicate in the forbidden domain, the muddy wallows of thought, but also that of leaving alone behind him his little chick or rather his beloved little pigeon who had taken advantage of his absence to fornicate in the most natural way in the world, in other words the way it's been done since the world began, taking for a partner not chlorotic reveries but merely a boy with a strong back, and when he realized it, it was too late; he no doubt saw himself there, naked – probably she had managed to undress him by taking advantage of that kind of daze, of paralysis – with that twenty-year-old pigeon cooing and rubbing up against him, and he (perhaps he noticed then the voluptuous disorder of the bed, or heard a sound, or else it was by instinct) pushing her away and walking with a firm step – although she clung to him now, pleading, denying, trying to hold him back, but probably it would have taken more than that, probably he could have dragged several more like her with him, he who had already been dragging for the last four days the heavy, rotten and stinking corpse of his disillusions – to the closet, opening the door, and then receiving in the head that pistol bullet fired at point-blank range, so that a kindly fate spared him that at least, that is, knowing what was in the closet, knowing that second and supreme disgrace, the farcical and vaudeville cabinet functioning providentially, the gunpowder doing its work, in other words putting an end to such painful and unendurable "suspense", producing the welcome relief, the salubrious reaction by, so to speak, blowing his brains out . . . '

And Georges: 'No!'

And Blum: 'No? No? No? But how do you know? How do you know they didn't lay him out there, stuffing the still-smoking pistol into his hand during the few minutes they had before the other servants ran in, not even bothering (the urgency, the haste, every second counting and she wide awake now, with all her wits about her and helped by that infallible instinct that allows a woman to see at a glance if everything is as it should be for the arrival of the guests, having enough presence of mind to post her lover in the hallway, ordering him to pound on the already broken-in door when he heard the others coming), not even bothering (not having time) to try to dress him again in that dusty uniform of which she had just now stripped him in the hope of . . . '

And Georges: 'No!'

And Blum: 'But didn't you yourself say that they found him stark naked? How can you explain that? Unless it was the effect of his reverence for Nature? Of his affecting Genevese readings? Wasn't he – I mean that melomaniac Swiss, the effusive *philosophe* whose complete works he had learned by heart – wasn't he a little bit exhibitionistic too? Wasn't he the one who enjoyed showing his behind to young gi . . . ' and Georges: 'Oh stop! For God's sake stop, stop! How boring you can get! Stop long enough to . . . ', then his voice breaking off (or perhaps he himself no longer hearing it) while he stared now without recognizing him, in other words without identifying the face as being Blum's, but only the countenance of misery, of suffering, of absolute nakedness, the mask with its emaciated features, drawn, famished, like a tragic denial of the gaiety, the clownishness of the voice, while he felt as if he were living it all over again: that lonely agony, those hours of the night, the silence (perhaps only, in the old sleeping mansion, the muffled echo of a horse whinnying in the stable, and perhaps too the black, silky, restless, wandering wind, whirling in sporadic gusts into the courtyard), and Reixach standing there, in that setting of a period print, stripping himself, tearing off, rejecting, repudiating those clothes, that ambitious and gaudy uniform which had now probably become for him the symbol of something he had believed in and now no longer saw any sense in (the blue frock-coat with the high collar and the gold-embroidered lapels, the two-cornered hat, the ostrich feathers: the pathetic and grotesque costume lying there, a crumpled mausoleum of what (not power, honours, glory, but the idyllic bosky dells, the idyllic and sentimental reign of Reason and Virtue) his readings had given him a glimpse of); and something inside himself finally disintegrating shaken by a kind of terrifying diarrhoea that fiercely emptied him of his contents as of his very blood, and not moral, as Blum said, but somehow mental, that is, no longer an interrogation, a doubt, but no longer any subject for interrogation, for doubt, saying aloud (Georges): 'But the General killed himself too: not only the one seeking and finding on that road a decent and disguised suicide, but the other one too in his villa, his garden with the raked gravel paths . . . You remember that military review, that ceremony, the soaking field that winter morning in the Ardennes, and he – it's the only time we saw him – with his little jockey's head, that kind of tiny, wrinkled, wizened and parboiled apple, his little jockey's legs in the tiny shiny boots that splattered indifferently through the mud while he passed in front of us without looking at us: a little old man or rather a little old foetus that had just been taken out of its jar of formaldehyde, marvellously well preserved, unchangeable, alert, expeditious and dry, quickly walking along the serried squadrons trailing behind him that group of beribboned, gloved officers, the hilts of their sabres at the hollow of their elbows, and panting as they followed him over the spongy field while he walked on without turning back, probably talking to the veterinary officer – the only one he would have spoken to – of the state of the horses and the bad case of thrush the ground gave them – or the climate – in this part of the country); and then when he learned, that is when he realized, finally understood that his brigade no longer existed, had been not annihilated, destroyed according to the rules – or at least what he thought were the rules – of war: normally, correctly, as for instance, by attacking an impregnable position or even by an artillery pounding, or even – he might have accepted this as a last resort – submerged by an enemy attack: but so to speak absorbed, diluted, dissolved, erased from the general-staff charts without his knowing where nor how nor when: only the couriers returning one after the other without having seen a thing at the place – the village, the woods, the hill, the bridge – where a squadron or a combat group was supposed to be, and even that resulting, according to all appearances, not from a panic, a flight, a rout – a mishap that he could also have acknowledged perhaps, at least have recognized as being in the realm of disastrous but, all in all, normal possibilities, comprising part of the anticipated, the inevitable risks of any battle and which could be remedied by means equally anticipated, as for instance a police barrier at the crossroads and a few summary executions – not a rout, then, since the order the courier was carrying, was supposed to transmit, was invariably an order to fall back and since the position the unit was supposed to be holding and towards which it was headed was itself a retreat position but which, apparently, no

one had ever reached, the couriers then continuing farther, in
other words towards the preceding retreat position, without ever
seeing, on either side of the road, anything but that inextricable,
monotonous and enigmatic wake of disasters, in other words
not even trucks or burned wagons, or men, or children, or
soldiers, or women, or dead horses, but simply detritus, something like a vast public discharge spread over kilometres and
kilometres and exuding not the traditional and heroic odour of
carrion, of corpses in a state of decomposition, but only of
ordure, simply stinking, the way a pile of old tin cans, potato
peels and burnt rags can stink, and no more affecting or tragic
than a pile of ordure, and just barely usable for scrap-metal
collectors or ragpickers, and nothing more until, still advancing,
they (the couriers) took – at a turn of the road – another burst
of gunfire, which made one more corpse at the bottom of the
ditch, the overturned motorcycle still sputtering or catching fire,
which made one more of those black cadavers still sitting on one
of those twisted and rusty iron carcasses (have you noticed how
fast it goes, that acceleration of time, the extraordinary speed
with which the war produces phenomena – rust, stains, putrefaction, corruption of bodies – which in ordinary times usually
take months or years to happen?) like some macabre caricatures
of motorcyclists still leaning over their handle-bars, riding at a
terrible speed, decomposing that way (spreading beneath them
in the green grass the bituminous and excremental brownish
blob – oil, grease, burnt flesh – consisting of a dark sticky liquid)
at a terrible speed – , the couriers, then, returning one after the
other without having found anything, or not coming back at
all, his brigade somehow evaporated, conjured away, erased,
sponged out without leaving a trace save a few dazed, wandering
men hidden in the woods or drunk and finally I had a minimum
of consciousness left, sitting in front of that tiny cone of gin
that now I no longer even had the strength to empty while
slumped down on the bench overpowered by my own weight I
was trying with that obstinate consciousness of drunkards to

get up and go away, realizing that they (Iglésia and that old man whom we had first robbed then almost killed and who had then offered to take us through the lines after dark) were just as drunk as I was, starting again without being discouraged to lean my body forward so that its own weight helped me get up from that bench to which I seemed to be nailed at the same time that my hands attempted to push back the table, realizing at the same moment that these various movements remained at the stage of impulses and that I was still absolutely motionless, a kind of ghostly and transparent double of myself – and without the slightest effect – repeating over and over the same gestures leaning my body forward the simultaneous effort of the thighs the arms pushing until it realized that nothing had happened coming back then melting back into my own body that was still sitting there which it tried to encourage once again but without any more success that was why I was trying to get my head clear thinking that if I could manage to settle clarify my perceptions I would also manage to order and direct my movements and then in succession:

first that door which I had first to reach and then walk through, seeing it reflected in the mirror over the bar one of those rectangular mirrors like the ones you can see or rather in which you can see yourself at the barber's the upper corners rounded the frame not enamelled white like in barber-shops but covered with a coat of brown paint, threadlike reliefs like noodles decorating the moulding like astragals asterisks starting with a central honeysuckle motif in the middle of each side, and since the mirror was tilted the verticals reflected in it were also tilted, starting at the bottom with the row of necks and spigots of bottles lined up on the shelf immediately underneath then the raw wood floor that seemed to tilt upwards at an angle of about twenty degrees, grey in the shadow, yellow in the rectangle of sunshine extending obliquely from the door open on to the street, the two jambs tilted too as if the wall were falling in, the doorstep a stone block then the pavement then the long rectangular stones forming the kerb then the first rows of cobbles in the street to which I had my back turned

and probably because of the drunkenness, impossible to be visually aware of anything but that that mirror and what was reflected in it my eyes clinging to it so to speak the way a drunkard clings to a lamppost as to the only fixed point in a vague invisible and colourless universe from which only voices reached me probably that of the woman (the proprietress) and of the two or three men who were there, and then one of them saying The front has collapsed but sounding to me like The runt has collapsed, able to see the little dead dog floating downstream with the current its pink and white belly swollen the hair stiff already stinking

then the rectangle of sunlight on the floor disappearing then reappearing then disappearing again but not entirely: this time I could see thanks to the mirror the bottom of the woman's skirt her two calves and her two feet in slippers all tilted as if she were falling over backward

then her voice coming from outside coming into the café over her shoulder probably talking with her head half turned in other words if the mirror had been high enough I would have seen her in profile; that way she could go on watching what she had just seen and still be heard from inside the café saying Here come some soldiers

and this time I found myself managing to get up clinging to the table hearing one of the conical glasses overturn roll across the table describing what was probably a circle round its base until it reached the edge of the table and fell hearing it break just as I reached the woman and looked over her shoulder seeing the grey car with the strange top like a kind of coffin with square-cut sides and four backs and four round helmets and Good God those are . . . Good God you

and she Oh you know I never pay any attention to uniforms and I Good God

and she I've already met one this morning on my way to get

the milk, he spoke French it must have been an officer because he was looking at a map sitting in a side-car, he asked me if this was the road I told him Yes It was only afterwards that I thought he looked funny

then crossing the café again shaking Iglésia who was asleep his elbows spread out on the table his cheek on his arm saying Wake up Good God wake up we have got to get out of here Good God let's get going

the woman still on the doorstep saying a moment later Here come some more

this time I was right behind her looking in the same direction in other words the direction opposite where the car had vanished so that the two cyclists looked as though they were chasing the car but they were wearing khaki

for a second I saw the soldiers of the two armies chasing each other round and round the block of houses like in the Opera or those comic films people dashing in those parodic and bur-lesque chases the lover the husband brandishing a revolver the hotel chambermaid the adulterous wife the bellboy the little pastrycook the police then again the lover in pants and garters running his body straight up and down his elbows pressed to his sides raising his knees high the husband with the revolver the woman in panties black stockings and camisole and so on everything went round in the sunlight I didn't see the step down to the pavement and almost landed head first I took a few strides my body almost horizontal at the limit of disequilibrium then I grabbed hold of his handle-bars

the face of the man under the helmet fat red unshaven and streaming with sweat furious his eyes furious and wild his mouth furious shouting What is it what Get out of here let go, then I saw the truck a dispatch car vaguely camouflaged hastily daubed with yellow brown and green paint off balance leaning on one side as it took the turn then straightening I waved my arms standing in the middle of the road

I saw from his insignia he was an engineer he must have been from the reserve staff he looked like an official with his steel-rimmed glasses, walking towards me as soon as he had stepped out of the cab furious feverish already shouting not listening to me and he repeating too What do you want what is it you want I tried to explain but he was still furious feverish constantly glancing over his shoulder in the direction they had come from holding his revolver first turning towards me then he forgot it waving it gesticulating holding me by a button of my jacket the work clothes the man had given me, shouting What are those clothes, again I tried to explain to him but he wasn't listening constantly turning round to look at the turn in the road, nervous, I took out my *livret* my identity disc that I had kept but he kept looking over his shoulder then I said That way, pointing to the place where the little grey car had disappeared and he What? and I They just went by five minutes ago four of them in a little car, and he shouting What if I had you shot? I tried to begin explaining again but he let go of me heading for the truck again still glancing in the direction they had come from (I looked too almost expecting to see the little coffin-shaped car appear that meanwhile must have had time to get round the block of houses) then he went back inside sat down closed the door from the window frame the window was rolled down he was holding the revolver now the barrel aimed at me his thin greyish sweating face leaning forward still looking behind him his myopic eyes behind the glasses the truck started up

running behind: there were about ten of them under the canvas sitting on the two benches on each side, I hung on to the back flap running trying to get in but they pushed me back they looked drunk too I managed to get one leg in one of them tried to hit me with his gun butt he was probably too drunk the butt coming down next to my hand then I let go still having time to see one of them head thrown back drinking greedily out of a bottle then he aimed at me one eye closed and threw it but they were already too far away and it fell at least a yard in front of my feet broke there was still some wine in it that made a dark spot on the cobbles with tentacles splinters of greenish black glass scattered around then I heard a shot but not even the bullet passing, drunk as they were and shaken up jolted in that truck it wasn't surprising then it disappeared

he had managed to wake up and was standing in front of the door in front of the woman his big bulging eyes looking at me with an offended expression, I screamed We've got to get out of here We've got to get our clothes back on He wanted to have me shot one of those boys took a shot at me

but he didn't move went on looking at me with that same expression of outrage reproving sullen then he raised his arm towards the café behind him, saying He said he'd cook us a duck tonight

and I A duck?

and he He's going to give us something to eat He said he

then I stopped listening, I headed overland climbing back up the hill the sun had that insistent obsessive presence of long afternoons in spring when it lingers endlessly lingering still high in the sky days that never end as if it were immobilized on the verge of setting but not able to move held motionless by some Joshua there must have been at least two or three days that it had forgotten to set since it had risen reddening at first softly tinting the sky purple the rosy-fingered dawn but I hadn't seen the moment when it had appeared only my shadow elongated and diaphanous, a quadruped's shadow on the road where there was nothing but those motionless heaps like rags and the idiot face of Wack lying back staring at me I had it right in my eyes now motionless in the white sky

turning round I saw he was following me; so he had finally made up his mind, he was still at the foot of the hill had just passed the last houses walking up the meadow staggering a little once he stumbled fell but got up again then I stopped and waited for him when he caught up with me he stumbled again and fell on all fours for a moment vomiting then he stood up again wiping his mouth on his sleeves and started walking.

157

Perhaps it was at this same moment that the General had killed himself? He had nevertheless a car, a driver, petrol. All he had to do was put on his helmet, pull on his gloves and leave, walking down the front steps of that villa (I suppose it must have been a villa: that's the usual place where a brigadier general's command post is installed, the chateaux being traditionally reserved to the division generals and the farms to mere colonels): a villa then, with probably a plum tree in bloom on the lawn, a gateway painted white, a gravel driveway turning between the aucuba hedges with their mottled leaves, and a middle-class salon decorated with the inevitable bouquet of holly branches or dyed feathers – silver or autumnal red – on the corner of the mantelpiece or the grand piano, the vase pushed back to make room for the sprawled-out maps, and from which (the villa) had issued for the last eight days, orders and directives almost all as useful as those given during the same period by the strategist of a provincial café commenting on the daily communiqué: he had, then, only to walk down those steps, climb calmly into his car with its flag, and drive straight ahead without stopping to the division headquarters or to his army corps headquarters, and to wait around there long enough for someone to give him a new command, as they did to the others. And instead of that, when his officers were installed in the second car, the motors already running, the motorcycles of the three or four couriers still sputtering, the car with its flags waiting with the door open, he blew his brains out. And in the racket of the motors and the cars no one even heard it. And perhaps it wasn't even the dishonour, the sudden revelation of his incapacity (after all perhaps he wasn't absolutely a fool – how could anyone tell? – perhaps it wasn't impossible to imagine that his orders weren't stupid but the best, the most pertinent, even inspired – but again how could anyone tell since none of them ever reached its destination?): probably something else: a kind of void a hole. Bottomless. Absolute. Where nothing had any meaning any reason for being – otherwise why take off his clothes, lying there that way, naked, unconscious of the cold, terribly calm probably, terribly lucid, carefully arranging on a chair (touching them, folding them with a kind of disgust and infinite precaution as if they had been rubbish or explosives) the frock-coat, the trousers, setting the boots down in front, crowning everything with that hat, that extravagant headpiece like a bouquet of fireworks, as if they had dressed, shod, hatted some imaginary and non-existent character, looking at them with that same dry, cold, astringent gaze, and stepping back to consider the effect, and finally knocking over the chair with the back of his hand, since in the print it was lying on the floor and the clothes . . . '

And Blum: 'The print? Then there really was one! You told me that . . . '

And Georges: 'No. There wasn't. Where did you get that idea?' And there wasn't any – at least he had never seen any – picture representing that battle, that defeat, that rout, probably because defeated nations don't like to perpetuate the memory of disasters; of that war there existed only one painting, decorating the main hall of the Hôtel de Ville and illustrating the victorious phase of the campaign: but that victory had occurred only a year later, and it was around a hundred years later still that an official painter had been commissioned to represent it, placing at the head of the ragged soldiers who looked like film extras an allegorical character, a woman wearing a white dress that bared one of her breasts, a Phrygian cap on her head, brandishing a sword and her mouth wide open, standing in the yellow sunlight surrounded by wisps of a glorious and bluish smoke, the gabions overturned and, in the foreground the grimacing and stupid face of a dead man shown in perspective, lying on his back, one leg half bent, his arms outstretched and his head down, staring with his bulging eyes, the features twisted into an eternal grimace, successive generations of electors listening to the speeches of successive generations of politicians upon whom this victory had conferred the right to make speeches – and upon the listeners the right to listen to them – on the dais draped with tricolours.

'But they had begun with defeat,' Georges said, 'and the Spanish had beaten them in that battle Reixach commanded, and then they had had to retreat on all the roads that led down from the Pyrenees, in other words, I suppose, a few faint paths. But, roads or paths, it's always the same: ditches lined with corpses, dead horses, burnt trucks and abandoned cannons . . . ' (It was a Sunday this time and the two of them, he and Blum, were sitting there trying to warm themselves in the pale Saxon sunlight, still wearing their grotesque Polish or Czech soldiers' overcoats, backs against the wall of their barracks and taking turns drawing on the same cigarette that they passed back and forth, keeping the smoke in their lungs as long as possible, expelling it slowly through their nostrils trying to imbue themselves with it more deeply, indifferent to the vermin swarming over their bodies, the dozens of tiny greyish lice the first of which they had once discovered with terror, desperately pursued their followers, and which they had finally given up killing, letting them run over them now with a feeling of permanent disgust, of permanent impotence and permanent decomposition, the shouts of the men from Oran arguing reaching them through the open window, Georges taking the last drag on what might have been the last quarter of an inch of the end that burned his fingertips, throwing it away or rather (for not even enough remained to hold on to it) flicking it away with his index finger from between his lips, then standing up, stretching his legs, turning his back to the sun, resting his folded arms on the window sill, his chin on his forearms and standing there watching them round the greasy table, their greasy cards in their hands, their impassive and hard gamblers' faces strained, implacable, gnawed by that cold, patient and attentive passion that isolated them in a kind of cage inside which they would have remained, sheltered in the violent and hard world (just as a swimmer is sheltered from the rain) by that bell, by an individual aura of risk and violence which they secreted like that ink squirted by

squids: the banker, the manager somehow of the game in which
whole fortunes in camp marks were won and lost, changed hands
from hour to hour (and for those who had no more marks,
tobacco, and for those who had no more tobacco, bread rations,
and for those who no longer had their ration of bread, the ration
of the next day, and sometimes of the day after that – and so
there was a man from Bône (an Italian) who gambled and lost
four days of rations, and starting the next day he came punctually
to hand the banker his ration of black bread and his coal-oil
margarine, and not a word between them, merely a nod, an
imperceptible movement of the head on the part of the man who
took the bread, added it to his own ration without even seeming
to see the other man, and the third day the Italian fainted, and
when he came to the other man took – still without looking at
him – the ration of bread and margarine which he had just
received and held it out to him, saying: 'You want it?', and the
Italian: 'No,' and, still without a look, the other man put the
bread and margarine back in his kit-bag, and the next day he
(the loser) brought his ration again (it was the fourth and last
time, and during the day, at work, he had fainted once again),
and the other man didn't look at him any more than the preceding
times, took the ration and without a word put it in his kit-bag
and someone who was watching said something like 'You
bastard,' and he (the banker) didn't move, kept on eating, his
eyes cold, dead, resting for a moment on the face of the man
who had just spoken, completely expressionless, completely cold,
then turning away, his jaws still chewing, while two or three
men helped the Italian stagger back to his cot), the leader, then,
the manager – or banker – a Maltese (or Valencian, or Sicilian:
a mixture, one of those bastard and synthetic products of har-
bours, of the islands of that sea, that old pond, that ancient
matrix, original crucible of all bargaining, of all thought and all
cunning) with a hawk's head, little dead reptilian eyes, a thin
dry black face, expressionless, ageless, and of course dressed like
the others in a vaguely military outfit but you wondered what

he was doing here (that is, in this war, that is, in an army, that is, why they had enrolled, mobilized a man with a face (and probably a court record too) like that one (or this one) and who obviously couldn't be used for anything except shooting an officer in the back at the first opportunity or else the treasurer of the battalion or the regiment and running off with the cash box – unless he had been naturalized, dressed up in a uniform and provided not with a rifle but with a military *livret* in the single and solitary anticipation of this eventuality – since it takes all kinds to make an army – , that future role of playing banker in a game in a prisoners' barracks); and facing him a calm, majestic, fat Jew (not adipose: simply fat, august, and probably the only prisoner in the whole camp – but how? for during those first two months, he had, like everyone else, not received a single package – not to have lost a single ounce of fat since he had been there), who was something like a pimp in Algiers and upon whom the absurd soldier's outfit, the ridiculous yellow coat, the shapeless cap, looked like a robe and a gold tiara, and who perpetually seemed to be sitting on a royal, biblical and assured throne, surrounded by a court of little bloodless brutes quarrelling over the privilege of lighting his cigarettes and whom he didn't even seem to see, although he was still capable of taking his scarcely touched mess-tin – Georges had seen him – and handing it to the most cadaverous of them, saying merely: 'I'm not hungry. Here!', interrupting the other's protests, saying: 'Eat!', in the tone in which you give an order, a command, and nothing else, taking out a cigarette, lighting it or letting one of the grubs light it and sitting there, placid, heavy, perhaps a little pale, exhaling long slow puffs of smoke while around him the others feverishly swallowed the disgusting bitter soup of which he didn't even seem to deprive himself, he who, no more than he had grown thin, had never been seen by anyone not only doing the least amount of work but even making the least pretence of working dragging to the yards the shovel that had been thrust into his hands and, once there, planting it in the ground in front of him, spending eight hours leaning on it, arms crossed, smoking (for just as he seemed, by a vestige of some royal privilege, to be able to do without eating, he always had, probably by virtue of the same privilege, something to smoke) or staring with not even a contemptuous expression at the prisoners working around him, and this without a sentry or the foreman ever making any remarks, and on Yom Kippur, he who had never in his life set foot in a synagogue nor observed, nor probably even known what the Sabbath was, and still less the Torah, and who didn't even know how to read (Georges knew that because – since he (the Jew) had either chosen not to let this weakness be known to one of the little wretches who gravitated around him, or preferred to have recourse to strangers for this task – it was Blum or Georges that he asked to write the letters he dictated to his mother (not his wives: his mother) and to read him the answers), on Yom Kippur, then, in the middle of a country where Jews were being massacred and burned by the hundreds of thousands, went on sick call in order not to work, and not only remained the whole day without doing a thing, clean-shaven, without eating or touching a match, but even was strong enough to oblige his kind (the members of that people of whom he once would have been – was still – king) to imitate him; both of them, then, the Sicilian and the king straight out of the Bible sitting face to face, and round them (or inside them, in other words inside what came out of them, inside that invisible cage they constructed or rather that constructed itself as soon as they sat down and took out the cards and on the sides of which it seemed that an invisible hand had written 'Private' as though on the door of the back rooms of casinos or clubs) the habitual row of the gamblers' heads, pimps, bullies, counter-jumpers, hairdressers with their hard eyes and coming to get themselves fleeced, their faces feverish and impassive, their lips scarcely moving, their hands scarcely moving to make each card slide just enough so that the right-hand corner appeared, and at the end of each deal that silent sigh, plaintive, orgastic coming not from the players, with faces still perfectly expressionless, but from the audience, and during one of those pauses, Georges rummaging, pulling out of his pocket, quickly counting out his tiny fortune, his tiny accumulation of bits of paper (wages which a victor, who somewhere else was murdering children with a clear conscience, felt obliged, and not ironically, and not out of facetiousness, but by virtue of a principle, a law, a kind of acquired or rather learned or rather implanted morality, irrational and apparently intransgressible, stamped by use with a kind of sacred character (although some hundred years before still perfectly unknown): that is, that all work must be paid for, with however little but paid for – the wages then which a victor who could have made them slave for nothing, and moreover did make them slave, but by a kind of homage – somehow superstitious although symbolic – rendered to a principle, believed itself obliged to pay out to them), set aside about two-thirds of the total, signalled to one of the spectators who stood up, took the bits of paper, approached the Sicilian, spoke to him, returned towards the window and held out two cigarettes which Georges lit, then, turning back, let himself slide down the wall until his buttocks touched his heels, then holding out one of the lighted cigarettes to Blum, and Blum saying: 'You crazy?', and Georges: 'Oh hell! After all, it's Sunday, isn't it?', and sitting down completely, inhaling an endless puff of smoke until he felt it reaching all the way to the bottom of his lungs, exhaling it as slowly as possible, saying:) 'So he was there, on that road, beating a pathetic retreat, with that hat, that two-cornered clownishly feathered hat, the flap of his coat draped like a toga over his shoulder, his boots muddy – or rather dusty – and lost in his thoughts, or rather probably in his lack of thoughts, in the impossibility of thinking, of putting together two coherent ideas, face to face with what he doubtless thought was the collapse of his dreams, without suspecting that it was probably the contrary – but luckily for him he didn't live long enough to realize it –, that is, that revolutions reinforce and confirm themselves in disaster to grow corrupt at the end, to pervert themselves and collapse in an apotheosis of military triumphs . . . '

And Blum: 'But you're talking like a book! . . . '

And Georges looking up, staring at him for a moment, perplexed, startled, and finally shrugging his shoulders, saying: 'You're right. Sorry. A habit, a hereditary taint. My father absolutely insisted that I get myself ploughed at the École Normale. He absolutely insisted that I profit at least a little from that marvellous culture which centuries of thought have bequeathed to us. He absolutely insisted that his son enjoy the incomparable privileges of Western Civilization. Being the son of illiterate peasants, he's so proud of having been able to learn how to read that he's deeply convinced that there's no problem, and particularly no problem standing in the way of humanity's happiness, that can't be solved by reading good authors. Not long ago he even found the way to keep for himself (and I can assure you that if you knew my mother you'd acknowledge the extent of the exploit, the amount of will and consequently the degree of emotion, of confusion it represents) five lines out of the insipid laments she spreads over her letters which are fortunately limited to the number of lines we are authorized to receive, to add to the concert his own laments by sharing with me his despair at the news of the bombing of Leipzig and its apparently irreplaceable library . . . ' (breaking off, falling silent, able to see the letter without needing to take it out of his wallet – the only one he had kept of all Sabine had written and at the bottom of which his father usually contented himself with writing under the inevitable 'We send you all our love' the tiny hen tracks in which only Georges knew the letters of the word 'Papa' could be found – , seeing again, then (still more hen tracks, still closer set, compressed by the lack of room and the desire to say as much as possible in the least possible space), the fine and delicate donnish handwriting, the clumsy telegraphic style: ' . . . let your mother give you our news which is good as you see . . . in so far as anything can be good today knowing you thinking constantly of you there and of this world where a man strives to destroy himself not only in the flesh of his children but even in what he can best achieve and bequeath: History will say later what humanity lost the other day in a few minutes, the heritage of several centuries, in the bombing of what was the most precious library in the world, all of which is infinitely sad, your old father . . . ', able to see him sitting, elephantine, massive, almost deformed in the dimness of the summerhouse where the two of them had sat that last evening before he left while from outside came the now furious now muffled drone of the tractor on which the farmer was mowing the big field, the pungent green smell of the cut grass floating in the warm twilight, surrounding them, the heady exhalation of the summer, the dim figure of the farmer perched on the tractor with his floppy, ragged-brimmed straw hat like a black halo reflected twice in the glasses, slowly crossing the curved and shiny surface of the lenses in front of his father's dim sad face, and the two of them opposite each other, having nothing to say, both walled up in that pathetic incomprehension, that impossibility of communication which had grown up between them and which he (his father) had just tried once again to overcome, Georges hearing his mouth which went on (probably had never stopped) talking, his voice reaching him, saying:) ' . . . to which I answered in return that if the contents of the thousands of books in that irreplaceable library had been impotent to prevent things like the bombing which destroyed them from happening, I didn't really see what loss to humanity was represented by the disappearance of those thousands of books and papers obviously devoid of the slightest utility. There followed the detailed list of the positive values, the objects of prime importance which we need much more than the entire contents of the famous library of Leipzig, including: shoes, underwear, wool clothes, soap, cigarettes, sausage, chocolate, sugar, tinned goods, ma . . .'

And Blum: 'All right. Fine. All right. Fine. We know. Fine. To hell with the Library of Leipzig. Fine. Right. But even so, to get back to your man, the one in the portrait, the glory and shame of your family, he wasn't the first general, or missionary, or commissar, or whatever you want who . . . '

And Georges: 'Yes. Of course. I know. Yes. Maybe it wasn't only the fact of that battle, a simple defeat: not just what he saw there, the panic, the cowardice, the runaways throwing down their arms, screaming treason as usual and cursing their leaders to justify their panic, and gradually the shots coming at longer intervals, then isolated, without response, without conviction, the battle fading, dying of its own accord in the late-afternoon languor. We saw that, we knew that: the slowing down, the gradual immobilization. Like the wheel of the country fair lottery, the dry crackle of the metal (or bone) tongue on the shiny circle of stoppers gradually decomposing so to speak, the clicking that made only a single continuous rattle separating, dissociating, rarefying, those last hours when the battle seems to continue only by virtue of the momentum it has built up, to slow down, start up again, break out in absurd and incoherent starts, only to collapse again while you begin to hear the birds singing, realizing suddenly that they have never stopped singing, any more than the wind has stopped swaying the branches of the trees or the clouds have stopped running across the sky, – a few shots, then, unexpected now, absurd in the evening's peace, a few last exchanges between rear-guards and pursuers, and probably not the Spanish troops properly speaking (that is, regular, royal, that is, probably composed not of Spaniards but of mercenaries, of Irish or Swiss hirelings and commanded by some boy of a prince or some old general with a mummified pharaoh's head, with papery hands covered with rusty blotches, equally (the boy or the old mummy) covered with gold, with medals, with diamond orders like reliquaries, like madonnas, with their immaculate white uniforms, their wide diagonal ribbons of sky-blue moire, their ringed hands, the boy prince astride his roan at the top of the hill, amusing himself watching through a spyglass he doesn't know how to work while the last enemy troops beat a retreat, the old papery mummy sitting in his carriage and by now already worrying about the billet, the farm, the dinner, the bed – and perhaps the girl – his officers will find for him), but fired (the sporadic shots) by those occult and mysterious allies which every victorious army seems to generate spontaneously around it, before and behind it, probably peasants, or smugglers, or high-waymen of the region armed with old blunderbusses and make-shift pistols, a chaplet of medals and ex-votos around the leader's neck, and almost the same head, the beak and the talons of that honourable gentleman of Calabrian or Sicilian ancestry who is running the poker table over there, disguised as a soldier, and who sells cigarettes at the rate of two for the price of about four days' work, and kissing (the peasants, the smugglers) an old, filthy cross pulled out from under their shirt before firing their old blunderbuss at point-blank range from behind a cork-oak or a thicket at a wounded man or a straggler with that kind of sacred rage, that holy and murderous fury, shouting at the same time as the bullet is fired something like: 'There, you bastard, eat that!', and he (de Reixach) apparently deaf and blind (to the shots, to the birds singing, to the sun setting), sullen, vague, letting his horse choose the way, the reins loose, already having reached or penetrated another state, another degree, whether of consciousness or sensibility – or insensibility – and then a man – a bareheaded soldier with neither insignia nor weapons – coming out of somewhere (from behind the corner of a house, from behind a hedge, from the ditch where he had been lying) and beginning to run beside him shouting: 'Take me with you, Captain, let me come with you!', and he not even looking at him, or perhaps the way you look at a stone, a thing, and im-mediately turning his head away, and only saying a trifle louder than his conversational tone: 'Get away,' and the soldier still running beside his boot – or rather trotting, and probably he wouldn't have had to trot, would have only needed to take longer strides to keep up with the horse, but probably the notion of running was the thing that spontaneously corresponded in his mind to his desire to escape, to flee – , panting, chanting: 'Take me with you I've lost my regiment take me with you Captain I don't have any regiment left take me let me come with you . . .', and he not answering now, not hearing him, probably not seeing him either, withdrawn, immured in that arrogant silence in which he was speaking now perhaps already as an equal with all those barons those dead ancestors all those Reixachs who . . .'

And Blum: 'But what do you . . .'

And Georges: 'No, listen': then the man stopped running and came towards us, or rather he merely stopped running, like a puppy, his head up, about as high as de Reixach's knee, stood there in the middle of the road and waited until we came up to him, saying at that moment: 'Let me ride that horse,' and Iglésia who was holding the bridle of that dapple-grey horse not answering him any more than de Reixach, not seeming to see him any more than de Reixach, and then I said: 'You can see there's no saddle, you can't stay on if we trot,' but now he was beside us and had begun to run or rather to trot again, moving at that jolting, jerky gait, his head jogging as if he were going to collapse at the next step, his eyes staring into mine, constantly repeating in the same monotonous, glum, pleading tone of voice: 'Let me ride let me ride please let me ride,' and finally I said: 'Oh ride if you want!', and actually I'd never have thought he could do it, weak as he was, but no sooner had I spoken the words than there he was hoisting himself up, clinging to the bridle with a kind of frenzy, his hips squirming and finally he was up, was on top, was sitting there, de Reixach turning round then as if he had had eyes in the back of his head, though at that moment he didn't even seem to see what was in front of him any more, shouting: 'What are you doing? I told you to clear out! Who gave you permission to ride that horse and follow me?' and the man beginning to whine again, starting his litany all over, saying: 'Let me go with you I've lost my regiment and they'll catch me let me . . .', and he: 'Get off right away and clear out!', then I didn't see the man on the horse any more: even quicker than he had got on he had slipped down and when I turned round I saw him standing at the side of the road, miserable, solitary, helpless, watching us ride away, and after a moment Iglésia said: 'He was a spy!', and I: 'Who?', and Iglésia: 'That fellow. Didn't you see? He was a German,' and I: 'A German? What's the matter with you? Why a German?', and he shrugging without answering me as if I were an idiot, and still the regular clatter of our horses' hoofs, and the stiff back of de Reixach straight on his saddle, scarcely swaying at all, and that sun, and that layer of exhaustion, of sleep, of sweat and dust that was pasted to my face like a mask, isolating me, and a moment later Iglésia's voice reaching me from the other side of that film, from far away, somewhere in the sunshine, the dust, the heavy air, saying: 'He was a German, I tell you. He spoke French too well. And didn't you see his head? His hair? His hair was red!', and I: 'Red?', and Iglésia: 'Oh Christ, what's the matter with you, can't you even . . . '

'And that was when that burst of machine-gun fire came,' he said (standing there, in front of her, while she went on examining him with that kind of bored, patient, polite curiosity, and sometimes something (not fear but something like a discrete and insolent suspicion awakened, like the thing that sharpens the indifferent stare of cats) something furtive, sharp, sudden flickering across her eyes, and immediately extinguished, the face changeless, that smooth, calm, magnificent and empty mask, 'Like those statues,' he thought. 'But perhaps that's all she is, perhaps I should never ask anything more of her than what I would ask of marble, of stone, of bronze: only to let itself be looked at and touched, if she would only let herself be looked at and touched . . . ', but he didn't move, thinking: 'But she was crying. He said she was crying . . . '), then he could imagine them both, she and Iglésia, standing in the confusion of the crowd, the incessant grating of the gravel strewn or rather soiled with losing tickets, and Iglésia's tiny monkey hands tearing up the little pieces of paper that were worthless now, both of them rigid, erect, facing each other: he with that leather-coloured, dazed, woebegone face, his white breeches, his doll's boots and that triangle of the brilliant rose-coloured silk of his jockey's uniform appearing between the tattered lapels of the jacket, and she no longer invented now (as Blum said – or rather, no longer fabricated during the long months of war, of captivity, of forced continence, starting from a brief and single glimpse one day at a horse race, Sabine's gossip, snatches of sentences (themselves representing snatches of reality), confidences or rather almost monosyllabic grumbles wrung by patience and guile from Iglésia, or starting from still less: from a print that didn't even exist, from a portrait painted a hundred and fifty years ago . . .), but as he could see her now, in front of him, as she really was, since he could (since he was going to) touch her, thinking: 'I'm going to do it. She'll slap me, throw me out, but I'm going to do it . . . ', and she still staring at him as if she were looking at him through a sheet of glass, as if she were on the other side of a transparent partition that was as hard, as impenetrable as glass although apparently as invisible and behind which, ever since he had come, she kept herself sheltered or rather out of reach leaving to her lips (only her lips, not herself – that is, that sharp or rather sharpened thing, subtle and lightning-like – and perhaps even unknown to herself – that moved so rapidly, flickering across her serene and indifferent gaze) the responsibility of raising like an additional barrier the series of indifferent words, indifferent formulas (saying: 'So you were . . . I mean: you belonged to the same regiment, I mean the same squadron as . . . ', not finishing, not pronouncing (as though by a kind of embarrassment, a kind of discretion – or merely laziness) the name (or the two names) which he himself had not been able to bring himself to write in his letter, contenting himself with mentioning merely the number of the regiment and the squadron, as if he too had felt that same embarrassment, that same impossibility), and then he heard her laugh, saying: 'But I think we're distantly related, something like cousins by marriage, aren't we? . . . ', hearing her pronounce six years later and almost word for word the very words he (de Reixach) had spoken himself one frozen winter morning while behind him passed back and forth the vague and reddish blurs of the horses coming back from the trough where they had had to break the ice so they could drink, and now it was summer, – not the first but the second after it had all come to an end, that is, had closed over, formed a scar, or rather (not formed a scar, for already no trace of what had happened was visible any longer) readjusted, mended, and so perfectly that you could no longer detect the least crack, the way the surface of the water closes over a pebble, the landscape that had been reflected for a moment broken, fractured, splintered into an incoherent multitude of fragments, of pieces of sky and trees (that is, no longer the sky, the trees, but confused patches of blue, green, black), recomposing, the blue, the green, the black regrouping, coagulating so to speak, organizing, still undulating a little like dangerous serpents, then motionless, and then nothing but the varnished perfidious surface serene and mysterious, in which was ordered the calm opulence of the branches, the sky, the calm slow clouds, nothing more now than that lacquered and impenetrable surface, thinking (Georges): 'So he can probably start believing in them again, lining them up, organizing them elegantly, one after the other, insignificant, sonorous and hollow, in elegant phrases that are insignificant, sonorous, polite and infinitely reassuring, as smooth, as polished, as frozen and as insubstantial as the shiny surface of the water covering, discreetly hiding . . . '

But Georges didn't even go back to the summerhouse any more now, merely defying it, spying on it without even looking at it (for he had no need to, he had no need to use his eyes for that, being able to see without needing the image printed on his retina, the mass of the body now increasingly invaded by fat, monstrous, more and more overpowered by its own weight, the face with the features more and more weighted down by the effect of something that was not only fat and which gradually was taking possession of him, invading him, imprisoning him, immuring him in a kind of mute solitude, a proud and ponderous sadness), the way he had defied him, spied on him when he came home, the scene occurring like this: Georges declaring that he had decided to work on the land, and supported (although he pretended not to hear her although he pretended to speak to them both together, and yet turning noticeably towards her alone and noticeably turning away from his father, and yet speaking to him, and noticeably paying no attention to her or to anything she might say), supported then by Sabine's noisy, obscene and uterine approval; and no more, in other words not a word, not a remark, not a regret, the heavy mountain of flesh still motionless, silent, the heavy and pathetic mass of distended and worn organs inside which or rather under which lay something that was like a part of Georges, so that despite his total immobility, despite his complete absence of apparent reaction Georges heard perfectly and louder than Sabine's deafening prattle, the imperceptible sound of some secret and delicate organ breaking, snapping, and after that nothing else, nothing except that carapace of silence when Georges would sit down at the dinner table in his filthy smock, with his hands not dirty but somehow encrusted with earth and grease the evenings of the slow and empty days during which he drove the tractor, following the slow furrows, watching his shadow at each lap, first distorted, extended, slowly changing shape as it slowly revolved round him like the hands of a clock, shortening, thickening, then extending, stretching out again, enormous, gigantic finally, as the sun sank over the forgetful and indifferent earth, the perfidious world once again inoffensive, familiar, deceptive, while the images sometimes passed in confusion, Blum's fleshless face, Iglésia cooking the pancakes, and the dim equestrian silhouette raising its arm, brandishing the sabre, falling slowly to one side, vanishing, and Corinne the way he, or rather they (but there was no one he could talk to about her now, and Sabine said she had behaved in such a way that they – that is, the ones who belonged or whom Sabine judged worthy of belonging to that milieu or that caste in which she included herself – no longer received her), the way they (that is, he, Blum – or rather their imaginations, or rather their bodies, in other words their skin, their organs, their young men's lusting flesh) had materialized her: standing with the sun behind her at the end of the afternoon in that red dress the colour of a gumdrop (but perhaps he had invented that too, that is the colour, the harsh red, perhaps merely because she was something he thought about not with his mind but with his lips, his mouth, perhaps because of her name, because 'Corinne' made him think of 'coral'? . . .) silhouetted against the apple green of the turf where the horses are galloping past; and often he seemed to see her as one of those playing-card queens that he too now slid slowly through his hands as he kept his face expressionless (thinking: 'In any case at least I'll have learned one thing from the war. I won't have been in it for nothing. At least I'll have learned to play poker . . . ' For he was playing poker now, joining in the back room of a café near the cattle market (going there just as he was, as he had eaten at his father's table, in other words in his smock, his hands impregnated with earth and grease), three or four men with the same expressionless, brief, economical gestures, and who played for high stakes, emptied (with the same gestures they used for playing, in the same silent, quick, and apparently uninterested way) bottles of the most expensive champagne while two or three girls with whom each man had slept in turn waited yawning and showing each other their jewellery on the shabby banquette): nothing but a piece of cardboard, then, one of those queens robed in scarlet, enigmatic and symmetrically doubled, as if reflected in a mirror, wearing one of those half-red and half-green robes with heavy and ritual ornaments, with the ritual and symbolic attributes (rose, sceptre, ermine): something without any more thickness, without any more reality or existence than a face drawn on the white background of the paper, impenetrable, expressionless and fatal, like the face of chance itself; then –

through one of the players – he learned that she had re-married and lived in Toulouse, and so now all that separated him from her was that glass from behind which she seemed to be looking at him, talking to him, speaking words, sentences that he (and probably she) didn't listen to, exactly as if he had been standing on the other side of the aquarium glass, looking at her, still thinking: 'I'm going to do it. She'll slap me, call someone and have me thrown out, but I'm going to do it . . . ', and she – that is, her flesh, stirring imperceptibly, that is, breathing, that is, dilating and contracting as if the air penetrated her not through her mouth, her lungs, but by the entire surface of her skin, as if she were made of a substance like that of sponges but with an invisible texture, dilating and contracting like those sea anemones those denizens of the deep halfway between vegetable and animal, those madrepores, palpitating delicately in the transparent water, breathing, and he still not listening, not even bothering to pretend to be listening, staring at her, while she tried again to laugh, observed him from behind her smile with that kind of circum-spection, that mixture of curiosity, suspicion and perhaps fear, as if he might have been something rather like a ghost, a phantom, he himself able to see himself in the cloudy depths of the glass behind her, with his sunburnt face, his starved dog's expression, thinking: 'Oh yes! That's just about what I must look like! As if I wanted to bite . . . ', and she still saying whatever came into her head: 'How tan you are Have you been on the beach a lot? Do you like the sea?' and he: 'What?' and she: 'You're so tan,' and he: 'The sea? Why . . . Oh! No, I work on the land you know I spend the whole day on the tract . . . ', then his own hand coming into his field of vision, that is, as if he had thrust it into the water, watching it move forward, away from himself, with a kind of astonishment, a stupor (as if it had separated itself from him, detached itself from his arm by the effect of that slight deviation of the light rays when they cross the surface of a liquid): the thin brown hand with the long, fine fingers, out of which he had not managed in eight years despite the handles of pitch-

forks, of shovels, of pickaxes, the earth, the grease, to make a
peasant's hand and which remained hopelessly slender and fine,
making Sabine say lovingly and proudly that he had pianist's
hands, that he should have been a musician, that he had certainly
spoiled, wasted a gift, a unique opportunity (but he didn't even
bother to shrug his shoulders now), excluding the image, Sabine's
voice, while he still watched his own hand now become something alien to himself, in other words belonging – like the trees,
the sky, the blue, the green – to that alien world, sparkling and
incredible, where she (Corinne) stood, unreal, incredible despite
her heavy perfume, her voice, breathing more quickly now, her
breasts rising and falling like those birds' breasts, palpitating, the
air (or the blood) rushing in rapid pulsations while her voice
sounded more urgent now, rose a half tone perhaps, saying:
'Well I'm happy to have seen you I have to go now I think it
must be rather late I have . . . ', but still not moving, his hand
far away from him now (like in cinemas when people sitting in
the balcony near the projection booth wave their arms, their
hands, the five spread fingers thrusting into the luminous beam,
projecting their huge and moving shadows across the screen as
though to possess, to reach the inaccessible shimmering dream),
completely detached now, so that when he touched her (the bare
upper arm a little below the shoulder) he felt at first the strange
sensation of not really touching her, the way it feels when you
take a bird in your hand: that surprise, that astonishment provoked by the difference between the apparent volume and the
real weight, the incredible lightness, the incredible delicacy, the
tragic fragility of the feathers, the down, and she saying: 'What
. . . what are you . . . ', and apparently as incapable of finishing
her sentence as of moving, only breathing faster and faster, almost
panting, while she went on staring at him with the expression of
fear, of impotence, and something between his palm and the silky
skin of her arm, something no thicker than a leaf of cigarette
paper, but something intervening, that is, the sense of touch
somehow slightly retarded, as when the fingers numbed by cold

come to rest on an object and perceive it only through a film, a kind of shell of insensitivity, and both of them (Corinne and Georges) perfectly motionless, staring at each other, then the hand closing over her arm, squeezing, and he could close his eyes now, smelling only that flowerlike odour, hearing her breathe, pant, the air passing in and out of her lips quickly now, then she uttered something like a sigh, a moan, saying: You're hurting me, saying: Let me go you're hur . . . Let me go . . . , until he realized that his hand was squeezing now with all its strength, but he did not let her go, merely relaxing his muscles a little, realizing at the same time that he was trembling now, continuously, imperceptibly, uncontrollably, and she saying: Please My husband might come in Please Let go of me Stop but still not moving, panting a little, repeating in a monotonous, mechanical, frightened voice: Please Now stop Please Please . . . , Georges merely leaving his hand where it was now, not doing anything more, and he too absolutely motionless, as if not between them now, but round them, enclosing them, the air had that fallacious consistency, the alarming fragility of glass, invisible and brittle, and then standing there (Georges) without making a move, without daring to move, trying to hold his breath, to calm the deafening murmur of his blood, the green and transparent May twilight like glass too, and in his throat that kind of nausea he tried to choke down, swallowing, thinking between two deafening rushes of air: It's from running too much, thinking: But maybe it's all that alcohol? thinking that he should have tried to vomit the way Iglésia did a little while ago in the field, thinking: But vomit what? trying to remember the last time he had eaten oh yes that piece of sausage this morning in the forest (but was it in the morning or when?), his stomach full of the gin he seemed to feel inside him like an alien body, unassimilable, a solidified ball or rather half-solidified and heavy, something like mercury, so a little while ago he should have put a finger down his throat and vomited, at least he would have been relieved, when they were in the house putting on their uniforms again, and then standing (again stiff, heavy, exhausted, in his stiff, heavy cocoon of cloth and leather) alone in the room, still wondering if he was going to vomit or not and where could Iglésia have gone, while out of the window he watched the engineers' trucks retreating down the road, no bigger than toys, following each other in a regular, hurried flight, then Iglésia there again without his being able to say when and how he had returned (any more than when he had vanished), Georges starting, turning round, looking at him with that same exhausted, incredulous look, and Iglésia: 'Those poor nags, after all they have to eat too,' and he thinking: 'Good God, he's even managed to think of that. Almost dead drunk. Like the other one this morning to let them drink. As if . . . ', then no longer thinking, not finishing his train of thought, no longer interested in it turning and looking at what Iglésia's bulging, yellowish, astonished and incredulous eyes were looking at now, both of them standing there motionless for a minute while in the distance beyond the sloping fields the little toy cars went on following each other: then jogging down the staircase, running across the farm's deserted courtyard and taking the lane they had followed that morning – but in the opposite direction and all he could see now (lying flat on his belly in the grass of the ditch, panting, still trying to choke down the terrible wheezing sound in his chest) with the narrow horizontal strip to which the world now reduced itself limited above by the visor of his helmet, below by the crisscrossing of the blades of grass in the ditch just in front of his eyes, vague, then more distinct, then no longer blades of grass: a green blur in the green twilight, thinning out then stopping at the place where the lane joined the road, then the stones of the road and the sentry's two black boots, carefully polished, with their shiny accordion pleats at the ankle, the axis of the boots forming the base of an inverted V in the opening of which, on the other side of the road, the dead horse appeared and disappeared between the wheels of the trucks jolting across the cobbles, still in the same place as that morning but apparently flattened out, as though it had gradually melted during the day like those snowmen who seem to sink imperceptibly into the earth, as though attacked at their base, gradually shrinking with the thaw until finally only the largest masses and the struts are left – broomsticks, laths – that have served as an armature: here the belly, enormous now, swollen, distended, and the bones, as if the middle of the body had absorbed the whole substance of the endless carcass, the bones with their round heads holding up as well they could the crust of peeling mud that served as an envelope: but no more flies now, as if they had abandoned it, as if there were nothing left to take from it, as if there were already – but that wasn't possible, Georges thought, not in one day – , no longer rotten and stinking meat, but transmuted, assimilated by the deep earth that hides beneath its hair of grass and leaves the bones of every defunct Rosinante and every defunct Bucephalus (and the defunct riders, the defunct coachmen and the defunct Alexanders) reverted to crumbling lime or . . . (but he was wrong: suddenly one flew out – this time from inside the nostrils – and although he was more than fifteen yards away he saw it (probably thanks to that nauseating and minute visual acuity drunkenness affords) as distinctly (hairy, blue-black, shiny, and though his ears were splintered by the incessant racket of the trucks moving at high speed, hearing it too: its impetuous, voracious, furious buzzing) as the nailheads in the four horseshoes lying on the edge beside the road and now, in relation to Georges, in the foreground) . . . reverted, then, to the state of crumbling lime, of fossils, which he himself was probably becoming out of immobility, watching, impotent, the slow transmutation of his own substance starting with his arm that he could feel dying gradually, growing numb, devoured not by worms but by a slowly mounting tingle that was perhaps the secret stirring of atoms in the process of permutating in order to organize themselves according to a different structure, mineral or crystalline, in the crystalline twilight from which he was still separated by the thickness of a leaf of cigarette paper, unless it wasn't a leaf of cigarette paper at all but the contact of the twilight itself on his skin for such, he thought, is the exquisite delicacy of women's flesh that you hesitate to believe you're really touching them, the skin like feathers, grass, leaves, transparent air, fragile as crystal, so that he could still hear her panting faintly, unless it was his own breathing, unless he was now as dead as the horse and already half swallowed up, taken back by the earth his flesh mingling with the moist clay, his bones mingling with the stones, for perhaps it was a simple matter of immobility and then you simply became a little chalk, sand and mud again, thinking that was what he should have told him, seeing him as he undoubtedly was at that same moment, in the dimness of the twilight summerhouse where through the coloured glass panes the world looked as though it were made of a single and simple material, green, mauve or blue, reconciled at last, unless it was one of those May evenings that were too warm to stay in the summerhouse, in which case they would have been – he and she – still sitting under the big chestnut tree where they took their tea, the chestnut tree in bloom then, its white clusters like candelabra glowing softly in the twilight, the heavy shadows tinged with blue, falling over them now, covering them like an opaque and uniform layer of paint, he and his eternal sheets of paper spread in front of him on the table beside the tray he had pushed aside, a saucer set on top of them to keep the breeze from scattering them for now he could probably no longer even make out the fine handwriting that covered them, probably contenting himself now or at least trying to content himself with the knowledge that those characters, those signs were there, the way a blind man in the darkness knows – recognizes – the existence of the protecting walls, of the chair, of the bed, though if need be he can still touch them to experience the certainty of their presence, – when the day, or the light (Georges thought, still lying in the ditch, watchful, stiff, now completely numb and paralysed with cramps, and as motionless as the dead nag, his face buried in the thick grass, the hairy earth, his whole body flattened as if he were trying to vanish between the lips of the ditch, to melt, to slip, to sink altogether through this narrow crevice to rejoin the original matter (matrix), remembering the evenings when they ate out of doors and when, at this hour, Julien brought the oil lamp and, while they set the table, his father went on working, enclosed – he and those scribbled sheets with their dog-eared corners that had somehow become a part of himself, a supplementary organ as inseparable from him as his brain or his heart, or his heavy old flesh – in that protective cocoon, that egg, that yellowish sphere the light of the lamp created in the darkness of the lawn and the humming of the mosquitoes), when the light, then, would bring no other certainty than the disappointing reappearance of the scribblings without any other real existence than that attributed to them by a mind (also without any other real existence) in order to represent the things it imagined and that were perhaps as lacking in existence, and in that case it was better to listen to her henlike cackling, her clanking necklaces, her perpetual and senseless verbiage which at least had the virtue of existing, even if only by sound and movement, supposing that sound and movement were not also futile and illusory forms of the contrary of existence: which is what he would have had to know, what he would have had to be able to ask the horse, and perhaps it was a problem Georges could have solved if he had been less drunk or less exhausted, and besides, perhaps the question would solve itself any moment now by the mere effect of a bullet, in other words by the fact that matter's natural inertia would be reversed for an instant (a combustion, an expansion, a projectile violently expelled from the interior of a tube), transforming him for good into a simple pile of horselike matter which only its shape would distinguish from that of the nag, provided it occurred to this sentry walking back and forth from one side of the lane to the other parallel to the road's edge to walk instead perpendicular to the latter about a dozen yards up the path, and of course he (Georges) could still try firing first which, granting that he managed to do so fast enough and then that he jumped fast enough over the fence, would give him time enough to taste for one last time that futile and illusory form of life which is movement (the time to cover some ten or fifteen yards in his turn) before knowing what the flies did not yet know, what they would know in their turn one day, what the whole world would end up knowing but which neither horse nor fly nor man had ever come back to tell to those who still didn't know it, and then he would be dead for good, and if the sentry were faster, he wouldn't even have time to get up, so that he would be in that same place, and the only difference from now would be that he wouldn't be completely in the same position any more since he would have tried to raise his gun to his shoulder and aim, and that was all, for ultimately it would still be the same calm and warm May evening with its green smell of grass and the slight bluish moisture that was beginning to fall on the orchards and the gardens: there would have been only one or two shots such as you hear in September after the opening of the hunting season, when a farmer has taken a gun and decided to go out walking in the direction of the place where he startled that hare the other day and this time the hare was at the rendezvous and he shot it, with this difference that no one would pick him (Georges) up by the ears, but he would still be there, in the same place, completely and definitely motionless then, with Wack's expression of stupid surprise, his mouth stupidly open, his eyes open too, staring blindly at the narrow strip of the universe that stretched in front of him, that same wall of dark-red bricks (the bricks short and thick, made of some grainy substance, the lightest ones rust-coloured the darkest ones the colour of dried blood, brownish purple occasionally shading into a dark mauve that was almost blue, as if the material they were made of had contained ferruginous slag, as if the fire that had baked them had somehow solidified – bloody, mineral and violent – like meat on the butcher's block (the same tinges shading from orange to purplish), the heart, the hard and purple flesh of this earth to which he was pressed belly to belly so to speak), the lighter joints made of a greyish mortar in which he could see the grains of encrusted sand, a wild weed of some delicate shade of green growing against the base of the wall (as though to conceal the line joint, the dihedron formed by the wall and the ground), and a little in front of it the heavy stems whose tops the visor of his helmet kept him from seeing (perhaps rose-mallows or young sunflowers?): almost as big around as his thumb, with stripes or rather longitudinal grooves of a lighter green, almost white, and covered with a fine down, not flat, but growing perpendicular to the stem, the leaves nearest the bottom already withered and dried, hanging limp like wilted lettuce leaves, their edges yellowed, but the higher leaves still firm, fresh, their veins distinct and branching like a symmetrical net-work of streams and tributaries, the substance of the leaves themselves elastic, downy, something (silhouetted against the rough mineral and bloody bricks) incredibly tender, immaterial, the blades of grass virtually motionless merely stirred occasionally by a faint shudder, the vigorous stems of the tall plants absolutely motionless, the broad leaves trembling gently from time to time in the calm air, while from the road that gigantic racket still continued to fill his ears: not the cannons (which could be heard now only in the distance, sporadically, in the calm and clear twilight, like the last shocks, without conviction, straggling and conventional, of battle – like that facsimile of work, that show of activity which employees lazily produce while waiting for the office closing time), but the war itself rushing on with an uproar like – only exaggerated – the noise of a railway station, echoes of clashing couplings, iron machinery jolting, unexpected and disastrous; then, farther to the left, springing just out of the ridge of the joint as though out of a fissure between the ground and the wall, was one of those weeds: a tuft or rather a corolla of leaves spread in a crown like a fountain cascading down, torn, ragged and bristling (like those ancient weapons, or those har-poons), dark green, shaggy, then the stem – the latter bent slightly to the right – of another of the same tall plants, then, fastened to the wall by an iron bolt (probably there was still another one higher up, but he couldn't see it either), the jamb or rather the wooden coping on which was hinged a chicken-wire gate to the hen-house: the bolt rusted into the brick wall, the cement round the thick iron tongue forming a creamy flange in which you could still see the traces of the trowel which in smoothing down the mortar had left a seam (a slight uneven swelling of the compressed substance), the coping – the door jamb as well as its frame – discoloured by the rain, greyish and flaky, like the ash of a cigar, the frame half coming apart, one of the two wooden pegs that held the lower corner together almost out of its fastening, the whole thing out of kilter, the lower crosspiece making an angle with the coping that was not right but slightly obtuse, so that it must have raked the ground when someone opened the gate, the grass round the base of the coping growing in thick, close-set tufts that were lower at that point, only a flat surface with a few blades lying on the ground's surface, short and stunted, then the bare earth striped with concentric curves corresponding to the bulges on the lower crosspiece of the gate where it had rubbed the ground around the coping, the chicken-wire not in much better condition, although it had apparently been replaced quite recently (more recently in any case than the wood of the gate itself) for it wasn't rusty yet (though the little horseshoe nails that held it to the frame were) but only staved in and distended, making a bulging surface, a deep sag (perhaps the consequence of the kicks necessary to close the hen-house gate) having formed in the lower part, distending or rather irregularly stretching the hexagonal mesh, the grass growing round the foot of the second wooden coping in close-set tufts, and continuing along the fence beyond, Georges's field of vision stopping there, that is, not distinctly: ending in that kind of fringe that extends to the right and left of what we see and inside which objects are not so much seen as glimpsed in the form of blurs, vague outlines, too exhausted (Georges) or too drunk even to turn his head: he saw no hens inside the fence, or perhaps they were already roosting since they're supposed to go to bed with the sun, and when he heard Iglésia whispering he didn't understand at first, repeating: What? Iglésia touching him on the thigh this time, saying: . . . the chickens. I bet they'll come to get some. It's dark enough, isn't it? . . . So they began crawling backward, their field of vision enlarging as they moved, the house gradually appearing, dark-red and squat, and to the left the hen-house and above the place where they had been lying the moment before a window with a blue enamel pot set on the sill, but the window, although open, empty, dead, black, and the two upstairs windows empty and black too, Georges and Iglésia still crawling backward in the ditch, then standing up when they reached the turn, dashing forward, balancing on top of the fence and falling on the other side, lying there for a second, motionless, listening to their own breathing that was uneven now, and for a moment unable to hear anything else, then – nothing happening – crossing the little garden bent double, crossing a second fence, and after that (it was an orchard) crouching again one behind the other against the hedge, and again their breathing, their tumultuous blood, but still not moving, the slow darkness gradually thickening, and behind him Iglésia's voice whispering again, hoarse and furious, stamped with that kind of childish indignation (and no need to turn around to see his big fish eyes full of that same stupefaction, sullen, outraged): 'Engineers' trucks! Hell! . . . ', Georges not answering, not even turning round, the indignant, reproving and plaintive whispering coming again: 'Christ. One more step and we'd have walked right into them. What were you looking at?', Georges still not answering, beginning to retreat along the hedge without taking his eyes off the corner of the brick house that was dark now between the shadowy branches of the apple trees: but no more trucks were going by now and all he could see was the light made by the pink rag hanging on the hedge not far from the horse, but not the horse, and not the sentry either, only the pink patch gleaming faintly in the darkness, then not even the rag any more because they had crossed another hedge, still walking backward, their heads always facing the road, bumping into the hedge, their hands groping behind them, raising their legs, straddling the hedge for a minute, bodies bent over, and landing on the other side without taking their eyes off the corner of the house, their heads and their bodies absorbed by different problems, each acting on its own account or rather dividing up what had to be done, their limbs spontaneously accomplishing under their own authority and control the series of movements to which their brains seemed to be paying no attention, the darkness almost complete now, the frightened cackles suddenly exploding in the hen-house in a burst of flapping wings, the absurd and discordant protest filling the twilight for a moment, terrified and furious, like a parodic appendix to the battle: men swearing, clumsy arms flailing the air among the vague reddish balls fluttering, colliding, squawking, until the unequal combat also subsided, ending on a last terrified, strangled, pitiful squawk, then nothing more, except in the empty hen-house the slow and silent descent of the scattered feathers falling, drifting down, and Iglésia's voice saying: 'Christ,' and a moment later saying again: 'That's at least a division that went by under our noses. I never thought there were so many. I never thought they could go so fast. If they're fighting the war sitting on those seats, what the hell are we doing with our damn nags? What the hell did we look like . . . '

3

Sensual pleasure, volupté, *is the embrace of a dead body by two living beings. The 'corpse' in this case is time murdered for a time and made consubstantial to the sense of touch.*

MALCOLM DE CHAZAL

He was still talking and cursing, but I dropped his lighter: we were groping in the dark now, stumbling up the wooden staircase, of course the old man hadn't come back and so there was no duck, that was to be expected probably he was sleeping off his gin, there was still something like a faint gleam of light in the room the kind that lingers on after the twilight we could see the reflection in the wood of the bed I bumped into the chair and knocked it over it made a terrible noise in the empty house we stood still listening for a minute as if someone could have heard it from the road then I groped again in the darkness to pick it up put down my rifle sat down then I saw that he had lain down on the bed I said the least you could do is take off your spurs, then there was nothing else, that is remembering nothing, I think I must have fallen asleep there maybe even before I was finished talking, maybe I hadn't even got to the spurs perhaps I had simply thought of it the nothingness the black sleep falling over me like a bell burying me while I was sitting on the chair leaning forward my hand groping trying to unbuckle the strap of my, thinking what a crazy idea it had been to put them back on since we had left the horses in the stable what good, their rowels were clogged with caked blood from having dug into their flanks on Sunday when we had covered those fifteen kilometres at a gallop almost the whole time to get over the bridge before it was blown up, once he told us that one of those old men in striped trousers grey stovepipe walrus moustache and rosette in his buttonhole had paid him to ride him (Ride him? I said, Yes ride him What like a horse Do I have to draw you a picture? – looking at me out of his huge astonished eyes as if I were an idiot or just about), Iglésia putting a string in his mouth, his crop in his hand, wearing his jockey silk and boots and he had had to put on the spurs, the man stark naked on all fours on the carpet of his bedroom he had to whip him saw at his mouth and scratch his belly with the spurs, telling this in his usual perpetually morose and naturally scandalized voice so that it was impossible to tell if he was really shocked: at most he might have merely found the thing a little incomprehensible but not so much as that after all, disgusting too, but not so much either, accustomed as he was to the eccentricities of the rich, according them that preoccupied indulgence (more astonished than outraged, and slightly but not very contemptuous) of the poor – whores, pimps or flunkies; that sleep fell over me as if someone had suddenly thrown a blanket over my head, imprisoning me, suddenly everything went completely black, maybe I was dead maybe that sentry had fired first and faster, perhaps I was still lying back there in the fragrant grass of the ditch in that furrow of the earth breathing smelling its black and bitter humus lapping her pink but not pink nothing but the darkness in the deep shadows licking my face but in any case my hands my tongue able to touch her know her assure myself my blind hands reassured touching her everywhere running over her her back her belly with the sound of silk then encountering that shaggy tuft growing like an alien parasite on her smooth nakedness, I kept running over her crawling under her exploring in the darkness discovering her enormous and shadowy body as though under a milk-giving goat, the goat-foot (he said they did it with their goats as well as with their wives or their sisters) sucking the perfume of her bronze breasts finally reaching that warm tuft lapping intoxicating myself clinging to the silky hollow of her thighs I could see her buttocks above me gleaming faintly phosphorescent bluish in the darkness while I drank endlessly feeling that stem growing out of me that tree growing its roots branching inside my belly my loins enveloping me like ivy creeping down my back wrapping round my neck, I seemed to be shrinking in proportion as it grew feeding on me becoming me or rather me becoming it and then there was nothing left of my body but a shrunken wizened foetus lying between the lips of a ditch as if I could melt into it disappear there engulf myself there clinging like those baby monkeys beneath the belly of their mother to her belly to her many breasts burying myself in that tawny clamminess I said Don't put on the light I grabbed her arm as it was reaching she tasted salty like shellfish I didn't want to know admit anything else, only to go on lapping her

and she: But you don't really love me

and I: Oh Good God

and she: Not me it's not me you

and I: Oh Good God for five years for five whole years

and she: But not me I know it's not me Do you love me for what I am would you have loved me without I mean if

and I: Oh no listen what difference does it make let me What difference does it make what sense does it make let me I want to

wet mould from which I had learned to stamp pressing the clay with my thumb the soldiers infantrymen cavalrymen and cuirassiers climbing out of Pandora's box (a race armed booted and spurred helmeted) spreading across the world the armed spawn they had a crescent-shaped metal plate hanging round their neck by a chain sparkling like silver, braid, silver fringe there was something funereal something deadly; I remember that field where they had put or rather penned or rather piled us: we were lying in successive rows heads touching feet like those lead soldiers stacked in a box, but when we first came it was still virgin undefiled so I threw myself on the ground dying of hunger thinking The horses eat it why not me I tried to imagine to convince myself I was a horse, I was lying dead at the bottom of the ditch devoured by the ants my whole body slowly turning by a thousand tiny mutations into a lifeless substance and then it would be the grass that would feed on me my flesh nourishing the earth and after all it wouldn't be so much of a change, except that I would merely be on the other side of its surface the way you pass from one side of a mirror to the other where (on that other side) things may go on happening symmetrically, in other words up above it would go on growing

still indifferent and green just as they say hair goes on growing
on dead men's heads the only difference being that I would be
eating the dandelions by the root our dripping bodies exhaling
that sharp pungent odour of roots, of mandragora, I had read
that shipwrecked men that hermits eat roots acorns and then
she took it first between her lips then far back in her mouth like
a greedy child it was as if we were drinking each other slaking
each other's thirst gorging on each other feasting famished,
trying to appease calm my hunger a little I tried to chew it,
thinking It's like salad, the harsh green juice putting my teeth
on edge a sharp blade cut my tongue like a razor, burning, then
somebody taught me how to recognize the ones you could eat
for instance rhubarb: they had immediately recovered their
primitive nomad instincts managing to make a fire and cooking
a dog they had stolen I wonder from whom probably one of
those fools one of those officers or N.C.O.s ambushed in
general-staff offices the kind you see occasionally their elegant
uniforms intact probably thinking they were well protected and
caught one fine morning by someone kicking open the door and
ironically shoving them with his machine-gun barrel to make
them line up in the courtyard hands over their heads stupefied
and not understanding what was happening, they said whole
general-staffs had been captured like that hair slicked down spick
and span, we took our time jeering at them but these men had
found it more profitable to steal their dog and put it in the pot
sharing it among them sitting there, ochre or olive, enigmatic,
scornful with their shiny white teeth their harsh guttural names
Arhmed ben Abdahalla or Bouhabda or Abderrhamane their
speech sudden, guttural and harsh their bodies smooth and shiny
as those of girls, and there were dandelions too but they kept
bringing up others whole herds exhausted and ragged some with
civilian caps their coats unbuttoned hanging at their heels
and soon the whole meadow was trampled and torn entirely
covered by the rows of bodies lying head to foot and in the grey
dawn the grass was grey too covered with dew which I drank

drinking all of her there taking all of her into me like those oranges that despite grown-ups telling me it was dirty that it was impolite noisy I liked to make a hole in and squeeze, pressing drinking her belly the globes of her breasts slipping under my fingers like water a pink crystalline drop trembling on the bent blade of grass under that light rustling breeze that precedes the sunrise reflecting containing in its transparence the sky tinged pink by the dawn I remember those incredible mornings never had spring never had the sky been so pure so clean so transparent the evenings so cold, we pressed close together hoping to preserve a little warmth wedged together head to foot I was thinking how he had held her like that my thighs under hers that wild and silky brush against my belly holding the milk of her breasts in my palms in the centre of which their tearose moist shiny tips (when I took my mouth away it was a darker pink, as though irritated, inflamed, of a grainy bruised texture, a bright thread still connecting it to my lips, I remember that I saw a tiny one on a blade of grass leaving behind it a luminous metallic streak like silver, so small it scarcely made the blade of grass bend under its weight, with its tiny spiral shell each scroll striped with fine brown lines its neck (grainy too and yet fragile and cartilaginous) stretching raising its horns that retracted when I touched them able to stand erect and to retract, she who had never given suck never been touched by any lips except the rough lips of men: in the centre you could make out something like a tiny horizontal slit with close-pressed edges out of which sprang, invisible, the milk of oblivion) rising pressing like the heads of nails driven into my palms thinking They've counted all the bones, able to hear my whole skeleton clattering, waiting for the cold dawn, seized with a continuous trembling waiting for the moment when it would be light enough to have the right to stand up then I carefully stepped over the interlocking bodies (they looked like corpses) until I reached the central lane where the sentries with metal collars like dogs walked back and forth: standing then still trembling for a moment, teeth chattering, trying to remember what that ceremony was in which they were all lying on the ground, row after row, head to feet, on the cold stones of the cathedral, ordination I think or the taking of the veil the girls the virgins lying full length on either side of the central aisle down which the old bishop passes in clouds of incense like a wizened mummy and covered with gold and lace, weakly waving his ringed hand in its amaranth glove and singing in a scarcely audible exhausted voice the Latin words saying that they are dead for this world and apparently a veil is stretched over them then, the uniformly grey dawn stretching over the field and in the low part a little fog hovered over the stream but they only let us stand up when it was broad daylight and meanwhile we lay trembling all our limbs shivering closely interlaced entwined I rolled on top of her crushing her with my weight but I was trembling too much feverish groping for her flesh for the entrance for the opening of her flesh among that tangled bushy moisture my clumsy finger trying to divide them blind but too hurried trembling too much then she put it in herself one of her hands sliding between our two bellies separating the lips with her middle and ring fingers in a V while her other arm seemed to crawl down her body like an animal like an invertebrate swan's neck creeping along Leda's thigh (or some other bird symbolizing the shameless the vainglorious yes the peacock on the net curtain falling back its tail spangled with eyes swaying oscillating mysterious) and finally slipping round passing under her buttock reaching me wrist bent back placing her palm bent back flat against me as though to push me back then taking it introducing it thrusting it in burying it engulfing it breathing heavily she raised her arms again the right arm round my neck the left pressing the small of my back where her feet were locked around me, breathing faster and faster now her breath cut off each time I fell back drove against her crushed her under my weight pulling away and driving against her she rebounding towards me and once it came out but this time she put it back very quickly with only one hand not letting my neck go, now she was panting moaning not loud but continuously her voice changed different from the way I knew it as if it were someone else a stranger childish disarmed moaning revealing something frightened plaintive lost I said Do I love you? I drove against her the spasm shaking her choking still she managed to say:

No

I said again You don't think I love you, driving against her again my loins my belly driving against her thrusting again deep within her choking for a moment she was unable to speak but finally she managed to say again:

No

and I: You don't think I love you Really you don't think I love you Then do I love you now Do I love you tell me! driving against her harder each time leaving her neither time nor strength to answer her throat her lungs releasing only an inarticulate sound but her head rolling wildly from right to left on the pillow against the dark blur of her hair meaning No No No No, they had locked a lunatic up in the pigsty they used as a guardhouse, a man who had gone crazy in a raid sometimes he started screaming endlessly meaninglessly and somehow calmly not stamping or pounding against the door he just shouted and sometimes at night I would wake up listening to him I said What's that, and he That's the lunatic, still sulky sullen he curled up again trying to bury his head under his coat, I could see them, see their black shadows coming and going noiselessly in the central lane huddled in their heavy overcoats with their metal dog collars gleaming sometimes under the moon, guns slung over their shoulders, swinging their arms to warm themselves, his voice reached me from under his coat muffled furious saying If I was them I'd give him a good smack across the mouth with my gun then maybe he'd stop braying like that all night long, shouting endlessly meaninglessly in the darkness, shouting then suddenly she stopped released me we lay there like two dead bodies trying to catch our breath as if our hearts had tried to leap out of our mouths with the air, dead inert she and I deafened by the racket

of our blood rushing flowing back booming into our limbs
rushing across the complicated ramifications of our arteries like
what's that called eagre I think all the rivers beginning to flow
in the opposite direction rising towards their sources, as if we
had been completely drained for a second, as if our whole life
had rushed out of us with the roar of a cataract wrenching
uprooting itself from us from me from my solitude freeing itself
rushing beyond spreading springing endlessly flooding each
other endlessly as if there were no end as if there were never to
be any end (but that wasn't true: only for a second, drunk thinking it was for ever, but only an instant in reality like when you
dream that so many things are happening and when you open
your eyes again the clock's hand has scarcely moved at all) then
it flowed back rushing now in the opposite direction as though
it had collided with a wall, some insurmountable obstacle that
only a small part of ourselves had managed to scale somehow by
deception, that is by deceiving simultaneously what opposed its
escaping, freeing itself and ourselves, something furious frustrated
then in our frustrated solitude, imprisoned again, colliding
furiously against the barriers the narrow and insurmountable
limits, storming, then gradually that subsided and a moment
later she turned on the light, I quickly closed my eyes everything
was brown then red I kept them closed I heard the water flowing
carrying away dissolving . . . (I could hear it silvery icy and
black in the night on the roof of the barn rushing through the
gutters it sounded as if in the darkness nature the trees the whole
earth was dissolving drowned diluted liquefied crumbled by that
slow deluge then I decided to go there myself to join them in
the house of the lame man who had invited us for the evening
instead of going up to lie down in the brown hay or going back
to the café to drink; Wack was still watching, he wasn't on stable
guard tonight and still he stayed there: he watched me pass
without a word and go out into the black rain but I still didn't
manage to see her, finding them already sitting down, three of
them with the lame man round the table, Iglésia and another

man arguing in low tones beside the stove; only she wasn't there, standing on the doorstep I looked round for her, but she wasn't there and finally I asked if this was the Soldiers' and Farmers' Soviet, but they turned their suspicious and disapproving eyes on me I said they shouldn't get up I said I had never been able to learn how to play anything except beggar-my-neighbour and I went to sit down beside the stove: on top was a big enamel coffee-pot and the table they were playing on was covered with a yellow oilcloth whose red pattern showed palm trees minarets riders with yataghans and women at a well filling or carrying on their shoulders elongated urns, each time one of the card players put down a card he held it in the air for a second or two then snapped it down with a (triumphant, furious?) gesture on the table which he pounded violently with his fist, then I saw her: not her, that whiteness, that kind of slow and warm apparition glimpsed in the morning in the dimness of the stable, but somehow her contrary or rather her negation or rather her corruption, the corruption of the very idea of woman of grace of pleasure, its punishment: a dreadful old crone with the profile and beard of a goat her head shaken with a continuous tremor and when I sat down beside her on the bench behind the stove she looked at me with two pale-blue almost white eyes that seemed to be liquefied staring at me spying on me for a moment still chewing, ruminating, her greyish whiskers rising and falling, then leaning towards me approaching my face until she was almost touching it her yellow and withered mask (as if I were spellbound, the victim of some enchantment there in that farmer's kitchen – and in fact it was something like that here in this forsaken landscape cut off from the world with these deep valleys from which rose only a faint tinkle of bells these spongy meadows these wooded slopes the autumn turned the colour of rust; that was it: as if the whole countryside (enclosed in a kind of torpor, a charm, drowned under the silent layer of rain) were rusting corroding gradually rotting with that smell of humus of dead leaves accumulated heaped up slowly putrefying and I the horseman the booted conqueror coming from the depths of the night from the depths of time coming to seduce to carry off the lily-white princess of whom I had dreamed for years and just when I thought she was mine, taking her in my arms, embracing her, holding her close, finding myself face to face with one of Goya's horrible old crones . . .) saying: I recognized him all right. Yes. With his beard!

and one of them interrupting the argument, looking at me, winking over the top of the stove, saying You made a hit

and I That's what I came for

and he Only maybe she wasn't quite the same age

and I About two hundred years less. But that doesn't matter. What was it you saw Grandmother?

she leaned over even closer glanced quickly towards the lame man, the card players still busy throwing their cards noisily on the table: Jesus she said. Jesus. Christ. But he's a sly one.

over the top of the stove I looked at him he winked at me again I know I said He's the slyest one of all Where is he?

On the road

Yes? How did he look?

He had his beard she said And a staff

I saw him too I said

He always has his staff He wanted to beat me

God damn it, the lame man shouted turning round Aren't you through telling your lies yet Why don't you go to bed

Christ the old woman said. The soldiers round the table burst out laughing, for a moment the old woman sat still watching the lame man waiting for him to pick up his cards huddled crouching over her bench her little faded red-rimmed eyes shining with a wicked hostile gleam, Cuckold! she said, (still talking between her teeth, still mumbling:) They're nasty I'm all alone, repeating Cuckold! and again Cuckold! but they had started playing again, she glanced at me triumphantly leaned towards me again, Chased him away with his rifle, she said. Took his gun but he's a cuckold all the same. I looked at him again over the top of the stove and he winked at me again

Didn't matter if he locked her in her room she said with a giggle She leaned over further nudged me with her elbow her little cadaver's eyes with their yellowish ooze laughing silently But there's more than one key she said

What

More than one key

What are you talking about now, the lame man screamed Go to bed! She started suddenly moved away huddled in silence at the other end of the bench still making gestures signals grimacing her eyes still staring at me raising her eyebrows while her silent mouth formed the words saying soundlessly Nasty, Nasty, twisting her hideous goat face) . . . then the bed sank again under her weight I still kept them closed trying to keep to preserve that limitless darkness under my eyelids it changed from brown to reddish then to purple then black with streaks vague blurry patches forming and fading slipping pale shaggy suns lighting up and going out I knew she had left the light on and that she was looking at me examining me with that piercing and close attention they have sometimes I buried my cheeks my forehead in her armpit able to hear the air enter her lungs now at each breath then come out, her heart still beating fast then gradually it slowed down, my eyes still closed I let myself slide down her body along her side her belly rose and fell fluttered like a bird's delicate throat (the whole peacock trembling with the curtain its curved S-shaped neck ending in the tiny blue head crowned with a fan of feathers, the curtain still swaying after she had let it fall back fluttering like something alive like the life hiding behind it, I had looked up a fraction of a second too late had I seen hadn't I seen only thought I saw half a face the hand that had suddenly been pulled back letting it fall back now only the bird's long tail still continued to sway then it too become motionless and the next day we didn't see her either, the horse had died during the night and we buried it in the morning in a corner of the orchard whose trees dripped in the damp air, their black branches shellacked by the rain, almost completely stripped of their leaves now: we hoisted the body on to a cart and dumped it into a ditch and while the shovelfuls of earth gradually filled it up I looked at it bony lugubrious more insect more praying mantis than ever with its front legs bent its enormous woebegone and resigned head that gradually vanished carrying under the slow dark mound of earth our shovels threw on it the bitter grin of its long teeth as if it were jeering at us from the other side of death prophetic strong with the knowledge of an experience we did not possess, the disappointing secret which is the certainty of the absence of any secret and all mystery, then the rain started falling again and when the order to leave came it was falling heavily interposing between the other slope of the valley and us a grey almost opaque veil while sitting in the barn with our packs on the horses saddled we waited for the signal watching the curtain the sheet of silver in the doorway that poured down from the roof hollowing a thin furrow in the ground parallel to the doorstep and a little ahead (directly under the roof line) where the pebbles looked naked washed bare, the air penetrating damp freezing a thick bluish mist escaping from our mouths when we talked, on the curtain the peacock still remained motionless enigmatic, while we were talking we glanced up at it furtively, Blum's pale face like an aspirin tablet under his black hair with only the two spots of his dark and feverish eyes he was holding his helmet in his hand his head his thin neck came out of his coat collar strangely naked against that soldierly equipment the stiff cloth the leather of the straps inside of which he seemed to be as fragile and delicate as though inside a carapace

we won't go Wack said It's already more than an hour we've been waiting I bet we don't go they'll make us stay here like this all day and then at midnight they'll come to tell us to unsaddle and go to bed

don't start whining Blum said

I'm not whining Wack said only I don't pretend to be smart that's all I

Good God I said I'd give a lot for that key

what key Wack said

The peacock still didn't move

The key to my heart Iglésia said. We were still looking through the sheet of rain at the silent house the windows closed the door shut the façade like an impenetrable face, occasionally a leaf from the big walnut tree slowly drifted to the ground almost black already consumed rotten

I bet it's the assessor Blum said

it can't be Wack said She sent him away She took down the gun when he went into her room

she did? Blum said Because he went into her room?

how should I know Wack said Why don't you go ask

he doesn't know Iglésia said So what are you talking about

nothing Wack said

Wack made friends with their farm-hand Iglésia said That chap who looks like a bear

bears always understand each other Blum said

spit on you Wack said

all right I said Don't get mad You helped him dig up his potatoes so he helped you find out what was happening Tell us about it

at least he didn't help me to kill a horse Wack said

all right Iglésia said you didn't have to ride it

and I didn't kill it either Wack said

oh shut up I said

let him alone Blum said If he enjoys it. He turned towards Wack: So it was the assessor?

why don't you go ask Wack said

was it?

he's an old friend of the family I said The best friend of the family He likes them very much He's always liked them very much

but she drove him away with a gun Blum said

it's a family of hunters I said

that's what the bear said Blum said That's not what the old woman says

that old fool Wack said

maybe she's confused I said Maybe she thinks it's still the other one

what other one? Blum said

I thought you knew everything Wack said

was there another one? Iglésia said

The sheet of water still flowed past, like threads of silver, like parallel metal rods barring the doorway to the barn, somewhere a gutter was overflowing with the sound of a distant waterfall: That's why he took his gun I said To keep him from coming in

coming where Wack said

don't you understand anything? Blum said In the house because he wanted to come back to the house too

but you said he had another key Wack said

but in broad daylight with everybody's knowledge with every right with the excuse of showing the rooms to the new conquerors you really don't understand anything do you?

he's an inside man Blum said He likes taking everything inside everywhere

I don't understand a word of what you're saying Wack said You think you're too smart I tell you you're cr

only the other one has to take care of his family I said

who

the lame man it's a question of honour

oh yes Blum said I didn't know that honour was split down the middle with hair round it

you moron Wack said

now there's the word I was looking for I had it on the tip of my tongue but I just couldn't find it These country boys you know they seem so ordinary and then all of a sudden

and these city Yids Wack said what do they seem

oh I said shut up will you?

you think you can scare me Wack said

A network of little rills ran across the pale sand of the road the shoulder gradually crumbled collapsed slid in tiny and successive avalanches that for a moment obstructed one of the arms of the network then vanished attacked corroded carried away, the whole world was collapsing with a continuous murmur of a spring, of drops running along the gleaming branches catching up with each other running into each other separating falling with the last leaves the last traces of the summer the days gone for ever that would never come again never what had I looked for in her hoped for pursued upon her body in her body words sounds as crazy as he is with his illusory sheets of paper blackened with hen tracks with words our lips pronounced to fool ourselves living a life of sounds without any more reality without any more substance than that curtain on which we thought we saw the embroidered peacock moving trembling breathing imagining dreaming of what was behind it not even having seen the face cut in half probably the hand that had let it fall back waiting tensely for the faint movement of a draught), she said What are you thinking about? I said About you, she said No Tell me what you're thinking about, I said About you you know I am, I put my hand on her right in the middle it was like down the light feathers of a bird a bird in my hand but also a bush an English proverb she said Why do you keep your eyes closed, I opened them the light was still on she was lying on her back one leg straight the other bent up like a mountain above me the foot flat on the rumpled sheet and behind, a little below the ankle the skin thicker at that place made three horizontal folds above the heels slightly tinged with orange, my cheek on the inner surface of the other thigh under the light I could see where it joined the body under the hairs that began there the swelling formed by the tendon that crosses the groin diagonally, the skin very white above the thigh, tinged with a pale ochre starting at the groin, the lips a more pronounced ochre at the place where the mucous membrane began as if there remained persisted there not completely effaced something of our savage primitive dark ancestors clutching clinging rolling naked violent and quick in the dust the thickets: in that position it was scarcely open at all, I could see a trace of pale mauve like a hem a lining, the ochre colour deepening accentuating more pronounced tawny as the eye moved down towards the folds like a cloth a pale-dyed silk pinched from inside by two fingers the upper part making something like a loop or rather a pucker a buttonhole of flesh, she said What are you thinking about tell me Where are you? again I laid my hand on her: Here, and she: No, and I: Don't you think I'm here? I tried to laugh, she said No not with me All I am for you is a soldiers' girl something like the kind you see drawn with chalk or a nail in the crumbling plaster of barrack walls, an oval split in two and the rays round it like a sun or a vertical eye surrounded with lashes and not even a face . . . , I said Oh stop it will you can't you understand can't you realize that for five years I've dreamed of nothing but you, and she: Exactly, and I: Exactly? and she: Yes let me go she tried to pull away I said What's the matter What's got into you? she still tried to pull away and get up, she was crying, she said again Drawings the kind the soldiers make, soldiers' jokes, I listened to them still arguing in the evening watching the daylight fade through the rain, Blum said he would like to drink something hot and Wack told him that since he was so smart why didn't he go knock on the door and ask her to make him a little coffee, and Blum said he didn't like guns that he was carrying one on his back but that he had never had much desire to be a hunter still less to be game and that the lame man looked as though he was awfully eager to use his, saying 'After all he has the right to shoot his off when everyone everywhere else is making his little bang. After all there's a war on,' but now I heard only his voice it was dark again and we couldn't see anything and all the knowledge of the world we could have was that cold that damp that penetrated everywhere now, that same obstinate omnipresent streaming that mingled seemed to unite with the apocalyptic and multiple trampling of horseshoes on the road, and jolting on our invisible horses it seemed that everything (the village the barn the milky apparition the shouts the lame man the adjutant the senile old crone the whole dim and blind and tragic and banal imbroglio of characters declaiming insulting threatening cursing each other stumbling in the darkness groping until they finally bumped into an obstacle a contraption hidden there in the shadows (and not even for them, not even intended particularly for them) that would explode right in their faces leaving them just time enough to glimpse for the last (and probably the first) time something that looks like light) had existed only in our minds: a dream an illusion whereas in reality we might never have stopped riding, riding still in that streaming endless darkness and still answering each other blindly . . . Then maybe she was right after all maybe she was telling the truth maybe I was still talking to him, exchanging with a little Jew dead years ago boasts gossip obscenities words sounds just to keep us awake to deceive ourselves into thinking we were awake to encourage each other, Blum saying now: But maybe that gun wasn't even loaded maybe he didn't even know how to use it People like making everything into a tragedy a drama a novel

and I: But maybe it was loaded it happens sometimes You see it every morning in the papers

Then I must buy the paper tomorrow there'll be something interesting to read at least

I thought that you were interested in this war I even thought you were actually involved

Not at four in the morning on horseback and in the rain

You think it's four in the morning You think it'll ever be daylight again?

Isn't that the dawn over there What is it that's a little lighter over there on the right

Where? Where do you see something in this soup

Every once in a while you see a lighter place

It might be water Maybe it's the Meuse

Or the Rhine
Or the Elbe
No not the Elbe we would have known
Then what is it?
Some river what difference does it make
I wonder what time it is
What difference does it make
We must have been in this car for three days
Then let's say it's the Elbe
The two faceless voices alternating answering each other in the darkness with no more reality than their own sound, saying things with no more reality than a series of sounds, yet continuing the dialogue: in the beginning only two virtual dead men, then something like two living dead men, then one of them really dead and the other still alive (so it seemed, Georges thought, and judging from appearances it wasn't much of an improvement), and both (the one who was dead and the one who wondered if it wasn't better to be dead for good since at least you didn't know it) caught, enclosed by that motionless and yet moving thing that slowly flattened the earth's surface under its weight (and perhaps that was what Georges went on feeling, something like a sliding, an imperceptible, monstrous and continuous scraping behind the faint and patient trampling of horses' hoofs: that Olympian and cold progression, that slow glacier moving since the beginning of time, crushing, grinding everything, and in which he seemed to see them, himself and Blum, stiff and frozen, perched booted and spurred, on their exhausted nags, intact and dead among the host of ghosts standing in their faded uniforms all advancing at the same imperceptible speed like a petrified procession of mannequins swaying jerkily on their pedestals, uniformly enveloped in that blur through which he tried to make them out, to examine them, repeating themselves endlessly in the green depths of mirrors), Blum's pathetic and clownish voice saying: 'But what do you know about it? You don't know a thing. You don't even know if that gun was

loaded. You don't even know if that pistol wasn't shot off by accident. We don't even know what the weather was like that day, if it was dust or mud that covered him, coming home empty-handed with his stock of good intentions unsold, and not only unsold but met with gunfire, and finding his wife (in other words your great-great-great-grandmother who's now nothing but a few crumbling bones in a faded silk dress in a coffin that's worm-eaten itself, so you don't even know if the fine yellowish dust in the folds of the material is bone or wood, but who was young then, was flesh, had a belly shadowed by dark hair, lilac breasts, lips, cheeks brightened by pleasure over these yellowish bones), finding his wife then busy putting into practice those nature-loving and effusive principles the Spaniards had wanted to have nothing to do wi . . . '

And Georges: 'No, he . . . '

And Blum: 'No? You yourself admitted your family always suffered from some kind of doubt: some embarrassment, some discreet silence. I didn't start talking about that engraving, that door broken in, that confusion, those shouts, that disorder, the torches in the night . . . '

And Georges: 'But . . . '

And Blum: 'And didn't you tell me that in that second portrait, that miniature, that medallion that dated from after his death, you hadn't actually recognized her, so to speak, that you had had to read the name and the date written on the back several times over to convince yourself, that you . . . '

And Georges: 'Yes. Yes. Yes. But . . . ' (she had put on a little weight between the two, in other words had acquired that kind of voluptuous flesh, had somehow developed, spread, flowered, as happens to young girls after their marriage, her whole person exhaling – in that costume that was like a negation of costume, that is, a simple gown, half transparent, leaving her half naked, her tender breasts exposed, emphasized by a ribbon and springing almost completely out of the impalpable pale pink stuff – something shameless, satiated, triumphant, with that tranquil opulence of the soul and the senses appeased and satisfied – and even gorged – and that indolent, candid, cruel smile you can find in certain portraits of women of that period (but maybe it was only the effect of a fashion, a style, the painter's skill, his *savoir-faire*, his trick of representing with the same brush or with the same voluptuous pencil the matrons and the lascivious odalisques lying seductively on the cushions of Turkish baths?) with their supple necks, their doves' throats, and certainly it was no longer the same woman as the one, a little dry, a little stiff, studied, corseted, whaleboned and embellished with hard cold jewels, who had posed in the heavy slashed dress, Georges thinking: 'Yes, as if she had been liberated in between, as if his death had . . . '), and hearing Blum's voice again (rising, ironic and even sarcastic, but without apparently addressing anyone at all, unless perhaps the bottom of his mess-tin, with which he seemed to be talking, conversing with affection and solicitude, and Georges wondering how far a man could waste away without disappearing, being annihilated by what would be the contrary somehow of an explosion: an aspiration of the skin, of the whole being towards the interior, a suction, for Blum was then really frighteningly thin, his eyes sunk in his head, his Adam's apple sharp enough to pierce the skin, his voice so ironic it sounded fleshless as it said:) 'But maybe he dragged around, along with his Genevan notions, some other blotch, some shameful malformation? Wasn't he also lame or club-footed or something of the kind: there was a lot of that kind of thing in those days among the noble marquis, renegade bishops or ambassadors. After all you never saw him except in paintings and then only from the waist up, with his hunting rifle on his shoulder, like the other bandy-legged village Othello. Maybe he limped after all. Maybe it was just that. Maybe that had given him a complex, and he . . . ', and Georges: 'Maybe,' and Blum: 'Or maybe he just had debts, maybe the hideous local Jew was pressing him with some good bill payable to order. The lords and masters, you know, lived mostly on loans in those days. They were

animated by pure and generous sentiments but they didn't know
how to do much besides getting into debt, and if Providence
hadn't created the usurous Jew with crooked fingers for them
they probably wouldn't have been able to accomplish much,
except perhaps the kind of exploits that are afterwards proudly
recounted in the family, for the nobility of the gesture, to astound
friends, for prestige, for tradition, so that a hundred and fifty
years later one of his descendants goes off to war taking with
him the man – a kind of servant or functionary – who had
straddled, covered his wife neither more nor less than a mare,
living beside each other for a whole autumn and a whole winter
and half a spring without exchanging a word (except when a
horse limps) until they finally found themselves, one still faith-
fully following the other, or one managing to get himself faith-
fully followed by the other, on that road where it was no longer
war, as you said, but murder, massacre, and where either one of
the two could have killed the other with a shot without ever
having to account to anyone, and even then, you say, they didn't
speak (perhaps just because they didn't feel the need on either
side: it's probably no more complicated than that), still keeping
their distance according to both rank and social station, like two
strangers, even in that courtyard of a country inn where he
bought you a cold beer about five minutes before the machine-
gun bullets hit him, as he might have bought a glass after a
winning race at the jockeys' bar, so that out of the holes in him
might have spurted not blood but beer, maybe that's what you
would have seen if you had looked carefully, the equestrian
statue of the Commander pissing spurts of beer, transformed
into a fountain of Flemish beer on the pedestal of his . . . ', but
not even finishing, only concerned with scraping the last shreds
of bitter, sickening, metallic-tasting soup from the bottom of
his mess-tin, and Georges not speaking, staring at him, staring
now behind the lowered head at the two tendons in the neck
like two stretched protruding cords, his voice, lowered now,
speaking into his mess-tin, saying: 'And it must have been nice

to have so much time to waste, to have so much time at your disposal that the suicide, the drama, the tragedy become a kind of elegant pastime,' saying: 'But back home we had too much to do. Too bad. I never heard about any of those distinguished and picturesque episodes. I realize that it's a lacuna in a family, a deplorable failure of taste, not that there weren't one or two or even several Blums who might have been tempted to do it one day or another, but probably they didn't find time, the necessary time, probably thinking I'll do it tomorrow, and putting it off from day to day because the next day they had to get up again at six and begin sewing or cutting or carrying bolts of cloth wrapped up in a square of black serge: after the war you'll have to come visit me, I'll take you to see my street, first there's a store painted yellow to imitate wood and written in gilded letters on black glass over the shop windows: Dry Goods Textiles Maison ZELNICK Wholesale Retail, and inside nothing but bolts of cloth, but not like those shops where an elegant perfumed salesman takes off the shelves a thin wooden plank on which is rolled a fine fabric which he unwraps with elegant gestures: these are bolts about the thickness of an old tree trunk and holding about enough on just one to clothe ten families, and ugly thick dark fabrics, and the shop where it's dark in broad daylight is lit by six or seven of those ground-glass globes hanging on the end of a lead pipe through which they have merely run an electric wire instead of gas but the same gas globes have been there for fifty or sixty years, and the next shop is painted red, and also differentiates itself from the first one by an imitation marble front, green with light-green veins, the name of the firm still spread over the same black glass plate with the same gilded letters, and this time it's: Wholesale Linings Woollen Goods Z. DAVID and Co. Dry Goods, and inside the same enormous tree trunks with their concentric spirals of dark, utilitarian, ugly materials, and the next shop is painted urine yellow again to imitate wood, and this time it's: Dry Goods WOLF Linings, after which there's a wide gateway with a horizontal scroll over it that says: Handcart Rental Coal, and above the scroll, in the narrow half-circle made by the top of the door, there's an almost square window which must correspond to a room located above the doorway and I've always wondered how a man could stand up straight in there though it must be inhabited there are net curtains and green plants in pots fastened to the little iron railing, next the wall itself is covered with brownish-red paint, as is the shop that comes after the gate, and its sign is written in Gothic letters: Fine Wines Old Cellar Liqueurs, then another shop window painted yellow to look like wood: Textiles Wholesale and Retail SOLINSKI Suits for Men and Boys, and next comes the corner of the street and the café opposite Café INFANTRYMAN Tobacco written in red on a white background, the window dark red with bright red panels, the door set in the corner of the building and always open except when it's very cold, so that you can always see two or three men inside leaning on the counter (but not men from my street: labourers, bill-collectors, salesmen) and the well-polished coffee urns shining, and the girl behind the counter, a blue pillar-box to the left of the door, and over the box, painted vertically in yellow letters against the red background, the word TOBACCO again and on the other side, that is, to the right of the door, a tall thin grey panel with a vertical red diamond on it in which the word TOBACCO is written again and underneath STATIONERY, STAMPS, then underneath two astragals drawn with a brush, two double loops, then below that TELE-PHONE, then after the café a shop or rather not a shop because there's no shop window just a big window and a door, the house wall painted brown up to the second floor and in big white letters: MANUFACTURER of Wadding Carded Cotton and Padding of All Kinds Wholesale Specialities for Tailors Furriers Milliners Florists Tanners Polishers Jewellers etc . . . , I could go on, recite it all to you by heart, backwards, starting at the middle or either end whatever you want, I've seen it for twenty years from our window from morning till night, that and the men in grey smocks walking along loaded up like ants with those enormous bolts of cloth as if they were spending their time carrying them back and forth from one shop to the other, from one store-room to another, and in every house the lights are on from six in the morning until eleven or twelve at night without a break, and if they are turned out it's because no one has yet found the way of spending twenty-four hours out of twenty-four pulling at a needle or snipping with scissors or carrying bolts of cloth or making shoulder padding or wadding, so even admitting that a lot of Blums have wanted I don't know how many times to commit suicide which is highly likely, how do you expect them to have found I won't say the time but even the space necessary to do it in, not even the . . . '

'Which doesn't keep it from happening,' I said. 'All you have to do is read the papers. There are things like that in the papers every day.' He looked at me, the fine rain falling in tiny drops of mercury on the cloth of his coat, a metallic grey dust where the shoulder stuck out beyond the roof line, while we listened to the discordant echoes, the incoherent outbursts, fragments of rage of passion detached from that permanent and inexhaustible stockpile or rather reservoir or rather principle of all violence and all passion that seems to wander imbecile and idle and object-less on the surface of the earth like those winds those gales without any other purpose than a blind and negative fury shaking wildly whatever happens to lie in their path; now perhaps we had learned what that dying horse knew, its long velvety eye pensive gentle and blank in which I had nevertheless been able to see our tiny figures reflected, that eye in the bloody portrait also long enigmatic and gentle which I questioned: Melodrama tragedy fiction, he said, you enjoy all that you add to it, and I No, and he And if need be you invent it, and I No it happens every day, we could hear that old half-imbecile woman groaning patiently interminably inside the house dry-eyed, swaying back and forth on her chair while the lame man was making his rounds with that gun loaded with buckshot and ready to go off by itself limping tramping through the spongy fields the soaking orchard where his footprints gradually filled with a faint sucking noise, and the general too followed by his general-staff trampling getting winded following him quick abrupt as dry and insensitive as an old stick of wood, putting a bullet in his head which couldn't have made much more noise than a rotten branch breaking, and lying dead with his little wrinkled jockey's head his shiny little jockey's boots Did I invent that I said Did I invent that? I imagined him limping gnawed devoured by that torment like a sick dog an animal obsessed by shame the insupportable affront endured in his brother's wife he who had been refused for war service who hadn't been entrusted with a gun, All right he said put down that gun that's how accidents happen, but he wouldn't hear of it, apparently he was fond of that hunter's weapon that rifle with which he had had himself represented a symbol or something, for a long time I believed it was a hunting accident I thought that was why she didn't want to buy me that carbine, because of repeating her sempaternal family stories, ancestor stories, the way she had always stubbornly refused to let me learn fencing with the excuse that I don't know how many members of her family had died from wounds caused by an unbuttoned foil unless she had even read that too in the newspaper the description of accidents of crimes the society columns about births and marriages the passions unleashed engendered by the delicate flesh of the sleeping beauty immured hidden behind the peacock's tail still swaying faintly but no Leda in sight whose peacock is it then, to which goddess does the vainglorious stupid bird belong formally displaying its many-coloured feathers across the lawns of castles and the cushions of concierges? I imagined her in the form of one of those Goddesses I could feel her breasts her silky belly revealed by that gown from which her neck rose like milk I said you hear I said the only thing that can give an idea of her is to crawl to lean over her as if she were a spring and lap, dresses like nightgowns, pale mauve and a green ribbon around her ... yes what a difference from that other portrait hard and cruel a kind of Diana then she should have had a greyhound lying behind her in the other picture, thin and smooth-haired while later on the contrary it was one of those little dogs with curly hair that you run your hand through and it quivers with ecstasy licking your fingers with its wet tongue rolling with pleasure moaning quivering, like what you see drawn on the walls she had said, the two hieroglyphs the two principles: feminine and masculine, sometimes the masculine is only a sign like a pair of closed scissors with two circles at the bottom like the rings in which you put your thumb and first finger and the point facing up the symbolic circles underneath and symbolically surrounded with lines like rays and the other one too, oval with its median line two rayed stars in the firmament of blackish walls drawn with the point of a nail, defeated now, yielding, merely making that childish noise that could just as well be sobs as the contrary, sometimes I moved back pulled it out altogether able to see it beneath me coming out of her thin at the base then swelling like a bobbin a fish (they say that they recognized each other by drawing the sign of the fish on the walls of cities and catacombs) with that kind of head at the end, that finial or cap with its slit at the tip, both mute mouth and furious dead eye like the eyes of the fishy creatures that live in underground streams caves, blind from living in the dark, the suppliant and furious carp's mouth carp's eye apoplectic out of water demanding pleading to return to the moist and secret hiding place, the dark mouth, it was autumn again but in a year we had learned to strip ourselves not only of that uniform which was no longer anything but an absurd and shameful stigma but even, so to speak, of our skin or rather our own skin stripped of what a year earlier we still imagined it enclosed, that is, not even soldiers any more, not even men, having gradually learned to be something like animals, eating anything and at any time provided we could manage to chew and swallow it, and there were great oaks at the edge of the forest near where we worked, the falling acorns strewed the path where the Arabs went to gather them, at first the sentry would yell and chase them away but they came back like flies stubborn patient tenacious and finally the sentry had to give up shrugged and decided to ignore them making sure that no officer came by, I joined them bent over the ground pretending to look for them and put them in my pockets watching out of the corner of my eye and when he turned his back then I was in the thicket panting running on all fours like an animal through the underbrush tearing through bushes scratching my hands without even feeling it still running galloping on all fours I was a dog my tongue hanging out galloping panting both of us like dogs I could see her hollowed hips beneath me, gasping, her throat choked, muffling her exclamations into the rumpled pillow and her child's cheek her child's mouth with the swollen crushed lips half open exhaling the gasp the rattle while I thrust slowly entering engulfing myself it seemed again that it wouldn't couldn't stop my hands resting pressing on her thighs parting them I could see it brown tawny in the darkness and her mouth going Aah aaaaaaaaah thrusting all the way into that foam those mauve petals I was a dog I was galloping on all fours in the thickets exactly like an animal the way only an animal could run regardless of exhaustion of my scratched hands I was that donkey in the Greek legend stiff now like a gold idol of a donkey thrust into her delicate and tender flesh a donkey's member I could see it coming and going shining anointed with what was streaming out of her I bent down slipped my hand my arm snaking under her belly reaching the nest the curly fleece that my finger parted until I found it pink wet as the tongue of a little dog wriggling yapping with ecstasy beneath which the tree growing out of me was thrust, her choking throat moaning now regularly at each thrust how many had how many men had entered her only I wasn't a man any more but an animal a dog more than a man a beast if I could reach it know the ass of Apuleius thrusting ceaselessly into her melting now open like a fruit a peach until my spine exploded the head exploding deep within her flooding her again and again flooding her flooding her whiteness springing spurting splashing flooding her, purple, the black fountain still spurting the scream endlessly spurting from her mouth until there was nothing left, inert, numb, both of us fallen senseless on our side, my arms still holding her crossing over her belly feeling against me her hips covered with sweat the same muffled blows the same battering ram shaking both of us like an animal coming and going ramming violently coming and going in its trough then gradually I began to see again making out the rectangle of the open window and the paler sky and a star then another and still another, cold, glittering, motionless while I was gasping, trying to move one of my legs caught under the weight of our intertwined limbs we were like a single legendary creature with several heads several limbs lying in the darkness, I said What time is it? and he What difference does it make what are you waiting for Daylight? what will that change You want to see our filthy faces so much? I was trying to breathe to shift that weight to find some air then I felt no more weight only furtive silent movements in the dark, something rubbing rustling I woke up completely I said What are you doing? she didn't answer, I was beginning to make things out vaguely but not much, maybe she saw in the dark like cats I said Good God what's happening what are you doing Answer me, and she Nothing, and I You . . . , I was wide awake now sitting up in bed and turning on the light she was dressed already holding one of her shoes: for a second I saw her her fragile face too beautiful tragic two shiny streaks on her cheeks, at that moment there was something haggard desperate then furious hard her mouth hard screaming Turn out that light I don't need any light, and I But what are you, and she Turn it out I tell you turn it out turn it out you hear turn it out turn it out, then the sound of the bed lamp breaking, tangled up with the shoe she had thrown and for a moment I couldn't see anything saying But what's the matter with you, and she Nothing, hearing the furtive silent noises again in the darkness realizing she was looking for her shoe wondering how she managed in that darkness, saying Now what is it, and she still looking for her shoe There's a train at eight, and I A train? But what's . . . You told me your husband wasn't coming back until tomorrow, and she not answering not moving round in the dark now she must have found her shoe and put it on, I could hear her imagine she was standing walking back and forth, and I Good God! I stood up but she slapped me I fell back on the bed she slapped me again, and out of her face that was very close to me came what sounded like a gurgle that she was trying to choke down I think she said Let me alone, saying You filthy bastard, and I What? and she Filthy bastard Filthy bastard you couldn't let me alone no one has ever treated me like, and I Treated? and she Nothing I mean nothing to you less than nothing less than, and I Oh, and she I who . . . I who . . . , and I Come on, and she Don't touch me, and I Come on, and she Don't touch . . . and I I'll take you home you aren't going to take the train I'll take you back in the car I, and she Let me alone let me alone let me alone, in the next room someone knocked on the wall, I stood up looked for my clothes saying Good God! saying Where's my . . . but she hit me again blindly in the dark with something hard, her bag I think, swinging several times with all her strength once she hit me in the face I felt the strange savour of the blows, violent as if the flesh splitting over the cheekbone spread inside at the same time as the pain, something like a green, sour juice not bad-tasting, spreading, thinking of the skin, the taste of plums, of greengages ripe dewy splitting and their sweet juice I let her go fell back on the bed feeling my cheekbone hearing her walking back and forth again with those quick precise movements women make when they are putting things away, stooping picking something up I wondered how she managed it but no doubt she could definitely see in the dark, then I heard the clasp of her bag then the clatter of high heels quickly crossing the room and for a second I saw her by the light of the hall bulb but not her face: her hair, her back, silhouetted, black, then the door closed I heard her quick steps fading diminishing then nothing else and after a moment I felt the dawn's coolness, pulling the sheet up over me, thinking that the autumn wasn't far off now, thinking of that first day three months ago when I had been at her house and had put my hand on her arm, thinking that after all she might have been right and that that wasn't the way, that is, with her or rather through her, that I will reach (but how can you tell?) perhaps it was as futile, as senseless as unreal as to make hen tracks on sheets of paper and to look for reality in words perhaps they were both right, he who said that I was inventing embroidering on nothing and yet you saw the same things in the papers too, so that you have to believe that in between the shops with yellow imitation-wood fronts and the black signs and the cafés, or between midnight and six in the morning, or between two bolts of cloth they sometimes found time enough and space enough to be concerned with such things – but how can you tell, how can you tell? I would have had to be the man hidden behind the hedge too, watching him advance calmly towards his death down that road, parading as Blum had said, insolent, idiotic, vainglorious and empty, or maybe not even having any idea of making his horse trot not even hearing the men screaming at him not to go on, maybe not even thinking of his brother's wife covered straddled, or rather of the woman straddled by his brother-in-arms or rather his brother-in-horsemanship since he considered him his equal in that, or else the other way round, since she was the one who spread her thighs, straddled, riding (or rather who had been ridden by) the same houri the same panting choking hackney, advancing then in the calm and brilliant afternoon asking me

what time do you think it is?

estimating that the road ran almost exactly east-west and that at that moment I could see his equestrian shadow foreshortened to the right and cast behind him at an angle of about forty degrees and that we were already in the second fortnight of May and with the sun opposite us and to the left (which is why our eyes were half closed, and with that gravel, that sandpaper under our eyelids from lack of sleep we could see only the shadowed surface

of the trees, the slate roofs, the barns, the houses sparkling like
metal like helmets in the middle of that dark blackish-green
foliage, the fields were green shading into yellow, in front of us
the asphalt was sparkling too) the sun was in the south-west,
then, which would make it around two in the afternoon but how
could you tell?

trying to imagine the four of us and our shadows moving
along the surface of the earth, tiny, covering in the opposite
direction a trajectory virtually parallel to the one we had followed
ten days earlier taking us towards the enemy the axis of the battle
having meanwhile shifted slightly the whole of the position
having thereby undergone a northerly movement of around
fifteen to twenty kilometres so that the trajectory followed by
each unit could have been schematically represented by one of
those bent lines or vectors indicating the movements of the
various corps (cavalry, infantry, artillery) engaged in battles on
the map of which, in big letters, figure place-names handed down
to posterity, the names of a simple village or even a hamlet or
even a farm or a mill or a hill or a meadow, place-names

the Four Winds
the Thorn
the Crawfish
Wolf Pit
The Bloomer Girl
The Hencoop
The Devil's Reaper
The White Rabbit
Kiss-Ass
White-Friar's Cross
Flea Farm
Folly Farm
White Farm
Wire Farm
Fallen Woods

Kings Woods
Long Woods
The Old Shoe
The Crucible
The Ashtray
The Reeds
The Maypole
Martin Field
Benoît Field
Haresfield

the hills represented on the map by tiny fan-shaped lines bordering the wavy line of the crest, so that the battlefield seems covered with sinuous centipedes, each corps represented by a little rectangle from which is drawn the corresponding vector, each bending back in this case to assume virtually the shape of a fishhook, in other words, the barb facing the rear of the part of the line forming, so to speak, the stem, the tip of the curve thus described coinciding with the point where contact had been made with the enemy troops, the whole of the battle which had just taken place therefore could be represented on the general-staff map by a series of fishhooks arranged in parallel and with their points turned west, this schematic representation of the movements of the different units not of course taking into account the accidents of the terrain nor the unforeseen obstacles occurring during the course of the fighting, the actual trajectories having the form of broken lines zigzagging and sometimes overlapping intersecting each other and which would have had to be drawn at the start with a thick vigorous line then diminishing thinning out afterwards and (like the maps of those wadis which are initially in spate and which gradually – unlike other rivers whose width constantly increases from source to delta – disappear vanish evaporated drunk up by the sands of the desert) ending in a dotted line the points spreading out farther and farther apart then vanishing altogether but what could you call that: not war not the classical destruction or extermination of one of the two armies but rather the disappearance the absorption by the primal nothingness or the primal All of what a week before were still regiments batteries squadrons of men, or better still: the disappearance of the very notion of a regiment a battery a squadron of men, or better still: the disappearance of any notion of any concept at all, so that finally the general found no further reason to go on living not only as general, that is, as a soldier, but even merely as a thinking being and then blew his brains out

struggling not to give in to sleep

the four cavalrymen still advancing among the pastures cut up by hedges the orchards the archipelagos of red houses sometimes isolated sometimes coming closer together gathering at the roadside until they formed a street then scattering again the woods scattered over the countryside patches like green clouds torn bristling

and still soldiers in so far as they were wearing a uniform and armed that is all four provided with a curved sabre about a yard long and weighing two kilograms the blade carefully sheathed in a metal scabbard itself protected in a brown cloth case, sabre and scabbard held by two straps called pommel strap and sabre strap on the left side of the saddle so that the scabbard made a slight bulge under the rider's left thigh the sabre's brass handle to the left of the pommel and able to be readily seized in case of need by the rider's right hand, the two officers also being furnished with a service revolver and the two cavalrymen with a short shotgun carried slung across the shoulder

and not altogether soldiers inasmuch as they were cut off from any regular formation and in ignorance of what they were to do not only because the highest ranking officer of the four (the captain) had received no order (save perhaps the order to reach a certain retreat point, an order most likely dating from the day before or the day before that so that it was impossible to know if that retreat point wasn't already occupied by the enemy (as was claimed by the wounded men or the people they met on the road) and if consequently that order could still be regarded as valid and should be executed) but even because it appeared that he (the captain) was no longer even disposed to give orders nor animated with the desire to be obeyed, as he had indicated not long before when two couriers who were still following had refused to go on and he hadn't even turned his head to listen to them nor opened his mouth to forbid them to desert nor made any gesture to draw his revolver to threaten them with it, but how can you tell?

the five horses advancing at an apparently somnambulistic gait four half-bloods the result of a breed known as Anglo-Arabian two of them stallions the captain's a gelding the fourth (ridden by the cavalryman) a mare, their ages varying between six and eleven, coats: the captain's almost black with a blaze on the forehead, the second-lieutenant's golden chestnut, the mare bay with a blaze and two white feet (right foreleg and hind leg), the captain's orderly's horse mahogany with a white left hind leg, and the lead horse (from a machine-gun team, the shoulder-straps cut (by a sabre?) and dragging on the ground) a requisition Percheron, chestnut or rather tawny or rather wine-lees, mottled with grey, the tail yellowish grey slightly curly, blaze on the forehead descending to the nostrils and the upper lip pinkish white, the manes of the five horses clipped according to military regulations, looking (save for the chestnuts') like hairy black caterpillars when the horses raised their heads high so that the skin on the upper ridge of the neck swelled in superimposed folds, the tails reaching to the hock, one of the five animals – the second-lieutenant's – forging, that is, knocking the front of its left hind shoe against the heel of its right front shoe at a trot, the orderly's mount limping slightly on the left hind leg from a wound in the hoof probably caused by a piece of slag from the railway bed along which the horse had been forced to gallop the day before when the group had withdrawn from an ambush, the animals not having been unsaddled for six days and probably having bad saddle sores caused by friction and lack of air

but how can you tell, how can you tell? the four riders and the five horses somnambulistic and not advancing but lifting and setting down their hoofs almost motionless on the road, the map the enormous surface of the countryside the fields the woods shifting slowly under and around them the respective positions of the hedges the groves of trees the houses changing imperceptibly, the four men bound together by an invisible and complex network of forces impulses attractions and repulsions interconnecting and combining to form by their resultants so to speak the polygon of sustentation of the group which itself constantly shifts because of the continual modifications produced by internal or external accidents

for instance the cavalryman riding behind and to the right of the second-lieutenant glimpsing for a second (at a moment when the latter turns his head to answer the captain) the second-lieutenant's profile which reveals a pretentious or stupid character, so that the indifference which the cavalryman felt or supposed a moment previously that he felt towards the second-lieutenant is transformed quite irrationally into a sentiment close to hostility and contempt while at the same moment, noticing under the helmet the youthful almost childlike neck, thin and even delicate and even apparently puny, his glance, moving down further, considers the body the shoulders the sharp shoulder-blades, so that the newborn hostility is balanced by a certain form of pity the two impulses pity and hostility neutralizing each other indifference re-established

the relations of the two officers probably quite distant though tinged with a certain mutual esteem and respect for a *savoir-vivre* that permitted them to maintain a banal conversation of no interest whatsoever particularly precious at this moment – near that of their death – when a common preoccupation with elegance and style made it necessary for them to exchange banal remarks of no interest whatsoever

the orderly following the captain at a distance of about four yards without the latter ever turning round to speak to the former whom, apart from that imperious concern with elegance, he would doubtless have preferred as an interlocutor to the second-lieutenant (but how can you tell?) by virtue of the older and closer ties that had developed between them in consequence of a whim (a need) of the captain's which had led him to marry a young girl half his own age whose whim had led him to buy a racing stable and hire a jockey whom a whim of the girl or rather of the girl's flesh . . . Unless it was a whim of her mind, considering the purely physical character of the jockey who seemed to offer nothing particularly seductive unless – without taking any more account of his outer aspect than of the qualities (such as his ability to ride race horses) that could make his unattractive physical character be forgotten, she had seen in him (but can you tell since subsequently – that is, when the war was over – she refused to admit that she could have maintained personal relations with him at one moment or another, not even attempting to learn what had become of him, not attempting to see him again (and he not attempting to see her either), so that there was perhaps nothing real in all this save vague rumours and gossip and the boasting which two captive young men, imaginative and deprived of women, encouraged him to make or rather which they extracted from him) – unless, then, she had seen in him only an instrument (so to speak phallic or rather priapic, like that device Japanese married women attach to their heels so that when they sit on it in an uncomfortable position peculiar to the erotic and more or less acrobatic science of the Orientals, it enters and penetrates their genitals, introducing into themselves (and filling themselves with) this proud and invincible succedaneum for virility), an instrument, then, convenient by his servile dependency and the ease with which she could meet him each time she desired to satisfy the elementary physical or perhaps spiritual needs – such as defiance revenge vengeance and not only with regard to the man who had married (bought) her and claimed to possess her but even to an entire social class the upbringing the customs principles and constraints of which she held in abhorrence

the relations between the captain and the former jockey further encumbered by that virtually unshakeable burden which an enormous difference of monetary resources constitutes between two human beings, and then a disparity in rank, aggravated by the fact that each of them used a different language, this raising between them a barrier all the more insuperable in that, save in regard to the technical problem that had united them (in other words, horses), they used not different words to designate the same things but the same words to designate different things, the captain perhaps nursing a certain resentment or a certain jealousy of the gifts evidenced by the former jockey for riding horses and other creatures and the former jockey feeling in a quite natural and unpremeditated fashion (having had the luck to be born in a social milieu where, lacking time and leisure that parasitic by-product of the brain (thought) had not yet had the chance to work the havoc, its ravages, the viscera enclosed in the cervical cavity remaining consequently suited to helping the man in the accomplishment of his natural functions), feeling, then, the kind of sentiments likely in an individual originating in a labouring class towards the person on whom he depends materially and – subsequently – hierarchically, in other words, above all (whatever impulses of esteem, of sympathy or of astounded commiseration that might have developed afterwards), deferential, admiring (this for the money and the power) and as respectfully, as completely indifferent, the captain existing for him only in so far as he paid him (to ride and train his horses), and later on was qualified to give him orders, any kind of bond or of feeling being thereby condemned to vanish at the very moment when for whatever reason (ruin, liquidation of the racing stables, choice of another jockey or of another trainer) the captain would cease to desire or be able to remunerate or (transfer, wound, death) command him

the cavalryman and the former jockey both free (though for

different reasons) of any concern for elegance and distinction, exchanging occasional remarks whose episodic brief and scarcely coherent character derived on the one hand from the naturally withdrawn and uncommunicative temperament of the jockey, and on the other from both men's extreme exhaustion, the cavalry-man therefore merely continuing to follow the (or rather letting his horse follow that of the) captain with regard to whom he harboured at present only a vague astonished and impotent fury

but how can you tell, how can you tell? About two in the afternoon, then, the moment when the birds stop singing when the flowers droop and shrink half withered under the sun, when people usually finish drinking their coffee, when the afternoon newsboys offer their first dose of headlines but still not the Sports-Final, the bell of the first race ringing, summoning the horses to the gate and as I passed I saw on a brick wall an old faded torn poster announcing Races at La Capelle up north they like betting, cockfights, the motley tails with their blue-and-green metallic feathers fluttering, scattered, a country of meadows woods calm ponds for the Sunday fishermen (but where were the fishermen the bathers the children splashing in striped suits the drinkers in suburban taverns with arbours and see-saws for little girls – but where were the little girls, with their short white dresses their awkward and cool bare legs . . .), Flemings and Flahutes, high-coloured faces and oxblood houses the yellow ANIS PERNOD posters on the brick façades, someone said that the posters for some brand of chicory had enemy information on the other side, plans, charts: perhaps we might have been able to escape the next day, not be captured if we had had one of them, if we had headed north instead of – but we would have had to know, be familiar with the lanes, the paths in the forest the spinneys (slipping again panting and furtive from hedge to hedge spying panting before crossing the fields the open places) the thickets quarry brickyard dale barbed-wire entanglement em-bankment slope the soil the whole earth closely inventoried described possessed in its least features on the general-staff maps

the forests represented by a scattering of circles crescents surrounded by dots as if they had been recently cut, the sprouts
starting in a pointillist scrub round the trunks sawed off at the
base (they would have to be coloured with that tawny yellow
of freshly cut wood) the trunks and the stakes growing denser
closer along the edges like a mysterious and impenetrable barrier,
we could see it stretching silky and dark green across the hills
to the south, which is probably why we headed that way thinking
that if we could reach it but first we had to cross the road again
nothing seemed to be moving there still we approached stealthily,
dashing across it, running and one last time I saw it I had time
to recognize it thinking that now it must have begun stinking
for good oh fine let it rot where it lies let it infect fester until
the whole earth the whole world is forced to hold its nose but
there was no one any more only an old woman carrying a milk
tin skirting the factory wall and who stopped as if she were
terrified or perhaps merely surprised to see us slink by like
thieves

something like the empty stage of a theatre as if a clean-up
crew had passed through pillagers or victors leaving behind only
what had been too heavy or too burdensome to be carried away
or really unusable not even the split suitcase was left and I didn't
see the pink rag or any flies either but certainly they must have
been at work in other words, at table, buzzing coming in and out
of the nostrils then still running we turned the corner of the wall
and I no longer saw it, after all it was only a dead horse, a piece
of carrion just good enough for the knacker: probably he would
come by here along with the ragpickers and the scrap-iron men
the dustmen picking up the forgotten or outmoded props now
that the actors and the audience had gone, the sound of the
cannons fading too, on the right now, to the west you could see
a tall grey bell tower but can you tell if they had taken the village
how can you tell, how can you tell, we could see their enigmatic
names on the street signs the medieval milestones, Liessies
Hénin Hirson Fourmies the whole brick-red villages the long

train of black bugs crawling along the walls (fourmies formicary) vanishing you wondered where in the staved-in doors the cracks the slightest crevice the least hole where even a cockroach wouldn't have managed to get in flattening out vanishing disappearing each time a shell exploded in a dusty dirty cloud you never knew why in this rubble this city where there was nothing left but that wretched procession of ants and the four of us on our broken-down nags, but apparently they had a supply a stockpile to get rid of, maybe they had loaded them during the night and now they were firing only to avoid the bother of unloading and putting the shells in the munitions truck, women protecting their children fruit of their womb pressed against them carrying bundles of red eiderdowns whose feathers whose down spread behind them dragging the entrails the white guts of the houses that unravelled like streamers garlands sometimes caught on the trees and who is that saint whose torment I had seen represented in some picture the muscular executioners winding the livid bloody intestines coming out of his stomach on a reel, for a second time I saw the same poster they must have been at least a year old but these were trotting races horses harnessed not ridden, it wasn't mine I was riding but the one belonging to some dead stranger probably it didn't matter much but I regretted my new torch and that ham I had managed to find yesterday in a house that was already pillaged from top to bottom, a bad business to be in the cavalry covering a retreat coming through last when the rest have already looted everything: all we had found to eat in the last eight days had been fruit salad, the only thing to eat they had left behind, drinking out of the jars, the sugary sticky juice running out of both sides of our mouths, still on horseback throwing the jar away three-quarters full watching it break on the roadside impossible to carry it with us because it would have leaked out everywhere, and I regretted my toilet kit I would have liked to wash to have a bath to feel the water streaming over me the dead were all disgustingly dirty their blood was like excrement as if they had let go of everything but you can't wash when you're at war on top of the left saddlebag, buckled on by straps, was the standard brass basin, flattened, folded like a paper lantern, for the horses to drink out of but we had mostly used them to shave in every time I think of those basins I see them full of water covered like a cataract with a bluish soapy film and against the rough sides clusters of bubbles, on the right was a shears for cutting barbed-wire, I wondered what that idiot of a dead man could have been carrying in his saddlebags they were swollen to the bursting point probably a dirty shirt maybe letters from a woman who was asking him Do you love me, what else did she want when I had done nothing but think of her for over four years maybe some socks too that she had knit for him in any case he must have been short because the stirrups were too short for me putting my knees too high and knocking them against the saddle-bags when I was accustomed to ride long not like those monkeys or jockeys I had been meaning to lengthen them since I had been riding I kept telling myself that I would have to lengthen them one and even two notches but that was already an hour ago and I still wasn't doing it thinking hoping from one moment to the next that he would still make up his mind to trot thinking Good God getting out of here crawling out of this ambush where all we did was parade ourselves through like targets but probably his dignity forbade it his race his caste his traditions unless it was simply his love of horses because he must undoubtedly have had to go at a terrific clip to get out of that ambush and maybe he simply decided that his horse needed rest even if it cost him his own life just as a little earlier he had cared enough to stop and let his horse drink: keeping his horse at a walk because he had ancestrally learned that you have to let an animal breathe if you've just demanded a violent effort of it, that was why we were walking aristocratically cavalierly at a majestic turtle's gait he continuing, as if there were no reason not to, to talk with that little second-lieutenant probably telling him about his equestrian successes and the advantages of a rubber bridle in races a magnificent target for those impenetrable Spaniards who were absolutely rebellious apparently allergic to the tearful homilies on universal brotherhood the goddess Reason the goddess Virtue and who were waiting for him ambushed behind the cork-oaks or the olive trees I wonder what smell what odour death had then if it smelled like today not of gunpowder and glory as in poems but of those disgusting nauseating whiffs of sulphur and burnt grease the oily black weapons steaming smoking like a pot forgotten on the fire the stink of burnt fat of plaster of dust

probably he preferred not to have to do it himself, hoped that one of them would take care of it for him, would spare him that nasty interval but maybe he still doubted that she (that is, Reason, that is, Virtue, that is, his little pigeon) was unfaithful to him, perhaps it was only when he came in that he found something like a proof, for example that groom hidden in the closet, something that convinced him, indicating in an irrefutable way what he refused to believe or perhaps what his honour forbade him to see, the very thing that leaped to his eyes since Iglésia himself said that he had always pretended to notice nothing telling about the time when he had almost caught them, when trembling with fear or unsatisfied desire she had scarcely had time to pull down her dress in the stable and he not even glancing at her going straight towards that filly leaning down to feel her hocks saying only Do you think that revulsive will be enough it seems to me that the tendon is still swollen I think we'd better give her a little heat, and still pretending to see nothing pensive and futile on that horse as he advanced to meet his death whose finger was already pointed at him laid on him his stiff bony body cambered on his saddle at first a blur no larger than a fly for the concealed sniper a thin vertical figure above the gun sight, growing larger as he approached the motionless and attentive eye of his patient murderer index finger on the trigger seeing so to speak the reverse of what I could see or I the back and he the front, that is, between us – I following him and the other man watching him advance – we possessed the totality of the enigma (the murderer knowing what was going to happen to him and I knowing what had happened to him, that is, after and before, that is, like the two parts of an orange cut in half and that fit together perfectly) in the centre of which he rode ignoring or wanting to ignore what had happened as well as what would happen, in that kind of nothingness (as it is said that in the centre, the eye of a hurricane there exists a perfectly calm zone) of knowledge, that zero point: he would have needed a mirror with several panels, then he could have seen himself, growing larger until the sniper gradually made out the stripes, the buttons of his coat even the features of his face, the gun sight now choosing the best spot on his chest, the barrel shifting imperceptibly, following him, the glint of sunlight on the black steel through the sweet-smelling hawthorn hedge. But did I really see him or think I saw him or merely imagine him afterwards or even only dream it all, perhaps I was asleep had I never stopped sleeping eyes wide open in broad daylight lulled by the monotonous hammering of the shoes of the five horses trampling their shadows not walking at quite the same gait so that it was like a crepitation alternating catching up with itself superimposing mingling at moments as if there were now only one horse, then breaking apart again disintegrating starting over apparently running after itself and so on over and over, the war somehow stagnant, somehow peaceful around us, the sporadic cannon-fire landing in the deserted orchards with a muffled monumental and hollow sound like a door flapping in the wind in an empty house, the whole landscape empty uninhabited under the motionless sky, the world stopped frozen crumbling collapsing gradually disintegrating in fragments like an abandoned building, unusable, left to the incoherent, casual, impersonal and destructive work of time.